B

A Jarvis Mann Detective Novel

By
R Weir

Copyediting by:
William Miller Solutions
http://kyrathasoft.wix.com/proofreading

Great Scott Editing
http://www.believepositive.com/greatscott-editing.html

Cover Design by:
Victoria Robinson
Cover Smartz
http://www.coversmartz.com
info@coversmartz.com

To Family:
The blood and sweat
we've shared

Thanks to all the beta readers,
who helped make Blood Brothers
the best it could be.

Chapter 1

Damn my ass hurt!

I was running as fast as I could, chasing after a suspect fifteen years younger than me. He was extremely quick. I was holding my own, yet not gaining on him. My fresh New Balance track shoes, loose fitting jeans and T-shirt kept me light on my six-foot frame. My rear cheek, where I'd been shot several months earlier by an angry former female client, was feeling the strain of the chase. The teenager was a breaking-and-entering suspect I'd been hired to catch in Highlands Ranch by a community watch group. There had been a lot of B&Es in the area. Residents were tired of coming home to missing jewelry and small electronic devices, and demanded action. I'd been working for about two weeks when I finally caught a break on surveillance and spotted him trolling the neighborhood. He popped a sliding glass door with a pry bar, quickly grabbed what he could easily carry in a white bag and took off. I took several snapshots for proof and got out of my car. When he saw me, the chase was on. I cut him off from his approaching escape vehicle driven by his partner.

My stamina was good, but the leg was holding me back. I'd rehabbed for two months, first hobbling with crutches, then limping without them, and finally walking normally. I had pushed myself hard to get back in form, but running on a treadmill is much different from sprinting full bore after a suspect. It wouldn't be long before I'd have to stop as fatigue grabbed at me, and my butt was throbbing.

Down several streets, cutting through a few backyards after hopping fences, and into some open fields we ran. He looked back at times, but I still was there. In full gallop, I saw him grab his cell from a pocket, punch some numbers, and yell into the phone. I couldn't hear what he was saying over my own heavy breathing, but I doubted he was calling for a cab or the police. He cut back down another street and I heard a car moving in, its wheels screeching. He leapt into the open window of the speeding Camaro and off the car went, his legs and feet sticking out as it drove away. There was no plate, and I stood there trying to catch my breath and soon had to sit down from exhaustion. In the distance, there was laughing, and I wondered who was making fun of me. Before me in the field, I saw several prairie dogs barking away with their chirp-like noises filling the air. Apparently, they thought I was funny. I was a joke to them too!

"Oh shut up," I yelled while flipping them off. That would show them.

If I'd been carrying my .38 I could have shot the driver or taken out the tires as they do on TV. Of course, Hollywood made life more dramatic than it actually was and I was trying to cut down my bullet usage after the pre-Christmas bloodbath. Besides, firing my gun in this case was overkill, though my clients might disagree.

"How did they get away again?"

"You let some kid out-run you!"

"Give us back our retainer!"

While sitting down, I felt the vibration of my cell phone. Noticing the number and name on the caller ID was from someone I'd not heard from in some time, I pressed the answer button, curious about what she wanted.

"Jarvis," said the voice on the other side.

"Hi, Helen," I said. "Haven't spoken to you in some time."

"I know. Do you have a minute to talk?"

"Can I call you back? I'm in the middle of something right now. Give me thirty minutes or so."

"Sure. It's fairly urgent. So as soon as you can."

The call ended and I sat there wondering what she was needing from me. It had been a few years since I'd talked to anyone back in my hometown. From her tone, it wasn't for some idle chitchat to see how I was doing. My danger senses activated, a tingle down my spine I'd felt before. I dreaded what my sister-in-law needed, full-well knowing what it was about. I shook my head to clear those thoughts, humming to myself the last tune I'd heard on the radio, to pass the time and calm my nerves. My phone rang again.

"We have a speeding car which rolled over," said the voice on the other side. "Appears to be a blue Camaro. Sound familiar?"

"Where is it?"

With the location, I dragged myself off the ground and hot-footed back to my car and drove over. The car, on its side, was the same car which had peeled off with my suspect. Both occupants had been pulled from the vehicle by the community security guards with minor injuries. I strolled over and glared down upon the young man who had run from me. His face was bloody from a few scrapes.

"I hope you got your seat belt on before crashing," I joked.

"They were going too fast, came upon another car, tried to avoid smashing into it and lost control," said one of the guards, an older fifty-something male. "Figured you'd want to see them since they got away from you."

I ignored the criticism.

"Do they still have the bag of merchandise they took?"

"Yep, inside. I left it there for the police. We called 911 and they should be here shortly. Appears you've apprehended our thieves."

"More like they apprehended themselves. But I get an assist."

That would show those prairie dogs who was boss!

Chapter 2

Once done at the scene, I contacted Helen. It had been more than thirty minutes and she was a bit perturbed, which was not unusual; many people are grumpy with me much of the time. I seemed to have a knack for pissing the world around me off. *A refined skill.*

"I need your help," she said, after getting over her anger. "I think your brother is into something, and I need to know what it is."

"What's going on?" I asked.

"He is distant and won't talk," Helen said. "Working late nights and weekends. Lots of overtime, but I don't see him bringing in any additional money. Our bank account has been shrinking. We are almost broke."

There could be a lot of explanations for what she was seeing. At least there would be no bartering on my fee, since they had no money.

"There must be something more?" I asked.

"You know his past. What more do I need?"

"How long has this been going on?"

"A couple of months."

"What does Flynn say when you ask him about it?"

"He brushes me off and says not to be concerned. He is working hard trying to bring in more money. I ask him what money and he says it's coming."

"Odd," I said.

Though with my brother, not necessarily, as he had a history of getting himself into situations, whether it be money or women. Loose with money, and the wandering eye had been his kryptonite. *Which was it this time?*

"He also says there is a big deal in the works which will pay off soon. This worries me, as he doesn't have the best financial sense. His investments in the past have rarely paid off. I was under the impression we had a fair amount tucked away, but when I checked a few days ago it was gone."

"What would you like me to do?"

"Can you fly out here and talk with him? Look around and see what is going on."

"We haven't talked in a while. I'm not his favorite person these days."

This had been true since we were kids.

"Jarvis, you know how he can be sometimes. I think he'll listen to you. He certainly isn't listening to me. At the very least, you might follow him around and see what he is doing. Isn't that what a PI does?"

"He won't like me following him around, either."

"He doesn't have to know. Please Jarvis, I'm scared for Jolene and me. I want the best for her, and we know this takes money. College is not that far off. We are family and need your help."

The magic words "please" and "family" always worked on me. I liked Helen and loved their little girl, Jolene, who wasn't little anymore. Heading back home wasn't at the top of my to-do list, but with this latest case wrapping up, I could spare a week to stick my nose into my brother's business. This thought pleased me.

"Give me a few days to wrap up some things and I'll fly out. Once I know what day, I'll call you. Do I need to sneak into town or can you come pick me up?"

"Would it be better he not know you're in the city?"

"Probably. That way I can snoop around without him discovering."

"Yes, you know how he gets sometimes. This way you can keep an eye on him without him suspecting."

"I'm good at being sneaky. Part of my business qualifications. I'll text you when I arrive."

"Thank you, Jarvis."

It would be like the old days when we were kids. Me following Flynn around and seeing what trouble he was getting himself into. This might be fun, at least for me. Though with late spring looming, a trip to the wet and humid Midwest was not thrilling me any, and was balancing out the enthusiasm index.

Chapter 3

A pair of shooting incidents right before Christmas had placed a strain on my relationship with Melissa, and lately she wasn't the most pleasant person to be around. Our trip to Hawaii had to be cancelled, because I couldn't walk without assistance for a couple of weeks. With her plans of studying to become a lawyer, we couldn't reschedule, and I insisted she not delay her dreams any more. Now she was back in night school, so between studies and work duties, there was little time for us. If we were lucky we'd get an evening together on the weekend. I'd been warned it would be difficult, and she had been right. I was doing my best to be supportive, though it was challenging. With me being laid up, I was stir-crazy and, to put it bluntly, all the free time left me moments to fantasize freely, leaving me lascivious. Of course, with a patched-up hole in my butt I couldn't do a whole lot for a month or more without lying there and letting her do all the work. Not so bad at first, although I enjoyed completely participating in our sex life and not lying there disabled.

As I became ambulatory, time still was an issue. On the one weekend night on which we managed to squeeze in moments together, mental fatigue gave her little energy to do much other than snuggle. Some weekends she didn't want to be together at all. We were drifting, and blame fell mostly on my shoulders. The shooting by Emily not only left a hole in my ass but also one in her heart. She was uneasy about the whole situation, as I explained to her in detail those minutes before the attack. I had been honest, though more so than I should have been. She said outwardly I wasn't completely to blame, although deep down, there was a sense she felt differently. And she was right. This was my fault.

Once the B&E case was settled, I made arrangements to fly home. I called Melissa to let her know I was leaving late morning Sunday, with the hope I could spend Saturday night with her. We had not seen each other for a couple of weeks and, though begging might have been too strong a word to use, I was figuratively on my knees before she agreed.

I grabbed a sandwich on the way, as she had already eaten. Upon arrival, I walked into her townhome and found her sitting at her desk, writing on her notebook computer. She was in old blue sweats, a CU sweatshirt and barefoot. Her hair was tied into a ponytail and didn't appear to have been washed. I wasn't holding out much hope of passion in her current attire. I sat quietly on the sofa, leafing through a magazine, allowing her to finish. About twenty minutes later, she closed her notebook and spun her chair around.

"Thanks for letting me complete my work," she said.

"How are you doing?" I asked.

She looked tired, with bloodshot eyes behind her reading glasses, which I'd rarely seen her use.

"I'm worn out and feel dirty and bloated," Melissa stated. "I'd like to take a long hot bath and soak."

I got up from the sofa, tossing the magazine on the end table.

"Let's get the water started."

"You do know my tub is not big enough for both of us?" she stated.

"I'll sit on the toilet and we can talk. I'll try not to leer at your naked body too much."

With a weak grin she came over and I put my arm around her, kissing her dirty head of hair. I got the water running while she stripped. Her nude body looked marvelous even though it appeared she had gained a few pounds from the work and personal stress. Being a smart man, I kept those thoughts to myself. I added the bath oil she liked, and down into the hot water she went. The air filled with the sounds of the tension sizzling out of her pores with the steam.

"So, what is going on where your sister-in-law needs you?" Melissa asked.

"I'm not certain. She says Flynn is working a lot but not making any more money, and they are broke. Her intuition says he is into something. Not unusual for him to get into a pickle. She wants me to come into town unnoticed and follow him around and see what I find."

"How do you feel about that?"

"Just another case. If he is doing something to jeopardize his marriage and family, she has a right to know."

"How will he feel if he finds out?"

"He'll be pissed, but he'll get over it. Won't be the first time he's been mad at me. I'm used to it."

"You haven't mentioned your brother much since we've been

together."

"Been a few years since we talked. He wasn't happy about Mom and Dad helping me out financially. Being the oldest, he felt he deserved more of their help. That and a long brotherly competitiveness created a wedge between us which has been challenging to overcome."

"Sounds complicated."

"Aren't all families?"

"Certainly true of mine. Well at least with my mother. What does your brother do?"

"He is a CPA and has his own business. He got the brains and I got the looks."

"Gee, he must be really ugly," Melissa said with a smile.

I had to laugh. Nice to know she still had her sense of humor, even when tired.

"Wow, my neck and shoulders are stiff," Melissa said. "Too much time staring at the notebook screen."

"Sit up."

I squatted on my knees placed my hands on her shoulders and began to rub them firmly. Stress filled her skin and more of it floated away with each squeeze. The water was rolling off her breasts. I wanted to run my fingers over them, but resisted, for now. I grabbed a wash cloth and some soap and started washing her back. The tense pressure in her whole body was going away.

"Oh, I love your hands on me."

She turned and kissed me with tenderness on the lips.

"Stand up," I said.

She did and I proceeded to bathe her by hand from head to toe. I grabbed the showerhead, rinsing her off as the water drained. Once she stepped out of the tub, I took a towel and dried her, wrapping the plush fabric and my arms around her, the heat of her body warming mine. I looked her straight in the eye and kissed her passionately.

"I'm too tired," she said after the kiss ended.

"We'll lie down on the bed together and sleep."

I picked her up and carried her into the bedroom. While placing her on the bed, the towel fell open and I enjoyed the beauty of her body freshly cleaned and smelling of flowery soap. I slowly undressed, lying on the bed beside her, pulling the covers over us. She curled up next to me and soon was asleep, the day of work being laid to rest. Another night of passion on hold; a closeness of body, but a distance in soul, remained.

Chapter 4

Flying had never thrilled me much. It was the fastest way to get somewhere, but I still didn't care for it. Other than the takeoff and landing, it was fine, so long as we didn't crash in the process. The up and down often affected my stomach, so I'd found foregoing a meal beforehand made the nausea less likely to occur. The little cup of ice water and small bag of pretzels they provided in mid-flight was all I could handle. Once landed, I was off the 737 United flight and through the concourse to my rental car. Soon, I was on the road in a black Dodge Challenger, heading for the hotel.

Even though it was still late spring, I felt the humidity pound me once outside, the threat of rain in the air. I hit a local Jimmy John's sandwich shop for a turkey, cheese and bacon sub and continued my drive to West Des Moines as the showers began. I found a decent hotel via an online reservation. One of the strong selling points was it served real breakfast each morning and hot snacks in the evening. With plans to stay a week, this trip was going to put a good dent in my cash flow, so it was helpful not having to pay for some meals. Thankfully, I'd been paid well for the B&E case, so at least I wasn't going into debt immediately.

Checked in and unpacked, I rested on the bed and sent a text to Helen I had arrived. I had been given Flynn's daily work schedule and where his office was these days, so I would follow him tomorrow and see where it led. Calling Melissa, I got her voicemail. I left her a lovely message of endearment hoping she would contact me back. All I got was a text an hour later saying she was up to her neck in studies and would try to call when there was some free time, which never happened. Her response was brief, sterile and a bit stand-offish. Our night cuddled together sleeping had not improved her attitude towards me any. I had become accustomed to it and did my best to shrug it off.

The bed was decent, as was the television. I hated the silence in the room, so I found a baseball game on ESPN pitting the Dodgers against Giants. I nodded off midway through the contest, which was easy to do watching the American pastime. Waking up a couple hours later, I silenced the TV and slept the rest of the night away, the air conditioning keeping the room cool and moderately free of humidity. Rain softly sauntered down the outside window.

Up at 7 a.m. the next morning, I showered and decided not to shave, a day-old beard serving as a moderate disguise. I ate a good breakfast of eggs, sausage and juice and was off. I had lived in Des Moines much of my early life before heading off to college in Colorado, and still remembered my way around. It hadn't changed much, though traffic seemed worse, the roads no wider than twenty years earlier, with more cars filling them. I found the Mann household and was parked down the street waiting, the sun replacing the clouds, the pavement still damp. Flynn liked to ride his Harley Davidson when the weather allowed it, and he pulled out in his leather chaps and jacket, three-quarter helmet covering his head. He zoomed down the road with the classic Harley roar filling the air, undeterred by the wet streets. Following at a safe distance, so he wouldn't suspect a tail, I patiently flowed with the crowd of vehicles. His business was in Urbandale, which was north of their house and even with the heavy traffic we were there in about fifteen minutes. The size of the Des Moines metro area was fractionally smaller than Denver, so it didn't take long to get anywhere, even in the worst of congestion.

The office was in a single-story building on Douglas Avenue. There were six other offices, with a small parking lot, making it difficult not to be seen. There was another space across the street, which provided an excellent view of his front door. I pulled in and got myself comfortable in the reclining seat and turned on some tunes, keeping the volume down. Douglas Avenue was a heavily travelled road, though the area wasn't overwhelmingly noisy. On the other corner was a Walgreens, so I had access to a bathroom and food when I needed to get out and stretch my legs. I sat back and passed the time thinking on the past, the music playing softly in the background.

My earliest remembrances were of starting school. Mom dropping me off that first day, nervous how I would be away from home, but I had no fear. I was psyched for the new adventure on which I was about to embark. At this age, I was a sponge trying to absorb all I could, wanting to learn at every turn. I grabbed books to read, what little I could read already, and listened intently to the teachers speak on the daily subjects. Some hated school, but I was loving it. This was true all through elementary and into junior high school.

Growing up, and being a few years younger than my brother, I, at times, worshiped him. He was older and cooler than I was, seeming to always be the center of attention, whether it was with other boys in the neighborhood or the few girls who seemed to be drawn to him. I'd follow him around, and for some time he didn't mind. As he hit his teen years, he wanted less to do with his little brother. He'd be off smoking his cigarettes he'd stolen from mom and dad, standing around talking as he puffed away, the coolest kid in the crowd. I'd still shadow him at times, and he'd get mad at me.

"Hit the road, butthead," he would yell out when he saw me. "I don't need my kid brother following me around and cramping my style."

His threats didn't worry me much, and I would still sneak around to see what he was doing. It may have been an early skill set I'd built for my future work. Many times he would not know I was there, as I was gathering intel for use against him. Knowledge was power, and I needed whatever I could use as leverage.

There had been few kids my age in the neighborhood, most being Flynn's age, so I was eager to discover new friends when he didn't want me hanging around anymore. I made a few, some whose names I've long forgotten, and others, like Joey Sheehan who had been as close a friend as I ever had. Someone whom I'd not seen or heard from since my middle years in high school when his family moved away. I had a few male friends, but always liked girls better, some as friends, others as more. I'd steal a kiss or two with a couple girls here and there, enjoying that sensational charge when our lips met. Like Flynn, I had an eye for the ladies. I watched and learned much from him and would use it as my confidence built. He would break a few hearts along the way, and so would I.

The morning turned to noon and the only real activity was Flynn coming out to smoke a cigarette. He had been a closet smoker for years, always claiming to have quit the nasty habit, while in reality he never could give them up permanently. Growing up in a smoking home hadn't helped and I was thankful I had not been lured into the horrible habit, as I hated the smell of them. I saw a couple cars pull into the parking lot, neither of the drivers going into Flynn's office.

Though I had an unobstructed view, it was hard to see well from this distance. As the day wound down, I decided binoculars would be on my shopping list.

Unlike Colorado, it took most of the morning and past noon before the streets had dried completely. With a St Louis Cardinals ball cap and sunglasses to provide a vague disguise, I strolled over to Walgreens twice for bathroom breaks, drinks and snacks. I would need to stock better food for the next day, as most of what they provided would slowly kill me with preservatives. As the afternoon wound down, Flynn came out, hopped on his bike and drove away. The direction he took was not for going home, so I followed as close as I could, thankful he was a careful driver and not hot-dogging, weaving through traffic as some motorcyclists did. We were heading west until he stopped at a Hy-Vee grocery store. I'd never known him to be the type of man to pick up milk and bread on the way home, so I suspected this could be a clue. I was certain when I saw him pull next to a brown Saab, the face of a pretty woman smiling at him through the rolled down window. Once he was seated on the driver's side, I saw the exchange of pleasantries and from there they headed north and on the corner of 86th and I-35/80 they stopped at a multi-story hotel. Flynn got out first and strolled in. I was able to pull up close enough to see her and, after checking her phone ten minutes later, she got out and followed his path. Though I couldn't say for certain, it appeared my brother had a girlfriend.

Chapter 5

The next day I was better prepared, with cooler pack with better food and snacks, water and a decent pair of binoculars. My phone would have to suffice for any picture taking, as I wasn't springing for a nice camera. The bank account was being taxed enough, and payment on this case wasn't likely forthcoming.

This day followed the previous, along the same path, only when leaving he headed east instead, on Douglas. This time he met up with her in the Target parking lot on the corner of Merle Hay Road. From there in her car, they headed north and went into a different hotel a few miles down the road. If anything, I had to give my brother credit for being smart enough not to fall into the same pattern. I had a few shots of them with my phone camera and one of her license plate. Since I didn't have any current police connections in Des Moines, I had called in the day before and left a message for April with the Denver Police Department. She called me back while I was sitting in the parking lot of the hotel playing the waiting game.

"Where are you at?" she asked.

"Des Moines, Iowa," I answered. "The heart of the bible belt."

"I'm surprised they let you in," April said.

"I was born here; they have to let me in since I sprouted from the Midwest loins no matter how far removed I am from the lifestyle."

"I was wondering, as the plate you gave me was from Iowa. Registered to a Casey Gaines. Lives in Johnston, wherever that is." She gave me the address, which I stored upstairs to enter later on my phone. "She's in her late-thirties and appears to be divorced from what I can tell. Not sure if Gaines is her maiden name or not. No arrest or driving record. Appears to be clean from what I can see. What are you chasing her for?"

"It would appear she is my brother's girlfriend."

"Well if he is anything like you then yes, that would be a crime, though likely not an arrestable one."

"My brother has a wife and daughter. He appears to be cheating on them."

"And the wife hired you?"

"All she could afford, for he is spending all his money on Casey, or so it seems."

"You must not care for your brother much to be doing this?"

"Don't dislike him. I just like her more. She shouldn't have married him in the first place, but she got pregnant and you know how that goes. Especially in the bible belt."

"Probably thought she could change him. All women believe it. He must have money or be a good lover for her to hang on. How long have they been married?"

"Fifteen years. Fortunately, they didn't have any other kids. He got a vasectomy shortly after Jolene was born. No worries about him getting anyone else knocked up."

"Well, that is a positive. I got to run. Enjoy the humidity and bring me back some sweet corn."

The call ended before I could tell her it was still too early in the year for ears of corn, though humidity was never out of season. I quickly tapped away the info in OneNote, so I wouldn't forget it, digital notes having replaced paper. There was little doubt in my mind what my brother was doing. Now, the hardest part was telling Helen. Shocking news was never easy and, when it came to family, even more so. I had received several text messages and a couple of voicemails asking if there was any news. So far, I had nothing concrete to tell her. My responses were "working on it".

I decided to wait them out tonight. There was a Perkins nearby, so I grabbed a to-go order and forced down the burger and fries in the car. I listened to sports talk on the radio, but got tired of the arguing and switched back to my rock music collection to keep me alert. At around 9 p.m. they came out, went to Target, and from there I tailed her as she headed north again. Johnston was a suburb of Des Moines, and we drove to an apartment complex where she stepped out and headed up the stairs to a top floor unit, confirming the address I'd been given. I gave her several minutes to get settled, walked up the stairs and knocked on the door. The door opened on the security chain a mere crack, where I could only see her hazel eyes and stylish hair. From what little I could see of her face close-up, it was apparent why my brother was attracted to her.

"Yes?" she asked.

"Pardon me ma'am, but I'm wondering if the man of the house is home?" I used my beaming smile and flexed my muscles through my t-shirt, which normally made woman fling open the door and undress before me.

"No man here. Peddle your wares elsewhere." The door slammed and I had my answer. No super power was ever universal.

Back in my car, I figured Flynn would be back home by now, so I sent a text to Helen saying I'd call in the morning and we could get together for lunch to discuss details in person, as news like this shouldn't be announced digitally. Once back at my hotel, sleep didn't come easily knowing tomorrow would not be a pleasant day.

Chapter 6

Helen and I decided to eat at The Tavern in the Historic Valley Junction District. This was my old stomping ground as a child growing up, my parents' home and antique business only a few blocks away. They had sold it and retired when their health started failing nine years ago. The business was still there today, only named differently than Mann's Classic Antiques.

The Tavern had been in business since the forties and still served the best thin-crust pizza around. The place had changed some, being much larger than I remembered, expanding into the building next door, and doubling their size. I found a booth while waiting for Helen to show up and ordered a soda with garlic cheese bread. It was close to noon when she arrived. She stepped through the door, removing her sunglasses when she saw me. I'd not seen her in years, but she still looked good. Slightly heavier on her 5'8" frame, but firm, with a good figure shown off well in beige jeans and a flowery print blouse, which clung to an average bust. Her long, dark, curly hair accented a deeply tanned face which, this early in the season, spoke of tanning salon trips. Heels added to her height and, as she walked over, I stood and gave her a sisterly hug.

"You're looking good, Jarvis," she said while sitting down, her huge cloth satchel covering half the table top. "Other than the hairy face."

"You look good too, Helen," I replied with a grin. "You haven't aged one bit."

"Nice to hear, though I know it's not true. Damn, I need a drink."

The waitress stopped to drop off my soda, and Helen ordered a Long Island iced tea. I couldn't help giving her a stare at the strength of the mixture so early in the day.

"I know, I'll make sure to stick with one only and drink it slow. I needed something before you give me the bad news."

"Why do you think it's bad news?" I asked.

"It's always bad news when it comes to Flynn. But let's talk about other things first before getting to that. A little food and drink to settle my nerves. How are you doing?"

"Good. Been busy with work. Mostly keeping out of trouble."

"How long has it been since we've seen you?"

"I imagine five or six years. Since Mom's funeral."

"Yes, that was a sad day. Hard to lose them both a few months apart."

"All those years of smoking will do it. A habit I'm glad I never acquired."

"I wish Flynn would completely quit. He thinks I don't know, but you can smell it. No amount of gum or mints can hide it. Fortunately, he knows better than to smoke at home."

I smiled knowing what she would do to him. Smoking was small potatoes compared to the news I was about to give her.

"Well, it's been too long since we've seen you," Helen said. "We heard about you and your encounter with some bad people, on the news. You were quite the hero around here for a while with folks that remember you. 'Former local boy in gun battle', I believe the headline said."

I wasn't real proud of all the carnage which happened last year, much of which I got credit for, but didn't do. The term 'hero' ran counter to how I felt. Fame did help my business, which led to a tinge of guilt about capitalizing on my moment in the spotlight. Though, it was nice not to be begging for clients.

"Part of the job."

The waitress returned with Helen's drink and the garlic cheese bread. We ordered a fourteen-inch cheese and sausage pizza, as I was anxious for the leftovers. I enjoyed the cheese bread dipped in marinara sauce. I had to say there were few pleasures I savored more.

"Modest as always," Helen said after a long draw on her drink. "You know one person who was proud and asking about you?"

"Who?"

"Roni. She called me up and wondered if I talked with you any. She always cared about you."

"I thought she was married."

"Was, but no more. Been divorced about three years now. Changed her name back to Berry, as she couldn't stand the jerk and wanted to be free of everything about him. You should look her up while you're in town. I have her number."

Helen wrote down the number on a napkin and slid it across the table. Roni had been a girlfriend of mine in high school. We had dated for about a year, but I broke it off when she insisted on a more exclusive relationship. I had seen several different girls off and on during our time together. I hadn't been ready to settle down then, though she did carry quite a place in my memory. She was a devout Christian girl, who wanted to wait until marriage before having sex, which I respected. We had never been intimate beyond kissing and some heavy petting. I hadn't thought of her in years. I took the napkin and looked at the number.

"Sure, if there is time."

"I gave her your number, too, when I told her you were in town. Don't be surprised if she calls you first. I always thought you two made a cute couple."

I entered the number into my phone contact list, so I would know it was her calling. I couldn't say for certain if I'd take the call or not. Being a long way from home and from Melissa, I didn't need the temptation. But I was curious to see Roni again all these years later.

"Of course, everyone said the same about me and Flynn," stated Helen. "And see how it turned out."

"You knew what Flynn was like when you started dating him!" I said. "There was no mystery he was a ladies man."

"I did. He told me many times he would go right up to a woman and tell her the most direct statement he could come up with. If she told him to 'take a hike' he'd go on to the next one. Might work on one out of ten women, but he didn't care. Rejection never bothered him. Hell, I was one of the ten. Hopped in bed with him that first night we met, and I was over the moon. The man knows how to satisfy a woman. Of course, now I'd be lucky to get any action with him once a month. I've often wondered how my life would be different if I hadn't screwed up on my contraception meds."

"Hey, it's not all bad. You got Jolene out of it."

"Yes, and I love her to death. She's not the same loving little girl from when you last saw her. She's a teen now and wants less and less to do with me, leaving me feeling lonely and rejected by those at home." She paused to take a long draw on her drink. "Well, at least the dog still loves me."

"Maybe she senses what is going on at home and wants to escape it."

"Possibly. Though she has a boyfriend and it scares me to death. He is a couple years older than her. I don't want her to get knocked up like I did by accident. When I try to talk with her, though, she won't listen. I probably should have you follow her too, and see what she's up to."

"I'll pass on that one. Following one family member is bad enough. Snooping on a teenager is a parent's duty."

The pizza arrived and Helen's drink was finished. She tried to order another, but I reminded her, so she settled for a soda. Unlike some women, she had a healthy appetite and ate three pieces of pizza, nearly matching my consumption. *Maybe there wouldn't be leftovers.* As we finished up eating, she bore into me ready to hear what I had to say.

"I'm sorry to say, Helen," I stated. "It looks as if Flynn has a girlfriend. I followed him to two different hotels with her the last two nights."

"What is the bitch's name?" Helen asked.

I hesitated in telling her.

"Come on Jarvis, I have a right. Especially if it's someone I know."

"Promise you won't do anything stupid?"

"Nothing stupider than what he is doing."

I couldn't argue that point.

"Casey Gaines."

I waited but there was no reaction.

"Damn, I don't know the slut. Where does she live?"

"I'm not telling. You will only make it worse. Deciding how to deal with Flynn is most important. And I implore you to think it over carefully and not make a rash decision."

"So, my first instinct to cut off his balls I should ignore?"

I smiled. "Yes, I would suggest it. Jolene doesn't need to visit her mother in the slammer."

"Hell Jarvis, I have no idea what to do. He was a hound before I married him, so what did I expect? This may not be his first affair since we've been married. My concern is how to go forward. I make decent money on my job, but hell, we're nearly broke right now. And I doubt I can make the house payments on my own. I'm so mad I can't even cry."

"Don't do anything rash. If there is anything I can do to help, let me know. He's been out late the last two nights. Does he stay out late every night?"

"Generally, three or four nights a week. Tonight, he is supposed to be home. We are having dinner out with a client and his wife."

"Are you going to go?"

"I'm uncertain right now. I should, because it's important to his business. Though, it will be hard to keep my emotions in check. I do believe I must confront him tonight, afterwards. I can't sleep next to him knowing what he's been doing."

"Do you want me to be there to provide support?"

"No. But thanks for offering. I'm certain I can handle him. I do appreciate you helping. Can't be easy to tattle on your brother."

I smiled again and had no comment. Guilt at ruining his marriage should rule the day. But since we were kids, I'd always enjoyed spilling the beans on Flynn. Being an adult didn't completely kill the pleasure.

Chapter 7

After we finished up, I paid for lunch and decided to walk up and down and view all the shops. I had grown up walking these streets. I knew them well, for they had changed little over time. Some of the other shop owners knew my parents, so they knew me, though as a youngster. Many of the shops were the same, though some had different owners. I walked in and out of a few until I came upon my parents' old business, now called Fisher Antiques & More. I walked in uncertain what I would find.

Behind the counter stood a fifty something woman with graying hair, big thick glasses and thick red lipstick. She saw me and said, "Hello" and I stopped and stared at her. She adjusted her glasses with her hand and squinted. My three-day-old beard probably threw her off, but then she grinned with recognition, coming out from behind the counter and giving me a hug. Sue Ellen and her husband, Nathan, had bought the business from my parents after working for them part-time for many years. When my parents' health issues began to take their toll, they were anxious to buy the business and call it their own. They were the first in line to express their sorrows at both funerals, being the good friends they were.

"My lord, I'm surprised to see you," said Sue Ellen. "Why are you in town?"

"Business matters," I said. "I needed to come in and say hi."

"So happy to see you. Nathan guess who is here?" Sue Ellen called out.

Nathan walked out stiffly, showing his age more so than his wife. What was left of his hair was gray and slicked down, the balding top shiny as if it had been buffed. He put out his hand and I shook it gently. I could see the arthritis twisting the joints of his fingers. Though the body showed the years, the eyes still appeared sharp and clear. Next to my parents', these two were the closet thing I had to family other than Flynn, Helen and Jolene.

"What's with the scruffy look?" said Nathan. "Is the big shot PI in disguise?"

I laughed at his humor. He was one of the funnier people I'd ever known. Much of my wit had been born from listening to him speak.

"No, I left the razor at home," I replied. "Who knows maybe I'll keep it."

"Oh, hell no," said Sue Ellen, her hand squeezing my cheek. "Why would you want to cover this beautiful face?"

"Trying to look like a tough guy," said Nathan. "Though a goatee would give you a meaner appearance. The bad guys would be running away and hiding in fear."

"Never find the right woman looking tough and mean," answered Sue Ellen. "Probably scared them off with that horrible day we heard about back in Denver."

It was closer to the truth than she realized.

"Oh heck, Sue Ellen, the scum probably had it coming to them," said Nathan. "Evil to the core and we are better off they are no longer walking on this earth. Is that right, son?"

"Yes, you are probably right," I replied.

"Hard to believe that young boy we knew all those years ago would be involved in something so gruesome," stated Sue Ellen. "I shudder to think what your parents would have said when hearing about it."

"I'm sure John would have slapped him on the back and said 'well done'. Since he isn't with us anymore, I'll do it for him…"

There still was some sting in his slap, but all I could do was laugh. We stood and talked for some time, chatting about the past, present and future. How their kids were doing, who I'd grown up with, who were married now and provided them grandkids. I had spent a good chunk of my life in this store and several of the others in the area. I had helped my parents keep the place going and got in trouble many times while growing up. Been in a few fights out on the streets and in the neighborhood. They were mine and I owned them, so I'd thought. I'd been wild and undisciplined; probably still was in some ways. This was where I became who I was.

Around the age of fourteen I thought I was the cat's meow, with way more confidence than I should have. I strutted my stuff and thought I was tough. I was still small in stature, around 5'6", a late growth spurt still a year or two in the making. Being a bit on the pudgy side, my weight was my advantage. When perusing the neighborhood, there had been times I'd searched for trouble. Someone left a bike out, I would debate stealing it. An unattended football or Frisbee and it was mine. A jacket left behind and it would be a new addition to my closet. I wanted to be in control and take stuff from others, exerting my perceived notion of dominance. I'm not certain why I felt or acted this way. I certainly wasn't raised like that. My parents often preached right and wrong, since the time I could understand them. Something had gone off inside saying I was better than others, deserving what I could take. If I was sharp and strong enough, then so be it. I got by on cockiness and sarcastic attitude. If they weren't strong enough to fight back, oh well. The problem, though, was I wasn't as tough as I thought I was. I'd often run into someone who could kick my ass and did. I came home with bloody noses and black eyes on several occasions. I could hold my own with the best of them, but not for long, losing the battle often.

One summer day, I ran into a kid older than me by two years, he and his buddies ready to push me around. They wanted my baseball glove and hat, along with my bike which I used to ride to the ball field to play for my team, the Braves. The kid's name was Corey and he shoved me to the ground, knocking me off my bike. It was a nice eighteen speed unit which I gotten for my birthday.

"Jarvis, you better stay down," he said after a couple of well place shots to the stomach.

"I'm not afraid of you," I answered defiantly while rising from the pavement.

"You should be..."

Between him and his two friends I didn't stand a chance, but I tried. In the end, I took a beating I'd never forget and the items were no longer mine. I didn't like what happened, but it didn't deter me any. If they could take from me, I could take from others, including my own family. I had plotted my revenge, but against someone other than Corey.

There were many types of shops up and down The Valley Junction. Several other antique shops like my parents', but also dining, bakeries, arts and crafts, jewelry; the variety was endless. Some of the shop owners knew me. I decided to secretly take an antique from my parents' shop and look to resell it at one of the others, where they didn't know me. I'd use the money to replace the stuff stolen from me. I worked out the details and was able to sneak out the back with an expensive vase one afternoon while my mother was busy with a customer. I immediately took it to one of the other shops to see what they would give me for it. I hadn't thought it through very well, and the owner took one look at me and the vase, asked to have it so he could study it in the back, and called the police without me knowing. They arrived a few minutes later, the black and white parking out front. When I saw them pull up, I panicked and ran out the door. They caught up with me and dragged me back to the store.

"Where did you get the vase, son," asked one of the officers with a stern expression.

I played dumb. "I found it."

"Where?"

"In a dumpster a block or so away. Thought it might be worth something, so I brought it here."

"What is your name?"

"Jarvis."

"I need your full name, please."

I hesitated. Should I lie? If I didn't, they would recognize the last name and could connect me to my parent's shop.

"Smith," I answered.

It was the best I could come up with, and wasn't real convincing. The two officers looked at each other in disbelief.

"I guess we'll need to take him in," said the second officer. "We'll leave him to stew in a cell for a while. Once he breaks, we can call his parents from there."

I was cornered now. They took me to the car and started to put me in the back seat. All I could do was fess up.

"It's not Smith. The name is Jarvis Mann."

They pulled me back into the store and told the manager. He looked my way and told the officers there was Mann Classic Antiques two blocks away. He got the number and made the call. In about twenty minutes my father showed up. When he stepped in and saw me, his reaction was of disappointment.

"What has he done now, officer?" he said.

This was not my first run in with the authorities, though it would be my last. For my father would bear down on me teaching me a lesson forever, with the help of a friend in the county sheriff's department, changing my path in life.

When I finished talking with the Fishers I walked up and down the streets of the whole area. The weather was good except for the humidity which was always high and many times matched the temperature. The buildings here had stood a long time, some in better shape than others. Still for being a hundred years old or more, they looked good. Few modern structures stood for as long. I window shopped here and there and stepped into one of the many food stores to pick up a bottle of water and some caramel corn. As I stepped out my phone rang and it was Helen.

"I'm sorry to bother you, Jarvis," she said. "But I didn't do as you suggested and did something rash."

I was afraid to ask but had to know. "What did you do?"

"I called a locksmith and changed all the locks. Then I took all his clothes, packed them into several duffle bags and suitcases, and put them on the front curb. I then called him and told him to come by and get them. Once I simmer down in a few days I'll let him get the rest of his stuff, including his car. Then I contacted a lawyer."

"What was Flynn's response?"

"He didn't deny it, only wanted to talk and explain. I told him no, not until I had some time to think."

"And what if he insists on talking?"

"He won't. For I told him if he does anything stupid I'd kick him in the nuts and call the police."

Nothing more chilling than a double threat like that to keep a man away.

"Does he know how you found out?"

"I didn't mention you. I only said I'd followed him and learned of the affair."

It all seemed cut and dry. Domestic cases were the worst and I was right in the middle of this one. I could try to convince her to step back and cool down, but it would do no good. I could hear the resolve in her voice.

"What will you tell Jolene?"

"The truth. Her father is a pig."

"Hopefully, something with a little more tact."

"We'll see. I doubt she will care much, though. She is pretty caught up in her own world these days."

"Do you want me there when he picks up his stuff?"

There was a long pause.

"I would say no. He knows better than to mess with me. I'm no wilting flower."

Yes, he did and so did I. She had gone against my advice, but what could I say? She might regret her actions later, but for now she appeared to know what she wanted. I sure as hell wasn't going to stand up for my brother. He was on his own and heaven help him. It was the Mann weakness of not being able to keep it in our pants, an ailment I battled every day. Like now; I was fighting the urge to call Roni.

Chapter 8

The next morning, for some silly reason, I wanted to check up on my brother. It was dumb, but I felt I must. I had looked at flights online and wanted to book something and get the hell back home. I couldn't bring myself to hit the reserve button. *Run away and don't get involved anymore* I told myself. This all seemed unresolved and I couldn't leave it. On the drive over to his office, I thought it was idiotic on my part to stop by, for he would know I was the one who'd spilled the beans. Of course, it wouldn't have been the first time I'd done so.

Before the vase incident I had gotten into a scrap at school with another student. The fight was over stolen lunch money, which I had taken from him. I had been challenged outside after school and the fight began on the school grounds. He was not much bigger than me, a little taller but thinner, so I'd used my weight against him. We mostly rolled around the ground, the majority of the punches going to the body, before a pair of teachers broke it up. Threats of suspension came, even though the school year was nearly over. But if it happened, it was possible I'd miss some final tests and not pass the year since my grades teetered on the brink of failure, the sponge-like student of the past no longer present. I was grounded again and couldn't leave to do anything, awaiting word from the school. My father was livid with me, uncertain what more to do, asking if I had truly stolen the money. Once I'd confessed that I had, his anger increased, for this wasn't the first time I'd been in trouble. I was cornered, knowing the punishment would be harsh. This is when I blurted out something to take the heat off me, information I'd learned on one of my stealth missions of following my brother.

"But dad, Flynn has been sneaking out at night," I said. "He's been meeting up with some friends, smoking, drinking and messing around with some girls. He hasn't been getting home until 2 a.m. or so."

His expression changed immediately. He was stunned to hear this. Flynn was three years older than me. He was the eldest, and the good one in his mind, having done an excellent job of mostly hiding his indiscretions. I knew better and tried to tear him down, breaking my father's illusion. This got him to storm out of the room searching for him. I was free from his wrath, I hoped, but of course this was wrong. It only delayed the inevitable. We now both would be punished, and my brother's trust in me was further tarnished. This was the last straw and would forever change our relationship.

I stalled some, driving around contemplating the best way to approach Flynn. No amount of thinking could come up with solid logic to use to explain my presence.

"Hi Flynn, I was in the neighborhood and thought I'd see how you're doing!"

Of course, living in Denver, this wouldn't work.

"Helen called and gave me the news. So, I got on a plane to see if I could help."

Yea right, he'd really believe that load of crap.

"Flynn, I wanted to let you know I spied on you for two days and then ran to your wife and gleefully told her of your affair."

This at least would be closer to the truth, but likely would get him to take a swing at me, like he had many times before. There was no good way to put things. But I felt I had to at least fess up and hear what he had to say. I'm sure there was a good reason to be screwing another woman while he was married. He'd used a couple of excuses in past relationships I was aware of; pretty good ones I'd even used myself on occasion. I'm certain he could piece something together which would be worth hearing.

It was raining lightly today, and when I pulled into his parking lot I saw his bike sitting there, covered to protect it. I took two deep breaths and got out and walked in. His office had a reception desk, but no one sitting at it. There had been a ding, announcing the door had opened. I heard his voice from the back say he'd be right there. I stood tall and waited for his arrival, expecting a stormy reaction. I still had my beard, so he might at first not recognize me, my Cardinal hat still in place, my sunglasses not needed on this cloudy day.

From behind me I heard two doors slam. I turned and saw a black SUV with dark, tinted windows. Two men came through the entrance in dark suits, looking ominous. I stepped over to the side, as each appeared mildly agitated. One stayed with me while the other went into Flynn's office. I wasn't sure what to make of it, but I was prepared for the worst.

"Beat it," said the one still waiting with me. "We have business with the owner."

He was a large man, maybe three inches taller than I was, a lean, taunt build displaying under his tailored jacket. No doubt his mean expression scared most he'd encountered. I, though, was unfazed.

"Are you a Michael Jackson fan?" I asked, with a tone of sarcasm. "Wow, isn't Eddie Van Halen some guitarist. Man that solo was smoking hot."

He appeared confused by my question.

"Oh, you know the tune *Beat It* by Michael Jackson" I continued. "I'm assuming you were referring to his hit song."

"Are you a smart ass?"

"Now, I don't know that one. Can you hum a few bars?"

He opened his coat to show his gun. It was meant to frighten, but I didn't cower. I'd have done the same, but wasn't wearing it since I didn't foresee gun play in my future.

"Nice piece," I said. "Is it a Glock? You must be overcompensating. It seems like some heavy hardware to bring to talk with a CPA."

Out of the back office walked my brother and the other suit, looking a little pale, his clothes wrinkled and his brown short hair a mess. I could see by Flynn's expression after a few seconds he recognized me. I winked at him, hoping he'd get the hint and keep his mouth shut.

"Where are you taking him?" I asked.

"I told you to get rid of him," said suit number two.

"He is a smart ass and won't skedaddle," replied suit one.

"Wow, I haven't heard that expression in years! Is it like narrow ties and making a comeback?"

I saw Flynn briefly smile. He was used to my wit, but was holding back a belly laugh.

"This is none of your business," stated suit two. "Mr. Mann here has a meeting he needs to attend. If you continue to meddle, I'll have you arrested."

He pulled out his ID and showed me who he worked for. The fancy FBI logo announced all I needed to know. I had figured he was working for some government agency by their dress and the monster SUV they drove. Now I knew which one.

"He's not going anywhere without me," I replied. "I'm his lawyer and he needs representation to protect his rights."

Both of the suits looked at each other, uncertain how to react.

"You don't look like a lawyer," said suit one, referring to my jeans, t-shirt, ball cap and filling in facial hair.

"I wasn't here for a lawyer meeting. I was here to go to lunch with my friend. Do I need to go back home and change my clothes? Now, you either let me go with you or I start calling your bosses at the Bureau and tell them how you were violating this man's civil rights."

"Show us some ID?" demanded suit one.

"Darn boys, I believe I left it in my work clothes," I stated while patting myself down. "Now, either I tag along or Flynn stays with me and we go get our lunch."

The civil rights statement, my forcefulness, and the fact these two weren't all that bright, got them to agree that I could tag along. While in the back of the black beast, a couple of times I could tell Flynn wanted to say something, but I reminded him to remain silent. The FBI office was west of the Valley West Mall, situated in an ugly brown building with no architectural imagination, looking more like a parking garage than an office building. They breezed us through security with their official IDs and soon we were on the second floor in the office of another agent, the sign on his door saying Bart Wilson, Organized Crime Division. The room was as plain as the building, with old beige carpeting, white orange peel textured walls badly in need of new paint, a plain particle board desk and high back black leather chair, both straight from OfficeMax. It was nice to know the Feds weren't wasting money on office space and furniture.

Behind the desk sat Agent Wilson, his name plate on his desk my first clue. His black jacket; or was it dark blue, it was always hard for me to tell, hung on the back of his chair. His yellow tie was loose around his neck, the sleeves of his white shirt rolled up on this wet, humid day, the material straining at his large biceps. He had a buzz haircut, strong cheeks and large ears which curled out from the sides of his head. If he wasn't ex-military I would be surprised. He shot us both a hard stare when we sat down. The first words out of his mouth were eloquently put.

"Who the fuck are you?"

"All those years of education and this is the best you can come up with?" I replied. "I'm his council, here to protect his rights."

"I doubt that. I know everything here about Flynn, and his lawyer is some over-the-hill ambulance chaser who'd piss his pants if I breathed hard on him."

"I said council. I never said lawyer. Your boys must have misheard me. Knew he needed someone to advise him when dealing with your bureau breath."

I was lying about saying lawyer, because I knew I couldn't get away with it at the Bureau. The two geniuses that picked us up weren't smart enough to push me to confess the truth. But I knew I could get in hot water if I kept it up.

"So, mister council, what is your name?"

"You can call me Mr. Smith."

When in doubt always go with a classic surname.

He smiled, though it wasn't a pleasant one.

"Are you sure it's not Jones or maybe Johnson, something else common?"

"Could have chosen Wilson, but it was already taken," I said with a grin.

"We got your picture in security. Facial recognition should have a name for me shortly."

With my newly formed beard, I wasn't sure if he'd get an ID or not. But I wasn't worried. I was here to find out what Flynn had gotten into.

"Well, we can exchange pleasantries waiting, or we can get down to why the hell you dragged Mr. Mann down here today."

"We didn't drag. He came of his own choice."

"Didn't seem that way to me. The two goons in black didn't give him any option. So then, we are free to leave anytime we want?"

"Sure. Once he explains why he is reneging on our deal."

"And what deal would this be?" I asked.

"Being his council, shouldn't you know?"

"As I said, he asked for my guidance only a couple of days ago. I haven't gotten all the facts."

"Well, he is doing us a favor in exchange for bailing his financial ass out of a mess with the IRS."

"What favor would this be?"

"He can explain it to you later. But he called this morning and said he wanted out."

"I told you, my wife is threatening to divorce me," said Flynn. "I have no choice in the matter."

"You do have a choice," said Agent Wilson. "Either you continue the job at hand or the IRS will put a lien on everything you own, including your house, your business and all your personal property. This will affect the little lady whether she is divorcing you or not. This is your mess and I gave you an out. End it now and you'll be ruined. Your whole family will be out on the street carrying a little sign begging for handouts."

This didn't sound good and I needed to stall for time and learn more from Flynn.

"Flynn and I need to converse and get back to you," I said. "Can we have twenty-four to forty-eight hours to make a final decision?"

Wilson thought it over for a minute. His phone rang, and he listened intently, before hanging up. I assumed he was getting the answer on what recognition software discovered. Leaning back in his chair, he rubbed at his temples as if his head hurt. It was an effect both Flynn and I had on people. He didn't allude to what he'd found, though, when speaking.

"I can give you forty-eight hours. But if the answer is anything other than what we agreed to before, we foreclose and shut you down with a snap of my fingers. Is this clear?"

"Sure," I answered. "Can we get a ride back in your black tank? That baby is so comfortable, and probably gets five miles to the gallon. I love burning taxpayer's money."

"Take a cab and expense it. I'll await Flynn giving the answer I'm looking for. Now, leave before I decide to revoke your building privileges."

Once outside, I turned and looked at Flynn.

"Well, this is another fine mess you've gotten yourself into, Ollie!" I said in my best Laurel and Hardy impersonation.

Flynn shrugged his shoulders and punched me in the stomach, doubling me over. I guess he didn't think I was funny.

Chapter 9

After the punishment had been handed out, it was a day or two later when Flynn came into my room and closed the door. Fire burned in his eyes. It appeared to be contained, though not for long.

"What's the idea, asswipe?" he said bitterly. It was the name he often called me when he was mad. "You get in trouble at school and to take the heat off yourself, you go and rat me out to dad."

I looked him in the eye and shrugged. There was little I could say.

"What I do is none of your business. So, keep your nose out of it."

Being as I couldn't help myself, and smartass was part of my nature, I saluted him.

"Aye aye, captain!"

"Watch your back," Flynn said. "When I get you outside and away from the house, I'm going to beat you senseless. So then next time you'll think twice."

I shrugged once more, since it worked so well the first time. I didn't fear Flynn any, even though he was older and larger than I was, and would likely carry out his threat. Probably too dumb to be scared. I refused to be intimidated by him, which only got him madder, so he stormed out of the room. Since we were both grounded, it was a month or so later before he got his wish and got a couple of punches into my abdomen before leaving me on the ground gasping for air. It wasn't the senseless beating he'd promised, but seemed to satisfy his anger. Getting up, I walked the rest of the way to school, thankful the light breakfast I had eaten stayed in my stomach, contemplating who I'd punch in return. I liked to spread the pain around, and got into a fight outside during recess, which required another trip to school for dad, further putting me in the doghouse with him and the Dean of Students. The end of the school year did not end well for me.

The ride in the cab back to Flynn's office was quiet. His punch had been a good one, though not debilitating. I'd recovered quickly. CPAs don't punch people often, and I saw him flexing his hand. He had felt it as much as I had. He was no longer larger than I was. My growth spurt years earlier had put me an inch taller. These days, he was leaner than I was, but didn't look in shape, appearing gangly and in disarray. When we arrived, he paid the driver with his credit card and walked into his office, not waiting for me. I stepped in and went past the front desk and into his back office. It was a mess, with papers all over his desktop, filing cabinets partway open, empty food containers and used drink cans everywhere. There was a sofa in the room with a sheet, blanket and pillow draped on it. He had apparently slept here last night.

"No place like home?" I said.

Flynn gave me a look, as if to say "why are you here?"

"You always have to have a smart-ass comment, don't you," he said.

I tried not to shrug but couldn't help myself.

"Yeah, that was your normal response when we were kids. Why the hell don't you leave me alone?"

"Because you are obviously in trouble and I can help."

"You've already helped enough by going to Helen and telling her what I was doing. Nosing into my business again where it doesn't belong."

"Flynn, she called me concerned about what you were doing, asking me to check up on you. I followed at her request and, as usual, you had to have a little tail on the side, instead of being happy with what you have at home. I reported back to her what I discovered. You can hardly blame me for doing what your wife asked me to do."

"I'm sure you got a great big thrill out of taking me down. Well, you can kiss off, or I'll slug you again."

I glared at him intently with the hardest expression I could muster.

"Flynn, we aren't kids anymore. You were older and bigger than me then, but no more. I do this for a living and you plug numbers into a spreadsheet. If you want to duke it out with me, you will lose and lose badly. Tuck away your anger and tell me what the fuck is going on. You are into something more than just screwing some sweet filly on the side. The FBI has you doing their dirty work, and I doubt it's about doing the taxes for the Governor."

Flynn backed down and sat in his chair. He put his head into his hands, as if he needed to escape. I stood there for ten minutes and he said nothing. After twenty, I decided to leave but made one last statement.

"You want to talk, call me," I said while tossing my business card on his desk. "No one can do it all on their own. I'm offering to help because I have the skill set to get you out of whatever it is you're into. I'll hang around for a couple more days. If you need a place to stay I have an extra bed in my hotel room. I'm at the Drury Inn over on Mills Civic Parkway. Believe it or not, I'm your brother, and I do care about you."

With that, I left him to his misery and went to get some lunch.

Chapter 10

The Drury Inn had an exercise room and a pool, which I took full advantage of. Dressed in my workout clothes, I was running on the treadmill. I needed it badly after sitting in the car for several days. They also had a few small free weights, which I lifted to burn off some aggravation. I then changed into my swimming trunks and did several laps back and forth, going from the inside half to the outside half and back again. Sufficiently exhausted, I sat in the hot tub with an older couple and made small talk while my muscles soaked up the warm jets of water. I made it back to my room, collapsed on my bed, and slept until the 5:30 kickback meal began in the dining area.

Meal options tonight were chicken tenders, hot dogs, baked potatoes and macaroni and cheese. I chose the chicken and potato, had my free complimentary beer, sat down and read the USA Today paper provided. Glancing over the paper, my mind went over the day's events. There was little doubt Flynn was into something bad. The FBI was squeezing him for some reason, threatening to repo all he owned. *But why?* Was he in major financial trouble, which they were using against him? It was the type of trouble my brother would get into. And one of the reasons Mom and Dad wanted to give me money to start my business, because he would use it for some get-rich-quick scheme and blow it all. *And what of the affair?* Agent Wilson didn't mention it, but was it connected to what he was working on? Again, I wanted to run away and let him fend for himself. But it was Helen and Jolene who would pay, and I couldn't abandon them. I had to stick around. The question was what more could I do? Unless I convinced Flynn, he needed my help, which was unlikely, my hands were pretty well tied. Following him now would be harder because he would be watching for me.

When I finished my meal, I wanted to go take a walk around, but the rain had started again. I was certain there was a ball game on I could watch, but what good would that do me? I got in my car and headed to Helen's house. I called her cell to tell her I was coming by, but got no answer. Tried the house phone number; still nothing. Oh well, it wouldn't hurt any to drop in unannounced. I needed to pick her brain to learn more. And I'd like to say hi to Jolene if she was home.

They lived in one of the older West Des Moines neighborhoods off 8th and Grand Avenue. A decent size white house with fenced in yard, two stories and a basement. The garage was separate and on the back side of the oversized lot. When I drove up, I saw a large black SUV in the driveway which looked eerily familiar. I pulled up and around it towards the back. Lights were on in the house and I saw Helen's car parked outside the garage. Their dog roamed the back, apparently agitated by something, the yellow lab not happy to be left out in the rain. Recalling her name, I strolled over to the fence and let Molly sniff me, as she lapped at my hand happily. It had been a while, but she seemed to remember my scent. Like most labs, she loved the attention.

Remembering Helen always left the back-side door through the kitchen unlocked, I walked quietly in, crept across the tiled floor, and listened at the doorway. The conversation seemed one-sided. I heard the familiar voice of one of the two FBI agents who had dragged Flynn and I down to their bosses' office. I stepped in, got their attention, and waved my index finger.

"Now Helen, being your advisor," I said, "I've often told you not to talk with feds without representation."

She looked a bit puzzled and then seemed to understand what I was doing.

"Yes, I know," she replied. "They came unannounced and didn't give me much choice."

"Well Thing 1 and Thing 2 here and I have talked before. Apparently, they didn't get it through their heads earlier today."

Agent number two stood up, his face seething with anger. His partner grabbed his arm to hold him back.

"Or are you the Men in Black?" I said. "Though neither of you are as handsome as Will Smith. And are a step down on the scale from Tommy Lee Jones. I'm going to ask both of you nicely to leave. Without a warrant, you must go, or I will call the police."

Agent two pulled from of his partner's grip and walked towards me, his gawking glare meant to scare me to death. I didn't flinch as he walked past and out the door, his shoulder brushing up against me with a slight shove.

Agent one remained cool and smiled. "Remember what we told you, ma'am. You have thirty-six hours to decide. Thank you for your time."

Out the door he went, winking at me on the way.

"Oh my," said Helen. "You're my advisor."

I went over and sat on the couch. "I'm trying to remain under their radar. In time, they'll figure out who I am, but for now…"

"You met with them earlier. What for?"

"Flynn."

"What the hell has he gotten himself into?"

"I'm not certain yet. Tell me everything they said."

"Mostly they asked me to reconsider and take Flynn back. It is causing a distraction for something he is working on. They asked me nicely at first, but I said no."

"And their reaction to this was?"

"Well, they got threatening then. Said they would take away my house, my car, and freeze all our assets and throw us out on the street. Told me my daughter would be growing up in a back alley and selling herself for money to eat. It was unpleasant to hear."

"Nice to see our government protecting their citizens."

"Are they really FBI?"

"Yes. We took a drive to their office and met their boss. He was a charmer too. Made similar threats to Flynn."

"So, I ask again, what the hell has he gotten himself into?"

"He wouldn't tell me. He's a little perturbed I told you about his girlfriend."

"You told him?"

"He put two and two together once he saw me. Since we have history of this, it wasn't much of leap to make. Of course, he knows I do this for a living."

"Jarvis, I don't know what to do. I don't want to lose my home. Can they really do this?"

"Depending on the hole Flynn has gotten himself into, yes they could. At his office, Agent Wilson mentioned the IRS. And they pretty much can do whatever they want. Any idea if you have any outstanding tax debts?"

"Of course not. Flynn handles all of this. But it wouldn't be surprising after what I've seen is left in our bank account. Oh my, Jarvis, what should I do? I can't have him back in the house after knowing what he's been doing."

Helen was tough and strong, but this was bringing her to tears. I gave her a couple of minutes to pull it together, while I found some tissue to give her.

"Here is what I propose. For now, can you tell him you two can discuss how to go forward, but you won't let him back in the house. Suggest he come stay with me at the hotel while you work things out. Give him some hope of a solution so we can bide some time with the feds. Hopefully, he'll open up to me and I can learn what is going on. If he won't tell me, I can surely find out as I dig deeper. I'm good at sticking my nose into other people's business. That is the hallmark of a good private detective."

"I doubt I'll want him back and I can't have him living in this house."

"I understand this. You'll only agree to talk with him, for now. I can be there if you want. They gave him forty-eight hours to decide, or they foreclose and put liens on everything you own. And we can't have that. So, we need him back in their good graces until we know what we're up against."

"What if I got a lawyer working on this?"

"Not enough time. They would have you out on the street before they could act fast enough. It might be a month or more before they could do much. And their fees would be enormous."

"Okay. I'll do as you ask. Should I call him?"

"Yes. Only tell him you're willing to talk. If you want me there, then tell him this as well. I'll contact him tomorrow and offer again to put him up in my hotel."

In the front door walked a young lady I hardly recognized. She was much taller now, nearly as tall as her mother, with darker, long hair, in blue jeans with holes and a tank top exposing her navel. When she walked in she saw me, uncertain who I was, and then noticed her mother's messy tear-stained face.

"Mother, what is wrong?" said Jolene. "Is it more dad drama?"

"Yes, honey," Helen replied. "I was here talking with Jarvis, figuring out what to do."

Recognizing the name, she turned to me and walked over. I stood up smiling, knowing it had been seven years since I'd seen her. She was a little girl then but, now had grown into a young woman.

"I'll be damned, it is you," she said.

She stepped into me, giving me a big hug. I put my arms around and sighed. *Would wonders never cease? She remembered me.* At least someone in Iowa was happy to see me.

Chapter 11

We talked for a while, going back in time, reminiscing. It was nice to connect again. Helen seemed thrilled to have Jolene to converse with, beyond the "I'm a teenager and I don't want anything to do with you" shtick. It likely wouldn't last, but she was happy for the moment.

Going into the other room, Helen called Flynn, and let him know she was prepared to talk. She had made it clear it wasn't a reconciliation, but she was willing to listen. They would get together the next day for dinner. I was invited, but she didn't tell him this. My plan now was to find him again, for it was a new day, and convince him he needed help. If necessary, I would pop him a few times to rattle his brain.

I was back at his office and sitting inside, waiting. So far, in all the days I'd been here I'd seen not a single customer walk in. Not a good sign for someone running a business. Only those he didn't want to see had come to say hello. He stepped out of his back office and saw me, with the look of someone about to get their teeth pulled at the dentist. He smelled of someone who had been bathing in the restroom sink with lots of cologne and deodorant to cover the fact he hadn't showered in a couple of days, his dark hair slicked back from lack of cleaning. Living out of your office was the pits, and his face showed it.

"You won't give up, will you?" said Flynn.

"No. Let's go to lunch. I'm buying."

"I have too much work to do."

"Flynn, I've been on you since Monday and haven't seen one client. If there is work to do, it must be filling in crossword puzzles. Now, let's go to lunch, or do I have to drag you out of here?"

"Okay, where to?"

"Felix and Oscars. I feel like deep dish pizza."

Flynn cracked a weak smile but conceded. I drove us over to the last remaining Felix and Oscars in town, the original over by Merle Hay Mall. The place wasn't busy. We were a little early for lunch, so we grabbed a booth and both ordered a draft beer and a large Sicilian sausage and pepperoni pizza. There were TVs to watch, but I ignored them for now. I looked across, trying to gauge him. He was always a hard guy to read, his emotions normally well hidden. He seemed a tad uncomfortable about me watching him.

"What?" he said after about five minutes of silence and staring.

"I'm waiting for you to tell me what the fuck is going on with you," I said bluntly.

"I doubt you would understand. You being the perfect son and all."

"That is bullshit and you know it!"

"Mom and dad clearly thought so."

"Certainly not in my teen years. Dad had to bear down hard on me to straighten me out. If he hadn't, I'd probably be in jail right now."

"He didn't want you turning out like me."

"You weren't a thug and a thief like I was becoming. You just couldn't keep it in your pants. I don't think dad had a real problem with that. He might have even been a little envious of you being such a ladies' man."

"Possibly. But he still bankrolled your business and now you are a hotshot detective and media hero."

I laughed out loud.

"Oh yeah, some hero," I replied. "Let me tell you about my last year. I met two beautiful women, one who I still see today, only because of her ability to forgive me. The other hired me to find a stalker and then turned out to be manipulating the supposed stalkers to do what she wanted with her perverted sex games. Then proceeded to seduce me in hopes of getting me to kill those men. I ended up shooting her in the woman's bathroom at Dave and Busters to stop her, only to have her shoot me in the ass several months later, in the midst of trying to seduce me again. A seduction which nearly worked because of the Mann brother weakness."

I swallowed down half my beer and continued.

"Then I get hired by two clients, one whose son is caught in a sex tape, the other who wants her husband out of her life because he is cheating. This puts me in the middle of two homicides and two different businesses running illegal operations. This leads to a showdown where numerous people were shot dead, which I am credited with, even though I wasn't the one to shoot them all. I'm a hero to some here, yet I never felt like one. But I ran with it and have parlayed it to raise my rates and gain new business, making me profitable for the first time in my life. So, as you can see, I'm hardly the perfect son. I'm a fuck-up too. I just happen to be a lucky fuck-up, other than getting shot in the ass."

Flynn looked up over the beer he was nursing.

"Wow," said Flynn. "Sounds like a wild year."

"It has been. And through it all, I still have Melissa, though I'm barely holding on to her. It's slipping away and I should go back home and work on it. But I'm here with you for some silly reason, even though you don't want me around."

"You're right, I don't," he said. "You are the last person I want help from. But you could be the only one who will help. I can't bring myself ask you to do it."

"Why not?"

"Pride I suppose. I'm afraid it will prove what a fuck-up I am. I feel like I have to be able to get myself out of these jams without help. I shouldn't need my little brother to save me."

"Well, let's recap what I know. You are having an affair with a woman named Casey Gaines, who your wife of fifteen years now knows about and has thrown you out of your house. You are living out of your office, sleeping on a sofa and in dire need of a shower. You appear to be working for the FBI on some operation, which you are trying to get out of, but if you do they'll throw the IRS at you and take everything you own away. From what I can tell, you are broke with no clients. Your only hope is to have avoided this mess in the first place. But it's too late now and brother, if anyone needs saving, I'd say you qualify."

After my sermon I was expecting an "Amen" from the audience, but didn't get one. Flynn appeared lost and I wasn't sure I could save him. The pizza came, along with two more beers. We dug in and he swallowed down the pie so quickly it appeared as if he hadn't eaten in days. After two pieces he still hadn't said anything else.

"Damn, you are stubborn," I said. "Got that from mom. Man, I do miss them both."

"I do too," said Flynn. "Being a couple of idiots, I'm sure dad would knock our heads together, even now, if he was still with us."

"We're all we've got, Flynn. We may not be friends, but we are blood and could still be brothers. Give me the scoop on what you're into. I may not be able to save your marriage, but maybe I can save your life. You're in danger, but too proud to admit it."

I looked up and saw tears in his eyes, as he started to cry. It was the first time I could recall since we were young kids. Not a tear had been shed, even at our parents' funerals. I was right, he was in danger and didn't know what to do. The question was, could he be saved?

Chapter 12

Flynn got it back together as we finished lunch. We went back to his office to get his bike. I was still working on convincing him to come back to the hotel and stay with me until we could work the situation through. He didn't speak much and when we arrived, there were two men standing outside his office. They both had blonde hair, mustaches, and were wearing baggy gym shorts, tank tops and Chicago Cubs ball caps. They appeared to be twins and there was an air of familiarity about them.

Flynn had not noticed them until getting out of the car. He paused when he saw them and took a couple steps back, a nervous look on his face. I walked around the back side of the rental and moved in front of him, sensing danger.

"Where is our money?" said the first of the two twins. His tank top was navy blue.

Flynn froze, unable to speak.

"We are tired of waiting," said the second one, his top a bright yellow.

"Damn, if it weren't for the shirts I would think I was looking in a mirror," I said.

"Who the hell are you?" said blue shirt.

I could play the lawyer-advisor angle again, but I had tired of the disguise.

"Do you date the same woman?" I said with a snicker. "Cause I doubt they could tell you apart, unless one of your dicks is smaller."

The two looked at each other and then stared back my way with a sneer of delight.

"Now we remember," said yellow top. "You are Flynn's wiseass brother."

"Guilty as charged."

"I bet you don't remember who we are," said blue top.

"Sorry to say boys, I do remember. The James Brothers; but not the famous ones from the westerns."

It was my freshman year in high school and only my second week. I was wandering the halls between classes, stopping at my locker to switch out books. I was feeling pretty good about my new school, my learning temple for the next four years. There was a crush of bodies, but as I turned two older students, likely seniors were behind me. They were dressed the same; jeans, t-shirt, each with a different heavy metal band logo, and crew cut blonde hair. The first came up to me and patted me on the shoulder and grabbed my hand, shaking it.

"We are here to welcome you to high school," he said. "We are so happy to have you here with us."

I was surprised at the welcome.

"Gee, thanks," I said. "That is really nice of you."

"Welcome from me too," said the second.

While I was distracted by the first brother, the second, as he spoke, stepped in, slugging me in the stomach so hard I buckled over and down to my knees. I was still a heavy kid, so I had plenty of gut to hit. I gasped for air, the wind completely knocked out of me. They high fived each other and walked away laughing. No one around me said a thing or even helped me up. I was alone to gather myself together, scared now of what had happened and if it would happen again. My brother was a senior too, but I doubted he would help me any. I stood up and closed my locker, slowly getting to class, arriving a few minutes late, the teacher pointing this out to all as I walked into the room. It was one of those moments in time I'd never forget.

The James Brothers were a famous western outlaw duo. Frank and Jesse were legendary criminals who robbed and pillaged, becoming larger than life. The two before me had been nicknamed the same around school, I'd learned later, though their story would never become the stuff of Wikipedia entries. Bruce and Crispin James were good at picking on people, whether it be boys or girls, always working as a team. Rarely would they poke and prod someone they couldn't best if they chose to stand up to them. And if they did, they would cheat, with one brother sucker punching from behind while the other was engaged. Since they were identical twins, I had no idea which of the two had punched me that day. I did my best to keep my distance later on, but it was difficult because they, in time, would become friends with Flynn, in a manner of speaking. They liked being around him because he attracted females and most of the girls at school couldn't stand the James boys. It was their chance to get his hand-me-downs. But as I got older, when I encountered them, I often wished to get even, though I doubted they remembered what they had done that day, since they had likely done it to others as well. I was nobody, a heavy kid they could easily trick, with little chance I'd retaliate. Until today.

"We are famous enough," said yellow shirt. I still couldn't tell them apart.

"And tough enough to take you both out if we don't get our money," said blue shirt.

Looking them up and down, their six-foot frames appeared to be in reasonable shape, maybe a touch soft, but I doubted they could fight as well as I could. My profession had taught me skills they wouldn't know about.

"Crispin and Bruce, though I still can't say who is who, you need to walk away from this. Not sure what Flynn owes you, but he is working on getting it back as we speak. You need to give him more time. Isn't that right, Flynn?"

He nodded his head, still strangely quiet for him. I wonder how much money he owes them, and if there are any others?

"We aren't leaving until we get some cash or a piece of his hide," said blue shirt. "If he doesn't cough it up, then I guess we'll take a piece of yours too."

Blue shirt stepped forward, put his hand on my shoulder and pushed me. I could have stood firm, for the push was nothing I couldn't handle, but I rocked back, using the momentum to lunge forward and drive my fist into his stomach. The sound of his breathe forced out, filling the parking lot, the grunt seemingly changing the air pressure around us. He was down to the ground in a heap, in a fetal position. If he'd been sucking his thumb you'd have thought he was a huge baby on the ground.

"What the hell?" said yellow shirt, stunned by what he saw.

"Payback," I replied. "Would you care to try me?"

He looked down at his brother, trying to decide what to do. They had always worked as a pair, so not having his wingman handy gave him pause. He decided to lunge at me with a sloppy left hand, which I dodged with ease, twisting to the side, shoving him at the shoulder away from me. Still uncertain, he turned again and charged me, but I rolled to the side as he crashed into his car, where I kicked him in the butt when he made contact, and put a couple of shots in his kidneys he'd not soon forget. He was winded now, trying to gather himself, rubbing his rear cheek and back, stalling for time. I soon found out why, as his brother was on his feet about to clobber me from the rear. But I had anticipated this, turned and elbowed him in the side of the head with enough force his head was ringing now and he was down again. I turned back and yellow shirt was moving to attack but stopped, holding his hands up that he'd had enough.

"Okay you win," said yellow shirt.

I was sweating thoroughly, thanks to the humidity, but I felt good. Flynn still stood in silence, a shocked look on his face at what I'd done. I wasn't the tubby brother anymore who was easily pushed around. I backed away and motioned for yellow shirt to help his brother. I reached into my pocket and pulled out a hundred-dollar bill.

"I don't know what all Flynn owes you," I said. "And I don't know why. He will make good on his debt to you, but you must leave him alone. Bother him again and I'll kick your ass even harder the next time."

I took the hundred-dollar bill and tossed it to yellow shirt, who, trying to catch it, nearly let his brother fall back down again, since he could hardly stand.

"Drive away boys," I said. "We'll be in touch."

Off they went in their old beat-up Chevy. I had to smile, for I'd exorcised one of my past demons, one of the few moments on the trip so far, I could call successful.

Chapter 13

After my scuffle I still couldn't get Flynn to talk, but did get him to agree to at least move his stuff out of his office and stay with me at the hotel. Once there, he showered and took a nap. While he did this, I went downstairs to make a phone call. I needed to find a police resource locally and the only one I knew was a retired Polk County sheriff. With a little quick internet research, I tracked him down, still living in the suburb of Clive. He remembered me and said I could stop by.

Clive was a quiet town nestled between Windsor Heights, West Des Moines and Urbandale. Small in size, with only about 15,000 people, it was known for its outstanding Greenbelt Park and trail system, and its tough little police force, which he'd been a part of in his early law enforcement career. I found his house off Franklin and NW 86th. I knocked on the screen door and heard a call to come in. I saw him sitting in his easy chair, the TV on, watching a replay of sports on one of the many ESPN channels. Time had taken its toll on the seventy-plus-year-old man. The hair on his head was mostly gone, signs of sunspots and skin cancer covered his wrinkled face and arms. On the phone, he'd spoken softly and carefully, and I could see hearing aids in both ears, a wireless microphone to amplify sound around his neck. There was a walker next to his chair to help him get around. He was much thinner now than I remembered him, his thick legs, arms and chest now mere toothpicks in comparison. It was much like I remembered my parents during their final days. I walked over to Bryer Campbell and softly shook his hand, the grip barely there anymore. It was hard seeing him like this, the once strong man weakened by life. For he was the man who, at my father's insistence, had helped shape my late teen life, getting me on a better path.

"Jarvis, it's been a while," said Bryer.

"Yes, you were at Mom's funeral," I said. "I was glad you came."

"I was moving better then. Damn stroke last year knocked me down. Nurse comes in a few hours a day to check on me since my wife passed."

"I'm sorry to hear."

"I miss her nagging me. Now all I have is news and sports TV to get me through the endless hours. How are you doing these days? Are you still gumshoeing?"

"Yes I am. Still living in Denver and doing fairly well. I had an adventurous year."

"I believe I heard your name mentioned on the news. What does it feel like to be a famous local boy?"

"Better than what I was before you and dad straightened me out. I still get myself into messes, but at least it's for the right reason."

"I'm honored to have made a difference. As I told you years ago, very few make it out of the system successfully. The key is to stay out in the first place."

He started coughing hard. I saw an empty water bottle on the end table. I offered to get him more to drink and he directed me to the kitchen. Finding one in the fridge, I opened it and handed it to him. He slowly drank it down.

"I'm sure you didn't come to see an old man wither away. What can I help you with?"

"Well, my brother has gotten himself into a pickle. It involves the FBI and I'm wondering if you still have any local police contacts that I can turn to for assistance. Preferably someone on this side of town, either in West Des Moines, Clive or Urbandale."

"Well there is someone in the West Des Moines police who is a pain in the ass but could be helpful. His name is Sterling Frakes. He is a detective, working the homicide and violent crimes division last I heard. I'd be happy to call him and see if he is willing to meet. I'm sure if you buy him a drink or dinner he'll listen. He is a pain, as I mentioned, but it's what makes him good at his job. What are you hoping he can help with?"

"Not sure. Right now, I'm pretty much in the dark, as Flynn hasn't told me much. Hopefully, I'll know what to ask when we meet. I've found working by the seat of my pants is pretty much my style."

"I'll give him a buzz after you leave."

"I'd appreciate it. If you can give him my number and have him call me, that would be great."

"No problem. I miss being a sheriff and, at the same time, I don't. It was better than sitting watching TV all day."

We talked a while longer before I left of days gone by and how we first met. At the time, it had been a dark, chilling day for me. One

I'd thought of often and would never forget.

Dad was determined to straighten me out after a string of events, culminating with the vase incident. There were conversations with mom on what to do and how to do it. They were both at their wits end. They knew I was on a bad path which needed to stop or else I could be lost permanently. It was a couple of weeks before they came to a conclusion. With summer upon us and school over, he took me for a long drive, his silence all the way giving me no clue of what he planned to do. The thought of being left in the woods to fend for myself crossed my mind. After a while we came to the Polk County jail, which sat on the Northeast side of town near Saylorville. The building looked modern, built recently to handle the surge of inmates, spread across a large acreage of land, the interstate buffering it on the south, a storage lot and rock quarry to the north and railroad tracks to the west. This would be one of many visits I would make to the jail over the next month. This was where I first met Sheriff Bryer Campbell, an old friend of my father. I would see, smell and touch what the life of a criminal was like when incarcerated. In time, it would scare me like nothing else ever had.

When we arrived, he came out to meet us. Though in his late forties, he was strong, tall and handsome, carrying the uniform with a confidence. He shook hands with my father, showing a smile, then turned to me with a chilling look.

"So, this is Jarvis, the troublemaker," he said sternly. "Son, it's time to teach you the facts of life about where you are heading. You are going to come with me, but first turn around and put your hands behind your back."

I looked at my father uncertain what to do. He grabbed me and spun me around, Sheriff Campbell grabbing my hands and cuffing them. My face turned from shock to fear at lightning speed as he marched me towards the prison. My father got into his car and began driving away.

Oh my god, I thought. I'm going to jail!

Chapter 14

I was driving Flynn for his meeting with Helen, the air of tension filling the passenger side of the car. We were meeting at The Tavern, with my job to act as a referee if necessary. If I'd dressed in a black and white striped shirt while carrying a whistle and yellow flag, it would have been perfect. But I stayed with dark jeans and a black polo taken from my limited packings. I, of course, had to break the silence by giving my two cents whether he cared to hear it or not.

"Be patient with what she has to say," I said. "Listen and don't lose your temper. She has a right to be upset with you."

If there was a reaction, he kept it hidden under his stone face.

"The idea is to come up with a plan we can go back to Wilson with. We are trying to keep you, her and Jolene off the streets."

I don't think he heard a word of it, as he remained quiet. Once inside, he saw her sitting at a booth and walked over. I could tell he wanted to embrace her, but she remained seated and he slid onto the cushion across from her. I took a seat at the bar, trying not to stare, and ordered a sandwich and a beer. There was a baseball game on the TV, which I tried to watch, but it was the Chicago Cubs, not one of my favorite teams, even though for once they were pretty good after years of being a cellar-dweller. Since their triple A minor league team was based in Des Moines, they were the team which was normally broadcast locally, much to my chagrin. But I persevered through it, for my pain was miniscule compared to Flynn and Helen's.

As I sat trying to watch the game and not watch them, I felt someone take a seat next to me. I could smell her first, the hint of perfume providing the right fragrance to arouse the senses. She stood two to three inches shorter than I, on flat shoes, with smooth skin with makeup, short brown hair parted in the middle. She was slender with nice hips and modest chest, her dark blue slacks and blouse covered with a nice jacket. She turned and smiled at me, and I immediately recognized Roni Berry, looking older, as she should since it had been nearly twenty years since I'd seen her, but still appearing much as I remembered her. She gave me a warm embrace which I didn't shy away from, the pangs of how I felt when I first met her all those years ago, an attraction which was immediate then and now.

"Jarvis, so good to see you again," she said into my ear before pulling away.

"Roni. It has been a long time," I replied. "Wow, you look great."

"Thank you," Roni said with a slight blush. "So do you. You've filled out nicely since high school. Though I don't recall you having a beard."

"Trying it out to see how it goes," I said. "Gives me more of a scholarly appearance."

"Not sure if I like it or not. It is hiding the face I used to love looking at."

I smiled. "So, I'm guessing it's not a coincidence you are here."

"No, I came with Helen. I'm here to support her and entertain you. She didn't want you to get lonely sitting while they talked. And I jumped at the chance to see you again."

While exchanging smiles, the bartender came and took her order of a house salad and a vodka martini. I looked her up and down, seeing that time had been kind to her. Her body was much the same as I remembered, with maybe a little additional weight here and there. She had always been slender and the extra weight gave her more of a figure to admire. I pulled myself from the leering, trying to remember I was in a current relationship, even if it was a rocky one.

"So, tell me about yourself?" I asked. "You still are here in Des Moines. I've heard a little from Helen, but none of the gory details of what you've been doing since high school."

"Well, after graduating from Valley High, I went to Iowa State up in Ames and got my degree in graphic design and worked for several companies. I grew a little weary of this and went back and got a degree a few years back in culinary science, and now I'm a chef in my own restaurant. You'll have to stop in while in town. It is doing quite well."

"So, the owner will make something special for me?"

"Of course. Though you could come out to my house and I could cook something at home. It would be more intimate than at work. Give us a chance to talk more."

"Helen mentioned you were married?"

"Yes, but no more. A nice man when I married him, but became lazy and a jerk after our years together. I've been divorced for a few years now. Mostly married to my work."

"I'm sorry to hear this. Any children?"

"Thankfully no."

"As I remember, you came from a large family and wanted to have several children."

"It was part of my upbringing. My mother still bothers me about it. I did get pregnant twice with my ex, but miscarried both times. God, I believe, was warning me this was not the man. We stopped trying after that. It was for the best."

Her drink and salad arrived, as did my sandwich. We dug in and I checked over my shoulder at the booth with Flynn and Helen. So far, all seemed civil. From what I could tell, Helen was doing most of the talking. Not surprising, since she had the leverage and Flynn had little to defend himself with. He could only ask forgiveness, and was likely not going to get it.

"So, your turn," said Roni between bites. "I hear you are a private detective now and a famous one to boot. Saw them talking about you on the news."

"Hardly famous, mostly lucky," I said. "Can't deny it has helped my business. Though it was not the choice I would have wished for to invigorate my career."

"It must be exciting work."

"At times, though it can be quite boring too. Lots of sitting around watching and waiting. In my youth I'd have gone stir crazy, but time has taught me patience."

"As I recall from our conversations, you were on the other side of the law in your early teens."

"Still am at times. Being a PI means I don't have the same rules as the police. So, sometimes I'm still walking a fine line, though I hope I normally fall on the correct side, which didn't happen in my youth."

The bartender brought me another beer, and a martini for Roni. My meatball sandwich was quite good and I did a superb job of leaving the sauce on the plate. For some reason, I was worried about impressing the woman next to me and at the same time worried about what would happen in her company.

"So, have you been married?" asked Roni after the last bite of her salad.

"No. Never been even close."

"You still have the aversion to commitment?"

She was referring to the reason we broke up.

"Yes, I would say so, to some degree."

I wasn't sure why I said this as I was mostly in a committed relationship now with Melissa.

"Well, so am I, these days," said Roni. "When there is time to date, I keep it completely casual, and physical if the attraction is there."

"Wow, this is a change from the woman I knew. With her strong Christian values to wait until marriage."

"I was glad then I waited, but sad now I did. I believe I missed out on playing the field, so to speak. Really, my ex was hardly a good lover. I've discovered more about myself after the divorce, with men who believe in my satisfaction, as well as their own. Unlike my ex who only cared about his needs. I've learned I can still have those Christian values and be a sexually active woman. God invented sex to create life but in a way for us to enjoy, which I now do."

The tingle of desire ran though me with her words. Once or twice after high school I wondered what making love to her would have been like, discovering the passion underneath her calm, faithful exterior. The attraction was still there. Would I resist? Could I endure temptation?

"Are you currently involved with anyone?" asked Roni.

"No," I answered quickly, the lie coming out before thinking.

"Well, if you want to get together for dinner some time before you leave, we could reminisce, enjoy a little wine, and who knows…"

I wasn't sure why I didn't admit to being involved with someone. It was the good and bad in me having its usual internal struggle to see who would win. I was a hypocrite for criticizing Flynn's indiscretions when I, too, had a history of failing in this area.

"I will need to see what is going on with Flynn and Helen, so we'll see."

"The offer is on the table. Say the word and we can get together. I can cook my way into any man's heart."

She reached out and put her hand on my knee. I could feel myself caving when I heard a commotion from the booth behind us. I turned and could see Helen upset about something. I excused myself and walked over, trying to calm her.

"Easy now, Helen. What is going on?"

"It's Jolene," she said. "I don't know where she is."

"What do you mean?" I asked.

"I've been texting her since we got here and she hasn't answered me back."

"I thought she didn't communicate well with you?"

"She always answers her text messages from me. Maybe not happily, but she'll answer. She understands I want to know what she is doing."

"Maybe she is off with her boyfriend. You know, doing boyfriend-girlfriend things. Easy to lose track of time when… you know…" I figured it was best not to spell it out.

"That is what is troubling," Helen said. "I texted him as well, and she didn't show. They were supposed to meet up at the bowling alley on Grand and she never made it over. He has no idea where she is, and is worried too. It's not like her not to show up and she is pretty stuck on him right now."

This didn't sound good. Couldn't call the police, as she hadn't been missing for long. Roni came over and sat next to Helen, putting her arm around her.

"I'm sure she is okay," said Roni. "Nothing has happened to her. I can feel it."

"It's all his fault," stated Helen, while pointing at Flynn. "He told me of the mess he is in and it's spilling into our lives. If anything has happened to her, I'll never forgive you."

Helen was on the edge of hysterics and we needed to get her out of there. There wasn't much they could do but wait and stay positive, fighting a parent's worst fears of what could have happened. They were an uncle's as well.

Chapter 15

The four of us went back to their house and waited. Helen was crying. Roni sat next to her, consoling. Flynn was pacing and even went outside to smoke a couple of times. I racked my brains on what to do and couldn't come up with anything. I could drive around and look for her, but wouldn't know where to start. I decided to take the most logical path and drove to the bowling alley. I found her boyfriend, but he still hadn't heard from her. He would wait, for now, while I drove back again slowly, finding nothing. It was close to 10 p.m. when we heard a vehicle pull up outside. I was out the door to see who it was, finding the dark SUV I'd come to know too well. The doors opened, the two FBI agents exiting, one opening the back door. Jolene, looking none the worse for wear, stepped out.

Flynn was outside now, too, and made a run at the driver. I grabbed him to prevent trouble. He was not a happy man.

"What the fuck were you doing to her?" he yelled as I used all my strength to hold him. Flynn was extremely strong when worked into a frenzy.

"We were having a conversation about you," said agent one. "Making sure she understood what her daddy has been up to."

"You son-of-a-bitch," Flynn yelled again. "You had no right."

"And what are you going to do about it," said agent one. "Not a damn thing."

I turned around from holding Flynn. "Maybe I will."

"What will mister lawyer do, sue me?"

I smiled. "It crossed my mind."

"Be my guest."

He turned and I stuck my foot out and tripped him and he fell with a grunt into the fender of the SUV with his shoulder before righting himself. Straightening up, he faced me, resisting the urge to rub his shoulder. He was about to take a swing when his partner spoke.

"Don't do it, Fred," said agent two. "He is baiting you to make the first punch. You know Wilson won't be happy you got suckered into it."

Agent one, now known as Fred, bore down on me with his cold eyes. I didn't blink and was ready for him to strike. If he took a swing, then I was in my right to defend myself and I was more than up to the task. But he didn't make the move.

"Another time," he said.

He shrugged his shoulder, rubbing it. I had to smile.

"Name it and I'll be there."

Outside the door came Helen and she ran to hug Jolene.

"I'm fine, Mom," she said.

Helen saw the two men and mostly had the same reaction as Flynn.

"What did you do with her?" said Helen.

"Only talked and told her the situation. She has been enlightened."

"Don't you come near her again or I'll call the police. I don't care who you are. You have no right to bother her. Do I make myself clear?"

"Sure thing, Mrs. Mann. Flynn here knows what we want to hear. He has till tomorrow to give us his answer. Have a good evening."

They got in the SUV and pulled out. I took note of the license this time and quickly typed it in my phone. We all went back inside and sat in the living room. After Jolene called her boyfriend to say she was home safe, she began to tell us what happened.

"I was walking over to the bowling alley when this big SUV pulled up next to me on the side street. The two men inside got out, showed me their IDs, and then forced me into the backseat. I didn't want to go, Mom, but they were too strong for me. I was scared and wanted to call you, but they took my phone away. We drove around for quite a while and then stopped at this office building somewhere in West Des Moines. They took me inside and locked me in a room for a while. There was just a desk and chairs, and nothing else, other than a glass mirrored wall. I don't know how long I was in there before another man walked in and started talking to me, telling me things that dad was doing."

Flynn glanced around the room, a look of horror on his face. You could tell he wanted to say he was sorry, but somehow it wasn't enough.

"He started off by saying dad was in debt with several banks and to the government, the IRS. They were going to take everything we own, our money, our cars, and our home, and throw us out on the street. The only way this wasn't going to happen is if daddy continued to help them. If he didn't give them an answer by tomorrow, we would be living on the street with nothing but the clothes on our backs. It was a little scary to hear."

"Those bastards," said Helen. "Why would they tell her this?"

"To force Flynn," I said. "Like when they came to talk with you. They are giving him no choice in the matter by using you two as leverage."

"Look what you've done!" Helen yelled at Flynn. "What you've brought upon us! Did you blow all our money on that woman you're sleeping with?"

Flynn still couldn't speak. There was little he could say, no way to defend himself.

"I hate you for doing this to us," said Helen, who started to cry again.

Roni and Jolene did their best to comfort her. Jolene seemed shaken, but was holding up fairly well. It was a horrible ordeal to go through.

"Jolene, did they say anything else?" I asked.

"They mentioned dad's girlfriend, and that was about it. Mostly, they were trying to scare me, I think. They left me alone again for some time. The two goons walked back in and drove me home."

"How are you feeling about all of this?" I asked.

"It was frightening. I wasn't sure what was going on. Even though they had badges I wondered if they were going to hurt me. I tried to stay positive, but it was difficult. I never want to go through that again!"

"I'm so sorry, honey," said Flynn finally. "I never thought this would come down on you or your mom. I'll fix this, I promise. Jarvis and I will fix this. He'll help me. We'll make it right, no matter what it takes."

I wanted to say he needed to tell me what was going on before I could agree, but resisted. Having no idea what to do, I nodded 'yes' to helping. Whatever extreme measures were needed, I was willing.

It was getting late and everyone was tired. It was agreed Flynn would stay the night in the guest room. Since Helen had picked up Roni, it was up to me to drive her home. I was both happy to do so and worried. She lived over on the new side of West Des Moines, which had grown much larger over the years, stretching out onto what once was farm land. When we got to her apartment, we sat in the car and talked for a few minutes.

"Wow, that was hard to see and hear," said Roni. "Is this what it's like being a PI? Do you deal with this type of thing often?"

"Yes. Though I still don't completely know what I'm dealing with here. Flynn has not told me much. It's harder, though, since it's family involved. This will be a first for me."

"Yes, stressful, but now with family the magnitude increases. What will you do?"

"Help all I can. I'm good at this, so I can provide assistance once he tells me what the hell we're up against."

It got quiet and we sat and looked at each other. It was the awkward silence of that first time alone together, like on a first date. I remembered how it was with her all those years ago, wondering if I should kiss her or not. Even with age, the unknown between a male and female remained.

"I'll walk you to the door," I said.

Getting out, I opened the door for her and she put her arm in mine. She had a first-floor entrance. Standing outside, the tension between us was palpable.

"The offer for dinner is still good," she said. "I know you'll be busy, but if you need a break, call me. I would love to see you again before you leave."

I smiled, every urge to spring forward and take her in my arms coursing through me, but I held back.

"I'd ask you come in, but it's late," Roni said. "And I do need to work tomorrow. Besides, never on a first date, and who knows what will happen if I get you alone."

My heart skipped a beat and I wondered what I would do if she offered. She leaned over and kissed me softly on the lips, turned, and went into her apartment. The urge to follow continued, but I resisted. I wasn't sure if I'd be so lucky the next time. When I returned to the rental car and pulled out my phone, I immediately called Melissa. I got her voicemail, but hearing even a recorded voice of hers was comforting. I left a long rambling message before making it back to my hotel. Thankfully, I fell asleep thinking and dreaming of her and not of Roni; whatever temptation I'd felt was, for now, gone from my psyche.

Chapter 16

The next day, I went to pick up Flynn. Helen had agreed to allow him to get his car, so I could use it and return the rental, which we promptly did. He could ride his motorcycle while I drove his car. He, like me, was a Mustang fan, but drove a modern one, a 2010 model. His was bright red, sporting a 4.6 liter V8 with all the modern conveniences. It was nice, but not a stick shift, which I preferred. Flynn had never been a manual transmission fan.

Arrangements were made to meet with Agent Wilson at his office. We went through security, got our visitor badges, and soon were sitting in his office. Once there, it didn't take long for things to get heated.

"What is the idea of having your goons taking my daughter against her will last night?" said Flynn, now standing before his desk, pointing his finger.

Wilson grinned, as if to say "So what? I can do whatever the hell I want!"

"Before we go any further, you need to agree to leave my daughter and wife alone," stated Flynn. "Do this again and the deal is off."

"So, our deal is on again?" said Wilson.

"So long as you agree to stay away from them."

"Sure we can, not that you would have any say in the matter. I think we've made our point and can leave them be. Get us results and we'll leave you all alone."

Flynn sat down. "And Jarvis is now helping me with this, too."

"Ah yes, the brother. Took us a while, but we finally figured out who you were. The beard was throwing us off. Quite smart of you."

I smiled. Though it was not as if I'd planned it all along to foil them.

"You will cover his expenses and he'll help me through this," said Flynn. "His hotel room, food, and transportation costs."

"We can handle this, so long as he understands what we want. Results are all we care about. Is he going to fuck your pretty girlfriend, too?"

"You are an ass," said Flynn, shaking his head in disgust.

Wilson's grin was quite aggravating. I'd have knocked it off his face if given the chance. He was a desk jockey now, and likely not as tough as he once was. For now, I'd let it pass.

"Then we have a deal?" I said.

"Yes."

"You'll cover my cost of sticking around and helping?"

"Sure."

"I'll need some seed money to cover my current costs, plus some extra."

"How much?"

"Oh, let's say five hundred."

He thought it over for a minute.

"Okay, get with Jen down the hall. Show her your current receipts and I'll tell her to bump it by that amount. She'll get you a check."

"And no more harassment of his family."

"We won't come near them. So long as there is progress. Do I need to fill your brother in, Flynn?"

"No, I'll handle it."

"Good, then both of you can leave. I want a report from you in a few days. Or we'll have to track you down and have another chat. Close the door on the way out."

Once we took care of business with Jen – getting a fancy check, which pleased me – we drove to Flynn's bank to get the check cashed.

"So, are you finally going to tell me what is going on?" I asked, once finished at the bank.

"Yes. But at my office."

Once inside, I decided to look around.

"What are you looking for?" asked Flynn.

"Something to drink," I answered, but then motioned for him to follow along.

I checked in obvious places: on lights, on his phone, under desks and chairs, anywhere something extremely small could be easily hidden. I found three different listening devices, so small you would have never seen them unless you were looking. I showed him where they were and then wrote on a piece of paper what they were. He mouthed "Damn" after reading it.

"Let's go out and smoke," I said.

Once outside, we could talk without fear of them hearing us.

"How did you know?" asked Flynn.

"I didn't. It was a hunch. Could be how they figured out who I am. Probably need to check my hotel room. Wouldn't hurt to look under your car and bike too. Could have put trackers on. The FBI has some sophisticated electronics these days. Pick up a Wi-Fi or 4G signal and transmit it back to them. Anytime we talk around them, we'll need to be careful what we say. We should be okay to go back in and chat about what they have you working on. Nothing there will be news to them."

Back inside, he put the closed sign on the door on the minuscule chance a client would show up, and we sat in back. He grabbed a couple of bottles of water from his mini fridge and handed me one. He took his time, trying to figure out the best place to start. I didn't push him, but the beginning would be nice.

"I never meant to hurt Helen," Flynn started.

"No one ever does," I replied. "But you did. The question is why."

"Hell, you know me. I've always had the wandering eye. All through school, even when dating her. Then, of course, she gets pregnant and I'm stuck. I had to do the right thing and I did care for her. And don't get me wrong, the marriage has been good, and Jolene? I wouldn't trade her for the world. But I've always tired of the same woman. I crave variety. I made it through ten years, but once the sex life got boring I needed more."

"So, this Casey you are banging now wasn't the first?"

"No. There have been a couple others. One was my secretary at one time. Used to fuck on that couch there. But she grew tired of me, as well, and quit one day. Came to the realization it wasn't going to lead to anything. It was fun, but she wanted more, and I wasn't about to give it to her."

"How did you meet them?"

"The usual. Work functions, bars, online. Casey was at a bar. She was divorced and hot to trot. No strings, only good old-fashioned sex, however I wanted it."

"And how long have you been banging her?"

"A few months now. We get together three or four times a week."

"So, what does screwing her have to do with the FBI?"

"Her dad. He is a bigwig at a securities and exchange company. Feds have had surveillance on him for a while now. Had an eye on her as well, saw us together and identified me. They want me to use her to get inside his business to look at his books. Well, at his books the government doesn't see. He is keeping one for tax purposes and one where the real money is coming from."

"Where would that be?"

"From those whose money needs cleaning. They believe he is laundering cash for someone who is less than honest."

I was afraid to ask the question, for I suspected the answer.

"And who would this be?"

"They aren't certain. This is why they want me inside."

"Could be dangerous. People who launder money won't care for some CPA digging his nose in their business."

"I don't have any choice in the matter. They have my balls in a sling."

"The money you owe?"

"Yes. Several bad investments I lost my shirt on, which drained our bank account and leveraged our home mortgage. And now, I owe the IRS twenty thousand plus in back taxes. They'll erase the debt if I can provide them evidence."

"Flynn, these guys will kill you. Maybe even kill Helen and Jolene, if they discover what you're doing."

"I have no choice. You heard them; we are all out on the street if I don't do this."

"And when it's over?"

"Witness protection for all of us, if necessary. A clean slate, with enough money to live on."

"Helen will never agree to this."

"She has no choice and neither do I."

"So, she has no idea of this?"

"No."

I let out a couple swear words, so loud it likely popped the eardrums of those listening. Served them right, as this was the mess of all messes and getting out of it would require a miracle. Anything short of the hand of God wouldn't save us. *Hell, did I really think I'd live forever?*

Chapter 17

If I had any brains at all, I'd bail on this now. This was a no-win situation and living in witness protection was not on my bucket list. Walking away was the only option and yet, I couldn't do it. He was not likely leading his family to the promise land in this FBI scheme. No matter how much it worried me, even scared me, I had to see it through.

Deep down I knew there had to be more, especially after our confrontation with the James Brothers and their claim of him owing them money, but it was all Flynn would tell me for now. We went over it again and again, and each time he said it the same and wouldn't give me any more. We agreed he should go and see Casey tonight since it had been several days and she was anxious for his loving touch. I had a meeting with Detective Sterling Frakes this evening. So, we parted, him on his Harley, me in his Mustang.

I had not talked with Melissa for nearly a week, and needed to hear her voice. Text messages had come through, but were basic in nature, as if my mother was talking to me from beyond.

"Take Care."

"Hope you are doing well."

"I miss you."

My last voicemail and text encouraged her to call me, as I had something important to tell. She finally called me late afternoon, her day and work nearly ending.

"All of us are about to go out and celebrate," Melissa said, sounding rushed. "What is so important you need to talk?"

"Flynn."

"Did something happen?"

"Not yet, though likely soon..." I gave her a quick rundown on the events of the last couple of days, leaving out the Roni details.

"So, Flynn is seeing someone else and it led to all of this?"

"Well, the money troubles likely came second. The issues with women have been ongoing for some time."

There was a silent pause.

"I'm not sure I like hearing this after what happened last year."

"I know, and I'm sorry. I didn't think it would take more than a few days. Now, I'm likely going to be here for a while."

"How long?"

"I can't say for certain. But I feel I can't run away, for the sake of Helen and Jolene. If it was only Flynn I probably could. I have to see this through, hopefully to a viable conclusion."

"I'm busy now, but I should have a break coming soon where we could spend some time together. I hope you can come home by then."

"If there is a break, I'll fly home. If not, maybe you can come and visit me. I have a charming hotel room with two beds and a recliner to make love in."

"Going to Iowa in the humidity is not high on my must-do list."

"There is a nice pool and Jacuzzi on the first floor as well. Though they might frown on us making love in them. And there is a large mall down the street. What more could a woman dream of?"

There was a small laugh, though a cautionary one. I hadn't convinced her. After last year's fiasco, she had a fear of being near me on a potentially dangerous case.

"We'll see. If I get desperate, lonely and horny enough, I might show up for the sweet corn. Of course, there is always phone sex."

"My phone camera might distort my manhood proportions."

This time she laughed more enthusiastically.

"I've had enough close-ups to know its true size. Please take care."

"I will. I love you."

"I love you too."

And she was gone. Again, I wanted to fly home and see her. But business before pleasure.

My meeting with Sterling was going to be at the Fleming's Prime Steakhouse Wine and Bar, which was down the road from my hotel. It was on the same large expansion of land in front of Jordan Creek Mall. Walking in, I gasped at the niceness of the place. I was happy this would go onto my expense report for the prices would be out of sight. I was led to the table that Sterling had reserved, since the place was always packed. He stood up with a decent smile for a cop and shook my hand. He was in a nice three-piece brown suit and tie with freshly polished brown shoes. He was around fifty or so, with a full head of blonde hair parted in the middle, a pale face from too much time inside behind a desk, a trimmed mustache, and rectangular glasses on his nose. One couldn't argue with his taste in restaurants, but you had to wonder how he could afford this place on a cop's salary. Once I saw the prices on the menu, I gasped again.

"Wow. Do you eat here often?" I asked.

"Not on my pay scale," he answered. "I'm easy, but not cheap. Since you were paying…"

The waiter stood before us, dressed sharper than I was. I ordered Blue Moon Belgian White, while he ordered an expensive red wine I'd never heard of. He might wipe through my entire up-front money in one sitting.

"So, Bryer says you are looking for some information?" Sterling said.

"How long have you known Bryer?" I said. "He had nothing but good things to say about you."

"Many years now. I'm surprised he said that about me."

"Well, to be honest he said 'Pain in the ass' but very good at what you do."

"That sounds more like what he would say. He brought me through the ranks, teaching me a lot. He was a mentor."

"You worked in the sheriff's department?"

"For many years. He encouraged me to move on and shoot for being a detective. I've been on the West Des Moines force about twenty years now."

"I imagine not a lot of crime here."

"It's quite low. Maybe a murder every few years. Most of my caseload is rape, assaults and burglaries when there is a violent incident committed during the crime."

The waiter returned with our drinks and I wanted to ask him how he could afford to be dressed as he was on a waiter's salary. *Probably the restaurant provided their clothes, or maybe they were paid on commission.* Sterling tried the wine and was satisfied. No taste testing on the beer, but it was good. He had pre-ordered the prime rib. I wanted to ask to eat off his plate, but resisted, so I ordered petite filet mignon and baked potato. Petite didn't mean petite in price, though.

"Bryer tells me you are a PI out of Denver. What brings you to Iowa?"

"My brother. He has gotten himself into a bit of a situation with a local FBI agent. I was wondering if you may know him. Name is Bart Wilson."

"A little bit, mostly from hearsay. The FBI and the West Des Moines police don't cross paths much. I believe he was a marine before becoming a fed. He is a bit of an ass himself, and will do anything to close a case, even if it's against the rules and the law. Mostly true of anyone in the Bureau since 9/11."

"He has two muscle guys working for him, one named Fred. Do you know them?"

"No."

"Anything else you can tell me about Wilson?"

"Not really. Only that if you are on his bad side, watch out."

Dinner was brought out, and though the price was out of this world, the food was as well. The filet was as good as I'd ever had. I felt guilty dipping it in ketchup. This was about as gourmet as I ever got.

"If I give you a name, would you be able to give me info on her? I have some basic stuff, but need more detail. Name is Casey Gaines. I have her home address and know what she drives, and can give you her license plate. I know she is divorced, but uncertain if this is her maiden or married name."

"What else would you need?"

"I'd like to know who her father is. Ex-husband would be good. Anything else you can dig up. If not, no problem and I'll track it down myself. It would save me some time, though."

"Sure, text me the info. I'll see what I can give up. Tell me more about your connection to Bryer?"

"Well, it was a long time ago and I was a kid heading in the wrong direction. My dad and him were old friends and had gone to high school together. He helped me find a better direction than the life of crime and destruction I was leading at the time."

"And now you're a PI. A monumental shift from where you were. I checked into you some before agreeing to the meeting. Seems you were famous last year. Your ten minutes of fame."

"Believe me, it wasn't something I sought or planned on. Though the end results did help my clients, so I live with it."

"We would prefer not having a bloodbath here. Folks here won't stand for it."

"I understand. Sometimes shit happens. Just know, I'll protect those in my family I care for."

Sterling cut through his prime rib with ease, enjoying sips of wine in between bites.

"For Bryer, I'll help all I can, but keep me informed if all hell breaks loose. I'd like to know in advance when I'm going into the doghouse for helping someone I shouldn't."

"Absolutely. When it's about to go south, I'll call you for dinner. Only one request?"

"What would that be?"

"Let me choose the restaurant. I don't think my pocket book can handle another fifty-dollar prime rib dinner."

He smiled. "We'll see."

Bryer took me inside and ran through the whole routine with me. I was finger-printed, photographed, and even strip-searched, along with everything else which went with it. They found a prison outfit my size and soon I was dressed, with a new number assigned to me. With leg irons chained to the handcuffs, I was taken to a room for questioning. They sat me down on a metal chair, all my restraints now connected to a bolt on the floor. There was one other guy standing behind Bryer, who glared at me. I was scared beyond anything I'd ever encountered before. I had no idea what was coming next.

"We understand you've been committing some crimes," he stated.

I began to answer but he shushed me.

"Please don't speak until I address you to answer me back."

He pulled out his nightstick and began patting his legs with it.

"Stealing money from people is illegal. Stealing coats, hats and bikes is also. Over time, what you have stolen amounts to a felony. And felons end up here in our prison system. Someone your age will be quite popular. And not in a way you will enjoy."

His meaning was quite clear and unsettling.

"Jarvis, you have two choices here," he said in a booming voice which echoed in the room. "Continue to steal, to get into fights, to lie and cheat, and you will have a new home here with the other criminals. Or learn and understand the right way to act and live; respect others' property, their rights as citizens, so they can respect you. Be the person your parents want you to be, raised you to be. If not, you have a uniform with your number on it waiting for you, a small 8x10 cell you'll share with someone who'll make you his bitch any time he damn well pleases. And believe me, you won't like what

he'll want you to do, and the guards won't give a rat's ass when you're screaming for help when he sodomizes you."

He swung the nightstick downward and I thought he was going to hit my leg, my scream in fear filling the room, when he stopped short, then tapped me with it on the thigh. I wanted to leave and go home, ready to think long and hard about where my life had been heading, and what I was going to do to correct the course. When I finally walked out of there, I could barely stand on my wobbly legs, riding home in silence, with not one word heard from my father during the drive.

Chapter 18

I woke up the next morning in the hotel and Flynn hadn't made it back. Now that the cat was out of bag, he didn't need to get home and spend the night. I didn't see him at all over the next couple of days. I checked up on Helen and Jolene and got an occasional message from Flynn telling me things were in motion. On the third day away, he called.

"I'm in," he said. "I have a meeting with her father over drinks tonight. She has put in a good word for me and I think I've got a good shot. I'm coming in with an eye on his investments, looking to convince him I can run his operation on the accounting side. She says he is always looking for investors and good people to work with."

"Should I be there with you?"

"No, I will do this part alone. If I need backup, I'll let you know."

Didn't sound great, but I let him run with it. He did tell me when and where they were meeting so I could be available if necessary.

Detective Frakes got back to me about Casey. Mostly, he had nothing more than what April had dug up, other than she was divorced and the ex was killed in a car accident little more than a year ago. He was drunk at the time. Also, he was able to find out her father was Edward Wyche, since he was there when she identified the body. He had no arrest record and only a couple of traffic tickets. He lived out in Urbandale in an expensive home, for which Frakes provided the address.

I went to the first floor of my hotel and used their workstation computers to access the web. I put in Casey's name first and didn't come up with much. She did have a profile on Facebook, but there was no juicy information there, other than she was seeing a mystery man, to judge from some of the conversations. I looked up information on her ex-husband's death and found accident scene photos of what was left of his car and the final verdict on the cause. He and Casey had been divorced for a year with no children. Divorce records were sealed and I learned little else. I needed to learn more about her and her ex. He still had family in the area I planned to visit.

After this, I looked into the father, Edward, and found he ran a hedge fund worth tens of millions of dollars. It had not performed as well over the last few years, but still was pulling six percent earnings, which was pretty good in a flat market. He was divorced himself. His Facebook showed him hanging with a younger woman, about half his age. There were comments from her on his page and I found her name, Tina Bailey. Her page showed a wild drinking woman who loved to party with whoever wanted to party with her, whether it was her sugar daddy or younger men and women. I added much of this information into OneNote on my phone. I now had people to contact, talk to and follow.

I tracked down the younger brother of Casey's ex and he agreed to meet me at the Valley West Mall, where he worked at Foot Locker, which was on the lower level. When I got there, he was dressed in his black and white striped shirt with jeans, like all Foot Locker employees. He yelled to another employee that he was taking a break. We sat outside the store on one of the benches. He was a tall guy, about 6'3", quite skinny with long blonde hair, probably in his thirties. His name was Jeff Gaines and he seemed talkative when it came to his brother.

"Mentioned you were a private eye," he said. "That is so cool. I would love to have a job catching bad guys."

"Nothing like it in the world," I said.

"You carrying a piece now?"

"No, I left it behind. Figured I could risk it in here."

"Yeah, it's pretty boring in this mall. As you can see, half the space is empty. A lot of businesses come and go here."

"So, I'm mostly interested in your brother, specifically related to his ex-wife, Casey."

"Oh yes, the sweet-as-honey trust-fund woman. My brother was always the lucky one with chicks. And man, was she a looker!"

"How long were they married?"

"Not too long, maybe six years, if I recall right."

"Any kids?"

"Naw. He wanted them, but she didn't. Was afraid it would wreck her figure."

"Was this the reason they got divorced?"

"Not really. They fought a lot. She spent money like it was going out of style. Her dad's money paid for much of it, but still Taylor wanted to be the provider. He could never pull her away from daddy."

A security guard walked by and gave Jeff a high five. I smiled as he looked me over before moving on. *My dangerous face.*

"Do you know where the father got his money?"

"Some financial bank stuff, I think. I never cared about that shit. My bro didn't mind having the money, would have loved to spend it too, but her dad forbids her to spend any on him. Never seemed to like him much. As I recall, he paid for the wedding, but didn't attend."

"Did you ever meet her father?"

"No."

"What about the accident which killed him? Any thoughts on it?"

"Damn shame. I loved my bro and I cried like a baby when I heard. But yeah, I thought it was weird because he never drove drunk. Actually, I don't think I ever saw him drunk my whole life. I was the drinker. He'd have a beer with dinner and nothing else. Never anything hard. But hey, he was pretty depressed when she left him. Something like that can lead a man to drink."

"So, she left him?"

"Oh, yeah. Stupid me, I didn't mention that, did I? She had a new man in her life, some slick guy who threw around money like it was going out of style. Came home one day and said she was leaving him, out of the blue. With her dad's money and power, he didn't stand a chance, and it was over, just like that."

"Any idea who the guy was? Did you ever meet him?"

"Nada clue. Taylor said he was a high roller and a slick talker. Maybe he sold used cars. Well, I need to get back to work. And if you need any new sneakers, stop in and I'll get you a discount."

He put his hand out and I slapped it. Apparently, it was the seventies again, or had it simply come back into vogue? I sat there and thought over what I'd heard. It appeared Casey might be a bit of a gold digger, hopping from one man to another. The high roller didn't sound like Flynn, so who was it? I needed to crawl a little deeper into her past. I sat there a minute, looking at my shoes, then walked into the store to see what deal Jeff would give me.

Chapter 19

Sporting my new Nikes, I spent that afternoon digging deeper into Casey's past. She had been a member of Facebook for several years, so I paged down further through her profile, waiting for each section to refresh on the screen. I went back more than a year, writing down each name I found, both male and female. One looked promising: Samuel Rivera. They appeared to have been involved for many months after she left Taylor. There were some others, but no full names were listed. As I went through, I thought it was strange there was no mention of the car wreck and her ex's death. Even if you didn't like the guy, you still wouldn't be happy he died unexpectedly. Or did he? His brother did mention he'd never seen him drunk before.

With the help of the web and the good old yellow pages, I tracked down phone numbers and started making calls. Few wanted to talk to me in detail about Casey. A lot of "Yes, I know her, we hung out for a time, but I don't see her anymore" type of responses. An occasional "She was fun and had a pleasant personality" but not much more. I came at it from different angles – from an old friend, to trying to track her down for the lottery commission, looking to pay her for a winning ticket she'd purchased. When I got around to Samuel Rivera, I found he was a furniture mogul owning a chain of stores throughout the Midwest, his office based in downtown Des Moines. It was Sunday, but I called and someone was manning the phones. He wasn't there but would be in tomorrow, so I made an appointment. Fortunately, he had availability.

"And what would you like to meet with him about?" she asked.

"I have an investment opportunity. I run a chain of mattress stores in Wisconsin called Mann Mattresses. Hoping to combine our forces to increase profit."

"I put you down on his calendar for 10 a.m. tomorrow. Don't be late. He is a bit put off by people who are tardy for meetings."

Most of the rest of my calls didn't lead me anywhere fruitful, so I decided to show up at Flynn's drinks and dinner meeting, sitting in the background. I didn't want to sit alone at the bar, and wondered who to call. Those I knew, besides Flynn, consisted of Helen, Jolene, and the West Des Moines police officer, none of which were good people to bring, for obvious reasons. The only person left was Roni. I debated the merits of doing this. I convinced myself it was for the case and not for personal reasons. I often was good at lying to myself. I called her.

"I know its short notice, but are you available tonight?" I said.

"I can be for you," Roni answered.

"I need some cover for dinner. I'm keeping an eye on Flynn and don't want to be sitting alone in the restaurant, as it would look suspicious."

"Is that the only reason?"

"You'd be better company than a West Des Moines cop."

She laughed. "Sure. What time?"

"Eight. Does that give you enough notice?"

"Depends on how spectacular I need to dress."

"Business casual. It's all I packed and can afford. Can you meet me there in case I have to drive off in hot pursuit?" I gave her the name of the restaurant.

"I can probably pull myself together in that time. I'll see you there."

The restaurant was in Urbandale, and was called Irina's Restaurant and Bar. I'd never heard of it and looked it up, finding it served Russian and American Cuisine, with a vast selection of Russian drinks, namely vodka in various brands. I had called earlier to make reservations, just in case they were busy, which they were. Flynn was meeting Casey's father at 8:30, so I wanted to be there early. When I arrived, the place was busy and I waited at the bar while our table was readied. I ordered a Russian beer I'd never heard of and sipped it slowly. It was strong stuff and I needed to remain lucid. Roni walked in wearing a nice beige pantsuit, showing enough cleavage to leave you wanting more. Her hair, was slightly wavy, and her face bore modest proportions of makeup and lipstick. She had on black boots with tall heels. Her walk drew stares from most of the men she passed and several of the ladies. I tried not to drool, remaining cool, so as not to lead her on. She brushed up against me and took the stool adjacent to me. I calmed my breathing before saying hello.

"This is how you dress for business casual?" I said.

"I wanted to make sure you could find me among all the other beautiful women here."

"You are hard to miss…"

I'd seen her around school for some time now. Our eyes had met as we passed in the hall. There was a shyness on her face, but still a look of interest and attraction in her demeanor. It was early in our senior year, and Valley High School was putting on a dance. I was currently not seeing anyone, and went with a couple of friends. She was standing with two of her girlfriends, dressed in a conservative blue skirt and blouse, with flat shoes. Her hair was long and straight, parted in the middle, her skin a nice summer tan. Feeling daring in my sport jacket and slacks, I walked over.

"Hello," I said. "I'm Jarvis. Would you care to dance?"

She turned to her friends, and both nodded in approval.

"I'm Roni," she replied with high-wattage smile. "I'd love to!"

The DJ was playing some loud dance mixes of some popular bands during that time, the volume vibrating the gym floor. We walked out together and I did my best to shake it, though dancing certainly wasn't my forte. She, though, was quite good, and I watched her move to the music gracefully. I felt an instant pang in my heart, wanting to learn more about her. When the music ended, I leaned into her and whispered in her ear, so she could hear me.

"Do you want to get something to drink?"

"Sure."

I reached out my hand and she took it and we walked over, finding a bowl of punch that, fortunately, hadn't been spiked by someone. We took our drinks and walked out into the hallway outside the gym, so we could talk. There was a connection in the air drawing us together. We talked, learning more about each other. We danced some more and soon left together to begin a tender relationship I always looked back on fondly. We spent the school year getting to know one another, seeing each other whenever we could, never wanting our time together to end. But in time, there were others I was attracted to, and began seeing, limiting our time together. It would become a common theme in all my relationships going forward, much like Flynn.

There was little doubt she had made an impression on all in the room. Since I had limited wardrobe, I was in simple black slacks and gray polo. I'm sure all the men and most of the women wondered how someone dressed like her could be here to see me. But I was only here to keep an eye on Flynn. I kept telling myself this over and over.

They led us to our table and I chose the chair which gave me the best view. I did my best not to stare too much at Roni, my eyes scanning the room. She wanted red wine, so I ordered a glass for us both. They brought bread with the wine and I swallowed a couple of bites. She had been so easy to talk to on that first night so long ago, but here, sitting now, I wasn't sure what to talk about, for I was technically on the job.

"So, you keep scanning the room," asked Roni. "Not wanting to make eye contact with me. I'd be depressed if I wasn't such a confident woman these days. So, you truly are here keeping an eye on Flynn. Where is he?"

"Sorry, I didn't mean to be rude," I answered. "You do look wonderful, and all the other men in here would agree with me. Flynn just walked in and is sitting at the bar."

"Thank you. I'm glad you noticed. A woman always wants to make sure the effort is worth it."

"Most definitely. I'm glad you're here, but I want to make sure you understand this is simply a date of two old friends. And I'm mostly here to watch Flynn."

"So, is this related to his troubles?"

"Yes. It's the next step along the way. Best you not know all the details."

"Is there any danger?"

"None at the moment. I wouldn't have invited you if there was. I respect you too much."

"Too bad. A little danger can be exciting."

Our eyes met and I could see and feel a spark between us, much like at the high school dance. Being a long way from home and the one I loved made for danger. I pushed aside the feelings and we ordered our meals. She had the beef stroganoff and I the steak de-Burgo.

"So, have you ever eaten here before?" I asked.

"Yes. When one runs their own restaurant, you have to check out the competition. This place is highly thought of around town. They do have very good food."

"Definitely a step up from the places I frequent back home. If the food is not served in five minutes in Styrofoam containers or cut into ten slices, I often don't go there. Seems I'm on the run most of the time. All part of the life of a private detective."

"Do you like living in Denver?"

"Yes. It's a beautiful city and of course much larger than Des Moines."

"Do you miss Des Moines?"

"I've not lived here in many years, so not really. It is a beautiful place to live, other than the humidity. But Denver is my home now, and will always be."

"I've often thought of trying to leave Des Moines. If the right opportunity came up, I would. But it is home to me. Where my friends are. And I feel safe here. I'm sure the crime in Denver is much worse."

"Yes, it has its fair share of crime, like most big cities. But, in my line of work, that is a plus. The demand keeps me in new Dockers."

Roni was laughing when I noticed at the bar Flynn was approached by an older man in dark suit, with short blonde hair. They shook hands and he ordered him a drink. They were led to a table across the room. I could barely see them. The conversation seemed lively, with Flynn attempting to sell himself. He could be good at the seduction process, with men as well as women, but for different end results.

"You always could make me laugh," said Roni. "What about your social life? I sense my advances are being fended off because of someone you are seeing in Denver. Though when I asked before you said there wasn't."

"Yes, I'm sorry. There is someone."

"Exclusive?"

"Yes." I didn't say it with much vigor.

"I sense all is not well between you."

"It's complicated in many ways. I've wronged her in the past and have placed her in danger with my profession. There is tension and some distance between us. I'm fighting the unfaithful gene which runs in my family. It is a complicated process."

"Like your brother?"

"Yes. I'd like to think his is worse than mine, but I sometimes wonder. At least he was committed enough to marry, even though he strayed in time. I have never been with someone long enough to reach that point. With Melissa, I feel there is a chance at monogamy."

"We are creatures who never seem to be satisfied with what we have. My ex was like this as well. Even I was tempted, especially when our marriage was going south. But I didn't go searching for it. It is one reason why I stand committed to my business and only seek out companionship for my physical needs at this time. Hence, my forward nature with you."

"Though flattered and tempted, I must respectfully decline. I hope you understand. I enjoyed our time together when we were younger, and consider you a dear friend."

"But not one with benefits."

"I'm sorry to say no," I stated as convincingly as I could.

The conversation died down from there. Dinner was served and I kept one eye on Flynn. If he had seen me, he didn't let on in any way. He was all business, trying to sell himself to the man across from him. His mannerisms and gestures were over the top. I was concerned he was pushing too hard. And there was still much I was afraid I didn't know about where this was going. The unknown had a way of hiding around the corner until rearing up and biting you in the ass. You'd think I'd be used to this in my line of work by now.

"So, tell me about your restaurant?" I asked while cutting into my tender steak.

She began to describe the cuisine, her philosophy on cooking, and the dream she had for the business. It was Italian American, and aptly titled Roni's Italian Bistro. She enjoyed talking about it, a sense of pride in her words, the pressures and the thrills of running a business. The hardest part was finding the right people to work with, to run things when she wasn't there. She liked to work, but like most people needed a break to recharge. Word of mouth travelled the area and the business was holding its own, even making a small profit.

"Sounds as if it's going well," I said. "I'm glad you found your niche. You look at peace with your life."

"I am. I enjoy getting out of bed every day to go off to work doing what I love. Money is not an issue for me. I received a large cash settlement in the divorce. He had deep pockets in which to pay from. So, I can live comfortably without worrying about finances."

We talked on, taking our time to finish our meal. I was dragging things out, waiting for a sign Flynn was done. About an hour into the meal Edward and Flynn stood and said their goodbyes. Once he sat down, Flynn took the check and threw down his credit card, turned and smiled my way. Once he paid, he got up and went to the bar again. I excused myself and joined him.

"I knew you'd be here," he said. "Sometimes you are so predictable. When we were kids, I normally knew when you were following me."

"I wanted to try a restaurant I'd never been to before. If you'd met him at Burger King I wouldn't have come."

He laughed out loud, which was pretty rare for him, when it came to my humor.

"So, what is the verdict?" I asked.

"I'm in," he said excitedly. "Hired me right on the spot. I'm supposed to come to his office tomorrow and get started."

"That was easy."

"What can I say, I'm a charmer. And he loves his daughter. Her word was nearly good enough. He wanted to meet me to confirm."

"What will you be doing?"

"Don't know, but he said they could always use a good numbers man. I'll see once I get there."

"Anything else?"

"Yeah, I need about a grand for him to invest for me. I offered to sweeten the pot some. Wilson will have to float me the bills."

"I'm sure he'll love the request."

"No choice. He wants it bad enough, it's what it costs." He downed the rest of his drink in one gulp. "Man, I'm psyched!"

"Easy now. You have to still drive home on your bike."

"Naw I took a cab here. Casey will be by in a while to take me some place where we can celebrate properly. What about you and Roni? Are you going to do the horizontal mambo?"

"No, she is my cover for tonight. I didn't want to eat alone."

"Well bro, that is too bad. Because that was always one thing we had in common, putting it to the ladies. I'd hit the iron while it's hot."

I smiled but didn't comment.

"Well, she is here," Flynn stated after checking his phone. "Got to run."

He shook my hand and gave me a quick hug, which felt extremely strange, before running out the door. His confidence was disconcerting and I worried he was walking a path with blinders on.

Chapter 20

Flynn didn't make it back to the hotel room that night. I assumed he was off enjoying his dalliance with Casey, celebrating his good fortune. I had walked Roni out to her car and said goodnight. I got a long hug and kiss on the cheek and did my best to remain cool. Pulling away, I watched her get into her car and drive off, keeping control as the urge to drive after her gnawed at me. It made for a restless night. No amount of texting Melissa saved me this time. My dreams were of Roni, and of the sweaty kind.

With sleep escaping me, several things ran through my head as I searched for answers. Many items about the whole mess Flynn was in still eluded me. The questions persisted until I finally fell into a light sleep. I woke up as the light of the new day crept through the open curtains. I heard the sound of the digital click of the door lock as Flynn walked in, looking hung over, but smiling about his evening.

"You look like shit," I said.

He laughed. "But it was worth it. I need to shower and change. Can't be late for my first day."

He stripped down and walked into the bathroom, going straight into the shower. I stepped in hoping to get him to talk, sitting on the toilet seat.

"So, how was Casey," I asked.

"Insatiable. But so am I when I'm stoked."

"Did you go back to her place?"

"No, stayed at a hotel."

"Does she have something against you being at her apartment?"

"No. And how do you know she has an apartment."

"Remember, I'm a detective."

"Yeah, and a nosy one to boot. She has a roommate and feels she can express herself more freely if she is not in the next room."

I wondered if that was true. Something to look into.

"So, first day on the job. Do you have something to wear?"

"I have a jacket and tie. Good enough for them, as they are pretty casual. But I want to look decent for the first day."

"Where is the office?"

He told me the location, which I already knew.

"Don't be popping in, though," stated Flynn. "I don't need my little brother cramping my style."

"I wouldn't dream of it. Besides, I have other things on my agenda."

"Hopefully it's Roni. Since you were here, I assume you didn't take my advice, unless you beat me home."

"I don't kiss and tell."

He stuck his head out from behind the shower curtain.

"I knew you wouldn't share the gory details. No matter, as I know that is one trait we share in common. One woman is never enough for us."

I gave him a thumbs up. No need for him to know the truth. He could have been right, but I was trying to break the mold and walk a better path of fidelity.

"What about the money?" I asked. "Are you going to speak with Wilson?"

"No time today. I hoped you'd do it for me and report in like he told us too. Make it fifteen hundred, will you? I need a little extra."

Once he finished, I shaved off the beard since I no longer needed it, and showered. We had a carb-loaded breakfast, which Flynn ate quickly before he was off to his new job. I headed out, stopping by the FBI office before my appointment downtown with the furniture king. I had to wait downstairs for Agent Wilson to come down and meet me. We went outside and he wasn't real happy when I hit him up for the money.

"What are you trying to pull?" he said, the steam coming out of his ears.

"Flynn is in. Just like you wanted. But he needs fifteen hundred investment money to seal the deal. I'm only the messenger. I figured you understand this to be part of the plan."

"This isn't a blank check he can cash in however he pleases. If he is screwing me, it will only come down even harder."

"I think you and your thug twins have made this abundantly clear. I doubt he'll need much more once he is inside and you will get the info you need to bring them all down."

Wilson gritted his teeth, but conceded. I was out with the check and off to visit the bustling metropolis of downtown Des Moines.

It had been many years since I had been in this part of town, and the heart of it all hadn't really changed much. I found parking as close to the Ruan Center as I could find and then travelled the skyway bridges before entering the building. I found the offices of Rivera's Best Furnishings and waited patiently in the lobby for my appointment. Apparently, he was a busy man, as forty minutes after our appointment time I was finally sitting in his office, the decor mostly stainless steel and glass.

Samuel Rivera came around the shiny desk and shook my hand. He was maybe a little older than Flynn, shorter and a little thicker, but not on the heavy side. His jacket was hanging on the wall, the tie loose around his tanned neck, his thinning long hair reaching his collar, the strong smell of cologne filling the air.

"Sorry to make you wait," he said after sitting down. "Had some inventory issues with a store in Kansas City I had to deal with."

I smiled as if to say I understood, resisting the temptation of throwing back in his face what I'd been told on the phone about him hating people being late for appointments.

"So, I understand you are here to talk about a partnership or something along those lines. I don't believe I've ever heard of Mann Mattresses. Where are you located?"

"Wisconsin. We are small but looking to grow."

"Do you have a website?"

"No. We are more of a hands-on company."

"Why do you want to partner with us?"

"You are the top furniture company in the Midwest, but you don't have any saturation in Wisconsin. Could be a chance for you to move into the dairy state."

"I'm in Iowa, Missouri, Minnesota and eastern Nebraska. Why would I want to be in Wisconsin?"

"Why wouldn't you? The Badger State residents need furniture too. And you have the price and quality they desire."

He turned to his notebook computer and started typing. When finished, a frown came over his face. He picked up the phone and dialed someone. He spoke softly so I couldn't hear him. I knew the charade wouldn't last, but I always enjoyed playing a role until it played itself out.

"No sign of you listed anywhere on the web."

"Hard to find what isn't there."

"What is this about then?"

I pulled out a business card and slid it across his desk top.

"I'm interested in your relationship with Casey Gaines."

The door opened behind me and in walked a man who barely fit through the opening. If he had been dressed in white I would have thought he was the Michelin Man, for his arms and legs strained at his shirt and pants. I guessed he was not an attorney.

"This is my security man, Chad. He is here to make sure you walk out of here and never return."

"I take this to mean you don't care to discuss her?"

"No, I don't. Discussing her in the past has only brought me trouble."

"Hence, why you have Chad here?"

"Exactly."

"So, you won't tell me how you met?"

He shook his head firmly. "Now, please go quietly, as I would prefer to avoid force."

"You are certain he can remove me if required?"

"You appear confident in your skill, but Chad has a size advantage you won't be able to overcome."

I stood up, moving over about four feet from Chad. He was a very large man and did appear to be armed. If I wanted to press the situation I could probably handle him, since he likely would underestimate me, which was normal for larger men when they confronted me. The size difference gave them confidence I often could exploit. He had brawn and bulk, but did he have fighting skills? After careful consideration, I decided I wasn't itching for a fight and had learned something valuable by coming here.

"I'll go quietly," I said. "But understand that my business is to find answers and, by not simply answering my questions, you've given me reason to dig into this more deeply. Rest assured, in time, I will learn what you don't want me to know. I hope I've made myself clear."

"Please go," he said.

I walked to the door and patted Chad on the shoulder smiling. It was like petting a slightly animated granite statue. I'm glad I didn't test my theory I could handle him.

Chapter 21

The next day I saw Flynn only long enough for him to stop by, and get the check, then he was gone again. I decided to dig more deeply on two fronts. One, Casey and the statement about a roommate; two, Samuel Rivera's reluctance to speak about his relationship with Casey. Apparently, after speaking before, someone had paid him an unpleasant visit, and he now employed muscle to protect him.

Firstly, I decided to follow Casey around. Since I expected her to know Flynn's Mustang, I traded cars with Helen, driving her gray Ford Fusion. It was dull and boring and like most other cars on the road, so I knew I'd be lost among the throng.

I went up to Johnston early the next morning and parked outside, waiting to see if she emerged. I saw her Saab, so I knew she was home. Since she never took Flynn, there was little chance of him seeing me. I waited through the morning, listening to music and reading my USA Today paper the hotel provided. Close to lunchtime she made an appearance, dressed to workout, hopped into her car and drove off. I had an unobstructed view of her apartment, but saw no other sign of anyone there. I went to her front door and rang the bell several times, but no one answered. Checking the door, I found it locked, and I had no tools to enter and look around. I found the building office, catching the manager as she was about to leave for lunch. With a bigger than life smile, I convinced her to return to her desk to help me. She was in a dark pant suit which fit her well, time being kind to her fifty-something frame. She put on her reading glasses to size me up.

"You are looking for a resident of the complex?" she said gleefully.

"Yes, I was supposed to meet her and her roommate for lunch. But I'm afraid I must have written down the wrong apartment number. When I knocked, they said they didn't live there and didn't know her. I'm hoping you can help me. I don't want them to think I stood them up."

"What are their names?"

"Casey Gaines and Shirley. I don't know her last name, I'm sorry to say."

"Oh yes, Miss Gaines I know. But she doesn't have a roommate, or least she isn't supposed to. That would be a violation of her lease."

"Oh damn, I hope I didn't get her in trouble. Please don't mention it was me. I feel so stupid for writing down the wrong number."

"Well, she is in 5G. One of the upper level units. Let me point out where it is, then I must get going. I'm late for lunch with my husband."

She walked me outside and pointed me in the proper direction.

"Oh, thank you so much," I said while grabbing her hand with both of mine, cradling it softly. "Please go and join your husband. He is very lucky to have such a sweet woman in his life. I will find my way."

She pulled away while I walked over to the door again. I rang the bell a couple more times, but the manager was long gone. I walked back to the car and sat there thinking what I had learned. She had no roommate, but for some reason didn't want Flynn at her place. It meant something, only I wasn't sure what. But there was a reason and I needed to dig into it further. I drove off, got a sandwich, and returned, waiting for her to come home A couple hours later she was back, her skin straining at the spandex, though in an attractive way. She was maybe inside for an hour or so before coming out again, this time dressed for social time. I decided to follow her to see where it led me. We drove several miles into Des Moines, where she met some girl friends at a local bar. I followed her in and took a seat at the bar with a clear view of them at their table. They talked very animatedly. I decided to take a chance and asked the bartender to buy a round of drinks for their table on me, to see what reaction I got. Since Casey didn't know me and only briefly saw me in the dark the one night at her door, I doubted she would remember me, especially since I was now beard free, and certainly Flynn wouldn't have told her or shown a picture. Once the drinks arrived I was pointed out by the waitress and raised my glass at them. After a couple of words exchanged between them and a little laughter, they summoned me over. I walked over confidently like a man on a mission.

"Hello," said Casey when I reached the table. "Buying a drink for all of us is quite brave. Were you targeting anyone in particular?"

I grinned ear to ear.

"You are all lovely," I replied. "I figured my odds were good one of the three of you would be interested and I'd get a phone number. If I happen to hit pay dirt and get three, I'd be in heaven."

All three laughed out loud and I made sure I was eye balling all of them, but kept most of my attention on Casey.

"My name is Paul Smith, but my friends call me Smitty."

"Well, Smitty," stated Casey. "I'm Casey and this is Kayla and Jennifer. I don't think we've seen you in here before."

"I'm new in town. Getting the lay of the land. I saw this place and decided to stop in and get a drink. I saw you three and figured what the hell. Better than watching what they had on TV or shooting the breeze with the barkeep."

Casey was the looker of the group and seemed to be the alpha female. But the other two were nothing to sneeze at. Kayla was African American, dressed in silk blouse, dark jeans and heels, while Jennifer had short blonde hair, jeans and tank top barely containing her chest, with multi-colored sneakers which would make me cringe if I wasn't playing a role. Kayla and Jennifer both had wedding rings on their left hand, but that didn't seem to lower their flirt index any.

"What do you do, Smitty?" asked Kayla.

"Sales mostly. I've done it all: cars, men's and women's clothes, life insurance. Hell, even Amway. Anything to make a buck."

"And what are you doing now?" said Jennifer.

"Staring at three lovely ladies," I joked. "But I'm certain you mean work wise. I'm currently selling new and used cars. If you're looking, I can make you a great deal."

"Too bad you aren't selling women's clothing," said Casey. "I'd love to see what you had, try them on, model them and see what type of deal you could make me."

"Yes, it is too bad. It would be quite enjoyable getting you in and out of a dress. Maybe I should change professions and get back to you. If you'd let me call you."

Our eyes met and I could feel the heat between us. She didn't shy away at all.

"Of course, I wouldn't want to leave your friends out. The same offer goes for them as well."

"Thank you," said Jennifer. "It is tempting, but my significant other would frown upon me giving out my number."

"Perfectly understandable," I replied. "My loss."

"Oh pooh, Jennifer," said Kayla. "You are no fun. I have no qualms about calling you, Smitty. And damn, Casey you need to leave some for the rest of us. How many men do you need?"

"No need to argue. There is plenty of me to go around. How about I give you my number and if you have the urge to call me, feel free. At the worst, you'll get dinner out of me. At the best…"

I left the words hanging for them to interpret however they desired. I took a couple of paper coasters, got a pen from the bartender and wrote down my cell.

"This is my cell. It's an out of state number since I recently moved here. Feel free to call me any time." I reached out my hand and took each in mine one at a time. "Thank you, ladies. I will pay for your drinks. Have a pleasurable day."

After paying the tab, I walked to the door, turned, and waved back at them, their smiles of joy lighting up my soul. Always leave them wanting more. *Oh Jarvis, you still have it.*

Chapter 22

I put a call into Detective Frakes earlier in the day, hoping to get some info on the furniture man. He called me back on my way back to the hotel.

"Rivera is forty-nine years old, has homes in Des Moines, Kansas City, Omaha and St. Paul. Looks like he is married, with several children and likely some grandchildren, since his kids are older. The IRS has looked into his business several times for tax issues and he had to pay back money he owed. Other than a couple of parking tickets, he has no record."

"Anything about him filing a complaint on anyone harassing him," I asked.

"Give me a minute."

I could hear key strokes and mouse clicks over the speaker.

"Yeah, he did file a complaint a few months back, but then withdrew the charges. Claimed someone came to his office, pushed him around some, gave him a black eye and did some damage at his office. He pulled the complaint a few days later, saying it was a misunderstanding."

"Interesting."

"Anything I need to know?" Frakes asked.

"Not at this time. But if I gather other data which is important, I'll let you know."

"Sure you will," he replied and then hung up the line.

The data I had was growing, but nothing was forming a solid connection. I decided to go back to my hotel and call it a night. Before lying down, I took a shot at calling Melissa and, luckily got her, though for only a few minutes.

"I'm leaving class right now and heading home," she said. "Man, I'm beat and still I have more homework."

"I wanted to call and say I missed you. I don't like being out of touch for too long. I'm worried the distance is harming us."

"I know it's hard being apart. I've been so busy I doubt we'd see each other much anyway."

Her words didn't thrill me any. We tried to fill the airways with small talk, but neither had much to say, exhaustion clogging our brains.

"Well, as always, be careful. Keep an eye on Flynn and come home as soon as you can."

We said our "I love you" and the room was quiet again. The conversation wasn't a high point in our relationship. I struggled to sleep, but soon dozed off. All I remember after that was a dream from when I was younger.

The whole senior school year had been great. Roni and I had a terrific time when we were together. But I'd also had a terrific time with two other girls, one a senior too, the other a junior. Roni had put up with my choices and I never lied to her about them. As the end of year neared and Prom lay just around the corner, she wanted me to make a decision. She wanted me to herself. Prom could be a wonderful time together, the beginning of a committed relationship. I had been given an ultimatum.

"Jarvis, you are a wonderful person," she came out and said to me. "I have extreme feelings for you. You are someone I can see myself falling in love with. But you have to be on the same page as me. If we are to continue, you must go out with me and only me. If not, then it must end."

I felt cornered. And when I felt that way, it usually didn't end well.

"Roni, you are great," I replied. "But I'm not ready to settle down. I'm enjoying myself too much to limit me. Besides, with summer coming and college on the horizon, I have thoughts of moving on from here. And I doubt you'll want to leave Des Moines."

She stepped close to me as we stood outside in the warming sun.

"I would with you," Roni said. "Tell me I'm the one and I'll go off with you wherever the wind takes you."

I put my arms around her, hugging her as tightly as I ever had. She smelled great, was beautiful, warm and of a good heart. Yet somehow, at this time in life for me, it wasn't enough.

"I'm sorry," I said in her ear. "I do care for you. But I can't give you what you want right now. I hope you understand and I hope you'll still want to go out with me."

I knew the answer, as I could feel her body shaking, as she started to cry. She pulled away and started walking backwards, and I could see the tears in her eyes.

"Goodbye, Jarvis," is all she said, and I never saw her again,

until all these years later...

The next morning, I woke and saw it was already 9:30. I pulled myself out of bed when Helen called. She sounded a little panicked.

"What are you doing?" she said, out of breath.

"Dragging myself out of bed. What is wrong?"

"Can you come over to the house? I need to talk."

"Shouldn't you be at work?"

"I called in sick. Can you, please?"

"Are you in danger?"

"No. Please come over as soon as you can."

She hung up and I was up and moving as quickly as I could. After a shower and getting dressed, I grabbed donuts and juice from the dining area and made it to Helen's in about forty-five minutes. She and the dog, Molly, greeted me at the door. Helen looked tired and was still dressed in a robe. I scratched Molly's ears and then gave Helen a hug. We sat in the kitchen after she gave the yellow lab a bone to chew on.

"I did something stupid, Jarvis," she said after drinking some coffee. You could see her hands were shaking.

I kept quiet and let her continue. I hadn't a clue what could be so bad.

"Flynn called me yesterday afternoon. He was finishing up at his new job and wanted to see if I got the delivery. While I was on the phone, a man came to the door delivering flowers and a beautiful necklace. They were from Flynn. He wanted to come over after work and take me and Jolene out for a lovely dinner."

Now I knew where the extra money he wanted went.

"He took us out to a fancy steak dinner. Jolene didn't want to go, but I insisted, and in the end, she didn't have a bad time and actually smiled much of the evening. Flynn was his charming self, saying he was making progress and hoped soon all this craziness would be over. He hoped we could be a family again. And, over dinner, it was like we were."

I wasn't sure where this was headed.

"We got back home and he asked if he could stay the night. He needed some more work clothes and it was late, so I agreed. After Jolene went to bed we talked, and one thing lead to another, and he is so damn charming and sexy that we started making out and ended up in bed together."

I nodded my head. This wasn't a good thing for her emotionally.

"I woke up this morning and he was gone off to work. The whole experience was surreal. When he is with you, physically, he is completely involved in the moment, a master of what a woman needs. I know there have been others and there still is, but when he is with you there is no one else, if you understand what I mean. It is your pleasure as well as his. And I know today he is gone again and it's as if it never happened. I feel silly for being drawn down that emotional road again."

"I understand what you mean. He does commit to you, but only for a brief time and then it's over. It's a road I've travelled as well with some of the women in my life."

"I'm afraid I will never be totally free of him. I'm scared to go it alone, but know he will never be totally mine. Damn him, and damn me for not being strong enough."

Helen started to cry and I slid over in my chair and held her hand through the sobs. I never felt more helpless.

Chapter 23

I spent as much of the day with Helen as I could. We went for a walk with Molly, had lunch and talked when she felt like talking. When Jolene came home from school, I spoke to her and convinced her to spend the evening with her mom doing mother-daughter things. I didn't want to abandon her and I was certain Flynn would not be around again this evening, but I had to get away, at least for the night, with the promise I would return tomorrow if she needed to talk more.

On my way back to the hotel, my cell phone chirped with a vaguely familiar female voice on the other end.

"Do you know who this is?" she said.

"Possibly," I replied. "If I had one guess, I would say Kayla."

"You win the prize."

"Which would be?"

"You offered dinner and I'm game. If all works out well, the second offer you made might be worth exploring."

"Since I'm new in town where would you like to have dinner?"

"Do you know where Biaggi's Ristorante Italiano is?"

"No, but I can find it. I'm in West Des Moines right now and would need to go home and change."

"Can you make it by eight?"

"I believe I can swing it."

"Looking forward to it."

She called, but what was I going to do. I knew I wouldn't sleep with her, no matter how much I wanted to. The idea was to make her think that was a possibility, while getting other information out of her, preferably about Casey. I made it back to the hotel, showered again to wash away Helen's tears, got dressed as nice as my suitcase allowed, and headed to the restaurant, arriving right at eight. Kayla was sitting in the waiting area looking splendid with one-piece black dress, with a slit up her thigh, a gold chain around her waist, with black heels putting her and me at eye level. She had long curly hair which draped over her shoulders, with a lipstick smile and a slight rosy tint to her black skinned cheeks. I took her proffered hand and kissed it softly. She didn't flinch any, looping her arm through mine as we were led to our table. There was candle light to provide a romantic mood to the darkened space. I pulled out her chair as she sat and I took the seat next to her so we were cheek to cheek. I cautioned myself not to play it up too much. I didn't want to hurt her.

"I'm happy you called," I said.

"I almost didn't. Took me a while to get up the nerve to."

"Are you nervous?"

"A tad, yes."

"Maybe some wine would help."

"It wouldn't hurt."

The waiter took our drink orders, with two glasses of white Chardonnay delivered promptly.

"To our evening, and getting to know each other," I toasted.

She smiled while lightly tapping my wine glass. Her hand looked a little shaky as she took a long sip. Hopefully it would allow her to relax.

"Let's look over the menu and order something."

I grabbed the menu and slid a little closer, putting my hand on her shoulder. For an appetizer we decided on stuffed mushrooms, while she would have a salad and we would share Ravioli quattro formaggi. With the order placed, I put my full attention on her, my hand still on her shoulder, rubbing it softly.

"Are you feeling any better?" I asked.

"I'm still nervous."

She drank the rest of her wine and I poured her some more.

"I sense you've not done this before."

"What do you mean?"

"Meeting someone you barely know for a romantic dinner. You are obviously married, as you still have on your wedding ring. Pretty obviously a first for you."

"I couldn't get the damn thing off. It's been on so long it feels like it's welded to my finger."

"I wanted to make sure you were here for the right reason. Doing something you are comfortable with. No need to rush into something you will regret later."

She frowned.

"I know. It's why I almost didn't call you. I'm not sure how she does it. Maybe I'm not cut out for being unfaithful."

"Who are you referring to?"

"Casey. She can have two or three men on the hook at one time and it doesn't faze her. She is always telling Jennifer and me to find another man on the side."

"Is she married?"

"Not anymore. But even when she was she slept around."

"People who do it, do it for a reason."

"She likes men doting on her, spending money and making her feel special. And, of course, the hot sex. She brags to us about it in graphic detail all the time, telling us we are missing out."

"Should I expect a call from her, or is her dance card all filled up right now?"

"I believe she is seeing two other guys I'm aware of right now, some numbers guy and some athletic macho man who speaks French and Italian. She really gets off when he says dirty stuff to her in either language. I'm sure there are others and she could still call you. You seem her type. Good-looking and smooth talking. Someone who knows the right things to say to a woman."

I smiled at her kind words.

"Hard to believe she can find the time to balance all of this. Does she work?"

"No, she lives off her dad's money. A trust fund baby, so she doesn't need to. Gives her lots of time to play the field. She has a personal trainer to keep her in shape. Who knows, maybe she's bopping him too."

The stuffed mushrooms and salad were served, so we slowly ate while talking. I had learned what I wanted about Casey. Now it was time to turn my attention to other matters.

"Do you work?"

"No, I'm a stay at home mother."

"Any children?"

"I do. He is twelve years old." She pulled out a picture and showed me.

"He is very handsome. Where is he tonight?"

"Staying overnight at a friend's house."

"So, you could meet up with me."

"Yes." She seemed embarrassed by the answer.

"What about your husband?"

"He is working and won't be home until midnight."

"Are you here with me because he has been unfaithful in the

past?"
"No, he wouldn't do anything like that. I'm certain he loves me."
"And here you are?"
"I know it's silly. I guess I wanted to see if I could go through with it."
"No shame in not doing it. I'm fine with having dinner with a lovely woman. No reason for anything else to happen."
"Thank you. You are a desirable man and I really thought I wanted too, but…"
Dinner was delivered and we shared the plate, as I reveled in the compliment. She was quiet now, uncertain what to say. As we finished up I turned to her again.
"Can I give you a little advice?"
Smiling, she nodded her head.
"I'm sure this experience was a little nerve-racking but also exciting."
She blushed some, so I knew the answer.
"My suggestion is to take this excitement, go home, dress is some revealing outfit, put on some sexy perfume, and wait for him to walk in the door and seduce him right there in the living room."
"Oh my! What if he is too tired?"
"He is a man, he won't be. Will you do this for me?"
Again, a blush came across her face, followed by a smile and a whisper "yes".
"Then, when he wakes up in the morning, murmur a few choice dirty words in his ear and suggest he call in sick. Try a few out-of-the-ordinary techniques on him to spice it up some. Nothing like a day of making love to rekindle your passion for each other."
"What if I can't come up with any new techniques to try?"
"Grab a notebook computer and do a search together. Believe me, you'll find something which will peak your interest."
She was convinced and gave me a soft kiss on the cheek, her body flush with excitement. *Jarvis Mann, the Private Investigator of Love.* Maybe I should start my own radio talk show.

Chapter 24

When I got back to the hotel, I saw Flynn's bike, and him sitting next to it. When I walked over, he looked out of sorts and I suspected he was drunk. I helped him up and spotted a rising welt under his eye. Instead of being drunk, he had been beat up.

"What happened?" I asked.

"I got back here and some guy in a car came up behind me, gets out and punches me in the face. Before I could cover up he drove two more shots into my ribs. I hit the ground and tried to protect myself and he stopped."

I wondered if it was more people coming after him for money he had lost when investing.

"Did he say why? Was he wanting money like the James Brothers?"

"He told me to stop seeing Casey or next time it would be worse and he'd kill me."

This was his other weakness; women. I helped Flynn inside and we made it back to the room. He lay down gently and I gave him three Advil and a bag of ice to put on his eye. It didn't appear anything was broken and he wasn't spitting up any blood.

"Can you describe him?"

"I didn't get a good look at him, since I was cowering. But he had an accent. Sounded European."

"Likely one of Casey's other boyfriends."

"How would you know?"

"I'm a trained investigator and learned you aren't the only stud she's seeing."

"You've been following her?"

"No. Only getting some information about her."

I was lying, but he didn't need to know the whole truth since he wasn't sharing all with me either.

"I don't expect her to be exclusive."

"You knew she had others?"

"I suspected. I'm not with her every minute of the day and she is very vibrant."

"Is vibrant the same as horny?"

Flynn attempted to laugh, though it hurt for him to do so.

"She loves sex. Nothing wrong with that. So do I."

"Yes, I know. I talked with Helen."

Flynn pulled himself up, twisting slowly, his feet on the floor as he sat on the bed.

"Are you following me too?"

"No, Flynn, I'm not. She called me in distress. Telling me what happened. It really confuses her. She felt weak for giving in to you."

"Did she enjoy it?"

"Sounds as if she did. She says you are all into her when making love."

"Yes, and I want us to be together. For us to be a family again. But I must complete this task, so we can be in the clear from the financial mess we are in."

"You mean the one you put them in!"

He gave me a dirty glare.

"Are there others you owe money to besides the James Brothers?"

The dirty glare intensified.

"It's none of your business."

I was getting angry now too.

"Yes, it is. You've dragged me into this. I know you aren't telling me everything going on. It's time to come clean!"

"You know all you need to know. Nothing else matters other than getting the information needed so I can get my life back. Once that happens, everything else will be taken care of."

"You really believe so?"

"Yes."

"And last night with Helen, was this part of the plan too?"

"I needed to make her understand I'm still committed to her and care for her and Jolene. I did what I do best."

I let out a sigh.

"Wow, Flynn, that is really sad. You are saying seducing her is what you do best?"

"I didn't plan for it to happen. We had an enjoyable time and one thing lead to another. I'm sorry she took it wrong."

I looked in his eyes to see if he was sincere, but couldn't say for certain. When it came to women, he'd always had a good poker face.

"Agent Wilson will be thrilled too. With you spending money on necklaces, flowers and fancy dinners to seduce your wife."

"The cost of doing business with me. He understands."

"I doubt that, given his reaction when I asked for the money."

"I must keep Helen happy."

"But you aren't. If anything, you are making it worse. Flynn, you will never be the one-woman man she desires. If you would only commit yourself completely to her."

"I am committed to her, like I've never been with anyone else."

"But you won't sexually. You always seek out something more. You have to change for her or it won't work. She can't live on the rollercoaster ride you are putting her through."

Flynn grimaced in pain, as he clutched at his side.

"I've tried and I can't. You know what it's like. When have you completely given yourself to someone else?"

"With Melissa."

"Like hell. I've seen you with Roni."

"Nothing has happened between us."

"Not yet, but it will. It's only a matter of time."

"Yes, I'm tempted, and I fight the temptation. But I haven't crossed that line yet. And you have, especially being married to a good woman and with a child who strangely enough cares for her dad. You owe it to them to change and give up skirt-chasing."

He was mad and tried to stand, but hurt too much to do anything about it.

"I'm tired and need to sleep. Please turn out the lights."

He lay back down and ten minutes later I could hear him snoring. It must have been nice to be able to sleep so soundly in his skin. I wanted to strangle him and make him tell me everything. But I was tired too and tomorrow was another day.

Chapter 25

Flynn was moving slowly the next day and wasn't talking to me. But it didn't stop him from going into work, after a long shower and several Advil to ease his stiffness. I decided I would again follow Casey. She was my strongest lead; everything was trailing back to her. I was out in front of her apartment again in Helen's car, with ball cap and sunglasses so I wasn't easily recognized.

Her first stop was Merle Hay Mall, where she shopped at nearly every clothing store, including Victoria's Secret for some lingerie. She grabbed a quick bite at the food court, as did I, and met up with a tall, good-looking man. She gave him a long kiss and showed him what was in the bag, whispering in his ear something which brought a devilish smile. They got up and walked arm in arm, doing more shopping. He was about 6'4" and over two hundred firm pounds, with blacker-than-black hair, slacks and dress shirt. He looked younger than she did, maybe late twenties, and had a European look which told me he was her French and Italian speaking lover. And probably the one who had attacked Flynn.

They separated with a long hug and kiss, and I decided to follow him now. He headed back the way we had come and soon entered Younkers Department Store. It appeared he worked in the men's section in the causal business area. A bit surprising, as he didn't totally fit the type of man she seemed to normally go after. He likely didn't have lots of money, but still he was good-looking and, from what Kayla said, a hot one in the sack. I looked around for a while and then walked up to him. On his shirt, his name tag said Carlos.

"May I help you," he said in a deep voice with a hint of accent.

"Well, I'm in town and my stay has been longer than expected and I need to pick up some slacks and another polo or two. What do you recommend?"

He walked me over and showed me assorted styles. As he pointed out and grabbed shirts, I could see his hands were bruised. Unless he had punched someone else or a wall last night, this was likely the man. He seemed to know his clothing, pointing out the discounted prices, so I did buy a few things, paying cash.

"Must be a bear working retail," I said while he made change. "Hard on the social life, working until nine each day."

"It can be, but today I'm off at five. Going to meet my sweetheart."

"Since I'm new in town where do you recommend I go to meet some ladies? A good-looking guy like you must do pretty well for himself."

"Well, there are some good spots…" He went to list off several names, one of which was the place where I'd followed Casey when she met Kayla and Jennifer.

"I appreciate the tip."

He thanked me and I walked out of the store. Since I knew when he was leaving, I left, returning before five, following him to his car. It was a newer red Audi A3 convertible, which seemed out of his price range. He peeled out of the parking lot and I followed as best I could, his car roaring out west. He met up with Casey for dinner. Once done, they went to her place in Johnston and I had my answer of why she didn't bring Flynn there. This was her place for being with Carlos. Who knew, maybe he secretly lived there.

I put in a call to Detective Frakes, leaving him a message, hoping to get a name off of the plate. The glee in his voice when he called back was overwhelming.

"Carlos DePaolo. Lives in the center of Des Moines near Drake University." He rattled off the address. "Looks to be twenty-seven, with no record but a couple of speeding tickets, which haven't been paid yet. But something is bugging me about that last name. It seems I've heard it somewhere before."

"Can you dig a little more?" I asked. "It could be key to my case."

"Oh, well, if it's key then I'll get right on it, since I have nothing more to do right at this moment."

"Might be worth another prime rib dinner. Though I may have to sell a kidney to pay for it."

"I'll see what I can find. My shift is over, though, so it will have to be tomorrow."

Being impatient, I decided to punch in the last name on my phone browser and see what came up. It wasn't common, so there weren't ten million Bing results to sort through. The third one down was from eight years ago and might be something. DePaolo was the surname of one of Italy's main crime families. Reading through the news clipping, I learned the family had been shot down and killed in a power struggle. This included the father and mother, along with body guards and a couple of assistants. Arrests were made and the crime leader and associates who initiated the massacre where arrested, convicted and put to death. There were claims a son of the DePaolo family survived, as he was living in the US at the time going to college. No first name was given or where he was living.

It might not have been Carlos, but it was a wild coincidence if it wasn't him. If this was a clue, I wasn't sure where it led me. More pieces with no connecting parts. My puzzle was a mess.

Chapter 26

I was beat, tired and done with this whole predicament. Wanting to flee, but knowing I couldn't, I needed a break. Flynn had returned to the hotel, which wasn't a surprise since Casey was with Carlos. He said very little on the way in or out, only other than he was making progress. It was good to hear, but I doubted it, just as I was doubting the progress I was making.

The weather was warm and humid, so I put on my bathing suit, went for a swim, sat in the hot tub and then lay on one of the outdoor chaise loungers soaking up some sun near the pool. It was Friday and the hotel was quiet, but a new throng of weekend travelers would likely be coming in this evening. I was tired of the hotel life, living out of a suitcase, and wanted to go back home and see Melissa, if only for a day or two. I debated this, figuring I probably couldn't afford it, but physiologically I couldn't deny myself. If Melissa was free, I would escape, if only for a while. I called and texted her, but got no response. So, I resigned myself to enjoying the sun and resting the day away.

While lying there, I thought over all I had learned. I knew much, but didn't know anything. All the facts, but nothing connected. Most of it seemed tied to Casey. Flynn had met her, slept with her, and got the inside track to her father's business. The FBI was interested in the business implying it was a front for laundering money, though whose money was unclear. Flynn liked sex, which I already knew, as did Casey. Of course, most people like it, though it seemed those two were almost obsessed with it. Casey appeared to sleep around a lot, including with Carlos who had beaten up and threaten to kill Flynn. His apparent family history of violence was of major concern, given he was the surviving son of a murdered Italian crime family. And I had Helen and Jolene struggling to come to terms with Flynn's indiscretions and financial mismanagement. There was more clues and evidence, but my brain couldn't take any more. I jumped into the pool for a few more laps, lounged in the hot tub, and went up to take a nap.

Though certainly much less dramatic, dad drove me to meet with Sherriff Campbell at the jail several more times. Once, he gave me a taste of what one of the prison cells was like: small, cramped, and if you shared with someone, no privacy. No TV, no phone, no computer, no internet, and a lot of time to do nothing. If you were lucky, you might have a book or magazine to read.

Another time I got to see the activities outside when the inmates got some time in the fresh air. A little basketball, maybe a football to toss around; but mostly hanging out with a bunch of macho men trying to see who was the toughest of the bunch. There were pockets of them hanging together and occasionally a fight or two would break out, the various groups squaring off, before a guard would break it up, but only after some blood was shed. They never seemed to be in a rush to end the entertainment.

Then he took me to the weight room the guards got to use. It was small but had free-weights, a nautilus machine, a treadmill and a heavy and speed bag. Dad had told me to dress for a workout, so I did, in spandex and sweats. At first, I had no gist what to do. My idea of a workout was walking or riding a bike, or playing baseball. All good activities, but not done often enough to work off the excess fat.

"Kid, if you're going to end up inside," stated Campbell, "you need to get into shape or you won't last long in here. We need to turn some of your flab into muscle."

I was reluctant at first, uncertain of the benefits.

"I'm not sure what to do."

"Do as I do, as much as you can. In time, you'll look forward to it."

It would be the summer of my growth spurt, shooting up almost two inches. I was a little leaner, but not firm. He worked me to the bone, showing me the proper way to workout. I had to say he was right, this part I enjoyed the most, where I learned the importance of getting in shape. For a man pushing fifty, he was just that. I soon looked forward to coming there. We even started getting together to jog, running the open area around the jail. By the time the summer was over, I was leaner, fitter, and of the right mind. I had become a different person.

Several hours of sleep helped me to feel better, but didn't clear anything up. I called Helen to see if she and Jolene wanted to go to dinner. She was onboard, but Jolene had a date tonight. I would pick

Helen up at six and we'd go somewhere quiet to talk. On the drive over, Flynn called me on his cell phone.

"I think I've got it," he said excitedly. "I hacked in, and I think I found what I'm looking for."

"Where are you now?" I asked.

"I'm at my office."

"Don't say anything else and go outside."

I heard him walking out, the street noise coming through the speaker.

"Are you happy?"

"Remember, there are bugs in your office. You can't be blurting out statements willy nilly."

"Sure, sure. I forgot in my excitement. But I believe I found the financial records the feds are wanting. I was able to copy it onto a flash drive since I was on an unrestricted computer. I'm going to look it over now. I know I'm close."

"Take it straight away to Wilson. Let him go through it."

"I will. I want to make sure it's the goods."

"Let me come over and help you. You might need backup."

"I'm fine. You worry too much. I'll be in and out in no time, and be off to the FBI. Waiting for us will be a… dollar sign Smitty 723."

I was confused by the gibberish. I wondered if he'd been drinking or maybe he was losing it.

"Are you okay?" I asked. "I'm not sure what you mean by that last part."

"Never been better. I'm on top of the world. Remember what I said."

"Flynn, don't fool around with this. I mean it. You don't know what they will do if they find out. It won't be someone coming to beat you up for screwing their girlfriend. There will be no sweet talking your way out of this. They will kill you."

"Casey won't let it happen. I've got to run. My cell phone is dying. I'll call you tomorrow."

"Damn it," I said to myself.

I called Helen and told her I'd be late. I rushed over to Flynn's office. Friday traffic was a bear and a light rain was falling, so it took me twenty-five minutes to get there. When I arrived, the office was locked and no one was inside. I didn't see Flynn's bike, so I figured he'd headed to the FBI office, if he had half a brain. I couldn’t babysit him forever. I headed back to get Helen and enjoyed a quiet, uneventful dinner, never once mentioning my conversation with him to her, the tinge of worry nagging the back of my neck.

Chapter 27

Saturday and Sunday passed with no word from Flynn. I called his cell, but it always went to voicemail. A trip to his office showed nothing there. Helen hadn't heard from him and, when I followed Casey around, there was no sign of him there either. I wanted to grab her and ask where he was, but I resisted. I needed to remain calm.

The FBI office was open on the weekend, with a minimal staff, as crime never takes a day off, but Wilson was nowhere to be found and wasn't expected back until Monday. When I asked for a personal number to reach him, they only laughed and threatened to arrest me if I didn't leave. I called up Frakes to see if any John Does had shown up, either alive or dead, and he said no. I asked for him to put out a BOLO on Flynn's motorcycle and he said he would Monday if there was no word, since he needed to wait forty-eight hours. By Sunday evening, I had exhausted all avenues I could think of, so I called Melissa.

"What is wrong?" she said.

'Flynn appears to be missing."

"How long?"

"I haven't heard from him since Friday night."

"He's been out of touch this long before, hasn't he?"

"Yes, but normally he'd be with his girlfriend, Casey. I've been watching her and he has not shown up."

"What could have happened?"

"He said he'd found what he was looking for and was going to take it to the FBI. I don't know if he made it to them or not. I can't get hold of the agent we had been working with."

"Could they have him in hiding? Didn't you mention witness protection?"

"Yes, but then they should have gathered up Helen and Jolene as well, and they haven't."

"I'm sorry you are going through this. I wish there was something I could do. I imagine whispering sweet nothings won't help in this case."

"Thanks, but no. Is there such a thing as phone cuddling? I could use a good hug right about now."

"You've got my hugs across the airwaves. Please be safe and call when there is news. I should be available, as it's a light week at work and school."

I made it through Sunday night, getting some sleep, but uncertain what to do. Monday morning, I decided to retrace my steps. I went to the FBI office first and Wilson was there. He came downstairs again and led me outside.

"Have you heard from Flynn," I asked.

"He left me a message on Friday, but I wasn't here. Said he was coming in with something, but he never showed."

"So, no log of him by security. He'd have been on his bike. What about video of the parking lot?"

We went to security and they checked after 5 p.m. Friday and there was no sign of him.

"I'm sorry," said Wilson. "If he contacts me, I'll let you know."

I called Frakes and he'd put out the BOLO for the motorcycle and Flynn Sunday night. So far, nothing. He would keep me informed of any news.

I went to his office again. There was no sign of his bike and the front was locked. I checked with the building management to see if they had a master key and would let me in. When I explained the circumstance, and threatened to break the glass and enter myself, he agreed. As he opened the door, you could smell the foul air.

"Oh my, what is that?" he said.

"Don't go in, and call the police," I stated.

He ran back to his office and I used my elbow to open the door. I walked in, afraid of what I'd find. There was nothing in the front office, but in the back in his chair, was Flynn, dead. A trickle of blood flowed from the hole in his forehead. His face was bruised and several of his fingers tips had been cut off. I stepped back and slumped down to the floor, a wave of shock overwhelming me. I couldn't think and could barely breathe. My head slumped down. I couldn't look at the scene. I needed to get up and search for clues before the police arrived, but I couldn't move. The sight and smell nauseated me and the whole room around me faded into grayness.

I had been living in Denver for a few years now, enjoying the mile-high air, dry environment, and all the activities a big city life afforded me. I was finishing up college, getting the skill set I needed to work in the investigative field. I was employed at a private security firm doing guard work, which I didn't much care for, but it paid the bills. I was working when a call came in. It was Flynn, who I'd not heard from in some time, and he sounded excited.

"Jarvis, I have some great news," he said. "I'm getting married. You'll be getting an invite, so I hope you can come. It will be in a couple of months."

I was a little surprised to hear this.

"Who is the lucky lady?" I asked.

"Helen. I'm sure you remember her."

I did, as he had brought her to a Thanksgiving dinner at our parents' house the previous year. I'd been surprised, as he'd never brought anyone he was seeing to a family event before. This appeared to be a good sign at the time, and apparently it had been. She seemed quite nice, from the little interaction I had with her. And I didn't say this often about the girls he'd bedded. His choices left a lot to be desired.

"Well, I'm happy for you. I guess I need to start shopping for a gift."

"Damn right brother, and make it a good one!"

At the wedding he l so happy, as did she. I came to find out she was about five months pregnant at the time, but he seemed generally at peace with being with her. And, for one of the few times in my life, I was overjoyed with my brother's happiness. It was a wonderful time I would never forget.

Siren's disturbed the stillness. The past blurred into the distance. Bodies came and went, and voices spoke. I was moving, but it wasn't me, as my position changed. Something bitter shook my senses, and I came to life. I pushed away the horrible smell as my eyes opened. Two paramedics were checking me over and I sat up quickly, remembering.

"Oh God, no!" I yelled out, wishing I was unconscious again, remembering the happy times, and not the horror that stretched out before me.

Chapter 28

The next several days were spent in a fog. Conversations with police, FBI and annoyances from the press. The grief of telling Helen and Jolene, the horror on their faces when they learned, the process they had to go through to arrange a funeral and a burial. The moments moved slowly and quickly at the same time. I was there, and then I wasn't. I was helpful and then I was distant. Melissa flew out and was in my arms, the one moment I remembered clearly. She was in tears and I soon joined her, burying my face into her chest. There was sadness, grief and anger boiling deep down.

The funeral was peaceful, and respectful, with many people on hand. Familiar faces abounded, all of which spoke with kind thoughts, shook my hand and embraced me with sorrow. The Fishers, old friends I'd not seen since high school, neighbors past and present, co-workers; even former Sheriff Bryer Campbell showed, with the help of his nurse, to give his condolences. Roni was there to support Helen, but I barely noticed her with everything else going on. I tried to speak about Flynn at the funeral, but couldn't make it through. He was my big brother, my pain in the ass, who I hated and loved at the same time. There weren't words to describe our complicated relationship, though I tried and failed. I wanted to again sit down and lose myself as I had done when I'd found him.

A couple more days passed and Melissa and I flew home. I couldn't think while there, and needed to go away. I knew I needed to help Helen and Jolene, and in time would be fine, but I was of no use to them now. It was good to be home, sleeping in my own bed, making love to my girlfriend, though my heart wasn't completely in it and it was mostly to escape the void I felt. I wrestled with what to do and mostly sat and slept. Melissa stayed with me for as many days as she could, but had to get back to work after two weeks away. I thanked her for being there and prepared for a Monday to begin sleuthing again. Staring in the mirror, it seemed I had aged many years during this trying time, looking tired and not as stout and strong physically as I normally felt. I had to get on with life; find some normalcy. Being a detective was what I did.

I had flown back home to see my parents with a favor to ask. It was a big one, and something I didn't feel right doing over the phone. So, I was there at the house I grew up in, sleeping again in the bed I'd spent a great deal of time in, noticing the toll the years had taken on their health. They had sold the business, no longer able to handle the strain. Both moved slowly, a smoker's cough seemingly never ending. Their days in this world were becoming short. I worried for them, but knew they had no regrets in their lives.

"You look well dear," said mom when she first saw me.

I knew I couldn't say the same to her.

"Thanks, mom. I love living in Denver."

"Well, it seems to suit you."

We talked for some time about how my life was going. Mom wanted to know if I had someone special to share my time with, which I didn't. Dad was more interested in my career. I was working, but unhappy. It was time for me to take the next step, but I needed help. Dad was the money man, so as the evening cooled off, we went and sat outside to discuss what I'd come there for. The air was still thick, the bugs a flying, the fireflies lighting the darkening background. He was silent, waiting for me to speak, sensing a query coming.

"Dad, I want to start my own business. You know me. I need to be my own boss. Just like you and mom, run my own agency."

"Yes, that independent streak runs in your blood. What do you need?"

"To put it bluntly, upfront money. It takes time to build a clientele. I have a couple already, but it's hard to work security and gumshoe at the same time. To be as good as I need to be, I have to concentrate on it full-time."

"How much?"

I told him a rough amount. I'm not sure where I came up with it. I needed cash to carry me though, and it wasn't a small figure.

"Okay. It's yours."

"Wow, that was easy."

"I have faith in you, son."

"Thanks, dad. I know that wasn't always true."

"But it was. Even when you seemed lost, I knew you'd find yourself."

"Only with your help. And Bryer's as well. How did you know it

would work?"

He stopped to cough for several minutes, spitting out some ugly-looking grime that came from deep inside, into the grass.

"I didn't. Neither did Bryer. If that hadn't worked, we would have tried something else. I trusted that all would work out for the best, in the end."

"Thanks, dad. And thanks for all you did for me. I won't let you down."

"I know you won't."

When I got the cashier's check a couple days later, it was for twice the amount I asked for. And it was the last time I'd ever see him alive, for he passed away a couple months later, with mom to follow a few after that, neither of them getting to see the direction my life had gone in. Most of which would have made them proud; but some, not so much.

A potential client had an appointment and came to my office promptly at 10 a.m. I offered her a seat and a bottle of water, which she accepted. Mandy Bailey was in her twenties and dressed upscale, with satin blouse and skirt, big hoop earrings and rings on nearly all fingers, including a diamond the size of my left testicle. Her perfume was potent and alluring, her hair long, bleached blonde, and straight. She sat with her legs crossed, the skirt riding up her smooth stocking-covered thighs. Out of respect, I didn't leer too much.

"I would like to hire you to find who killed my husband," she said, straight and to the point.

"When did this happen?" I asked.

I had note paper and pen to jot down information, since my mind was still a bit jumbled.

"Two months ago. The police are stumped and haven't been able to crack the case. They believe it's random, but I don't. I want the killer found."

"Why don't you think it's random?"

"Because he was scared. He was a computer programmer, a software engineer who came across high-level theft going on, the stealing of personal and financial information. He feared someone would discover what he had learned, and take action."

"Did he share any of the evidence with you? Give you any clues to what he found?"

"No. I think he was afraid to tell me, for fear I would be hurt too."
"Any threats against you?"
"No."
"How did he die?"
"He was shot to death in his car at the parking lot where he works. Took his money and credit cards. Evidence pointed to it being random and only a robbery."
"Did he have much money on him?"
"No. Certainly not enough to kill him for."
"Did he put up a struggle?"
"They say he was beaten, so they believe so. But he was passive in nature, so I find it hard to fathom he would have fought back."
I thought over what options I had to solve this case. Being sixty days had passed made for a cold case. It would be difficult, but not impossible. My confidence had been shaken with all I had been through, but I knew I could help her if anyone could. Still, there was one roadblock, hurdle, and demon to exorcise. The clichés filled my head, but were all true. I still had an open case to solve, and this was back in Des Moines.
"I'd be happy to work on this for you and I'm certain I can help you. But it maybe a few weeks before I can get to it as I have another case I'm concentrating on."
She looked at me sadly.
"I'd be willing to pay more if necessary."
"No need to. I promise when this other case is completed I'll start right on yours and give it the full attention it deserves."
"You do come highly recommended. A Detective Mallard said if anyone could solve it, you were the one. Though he did caution me not to sleep with you."
I laughed, for the first time in a week.
"Yes, strictly business."
"Then you'll take the case?"
"As soon as I solve the current one."
"I will write you a check for the retainer we discussed over the phone. So, you are certain you can find who killed my husband?"
"Absolutely," I answered, with more confidence than I should have.
There was little doubt I would catch Flynn's killers as well. The only question is what I would do with them once I did.

Chapter 29

On the flight back to Des Moines, I had a companion. Hardly a friend, but someone to provide the protection I required. I had called Brandon Sparks and arranged a meeting at his office. He was a construction mogul, and likely a crook on the side, with more connections than a United States Senator. An odd bond had been formed between us and I needed a favor. Something I had done in the past with some regret.

"I need someone to protect two people while I work a case," I said to him. "They need to be formidable because I'm uncertain what I'm up against. Someone who won't wilt under any danger that may come our way."

"I still owe you from the Emily shooting," he said, sitting behind his desk in his expansive office. "You did not turn her in, as I requested. Where and for how long?"

Nothing noble about not turning her in, as I likely wouldn't be breathing anymore if I had.

"In Des Moines until the job is done. I need it open-ended. I'm uncertain for how long."

"I assume this in relation to your brother's murder."

He had been aware of his death and had even sent flowers to the funeral.

"Yes."

"I'm sure something can be arranged. When?"

"As soon as possible. I have a few things to coordinate, but would like to leave in a couple of days. They can join me on the flight if they are available."

"Costs?"

"I will pay for the plane ticket. They will be staying at my sister-in-law's house. Ground transportation and gas money will be provided. Meals will be covered."

"The man I have in mind is paid a healthy amount for his services. Who will cover them?"

"You can. I will be working on expenses for someone but that is all. I doubt they will pay his hourly rate."

"Yes, the FBI can be so stingy sometimes."

I was never surprised by what Brandon knew.

"One other thing, and I need your word on this: there will be no killing unless necessary. None of this 'he did it on his own and I have no control over it' bullshit. If someone comes to hurt them, they are in their right to do what needs done. No random killing. And he needs to follow my orders. I'm in charge."

"You make some things so complicated, Jarvis. We could send him in, kill them all, and be home in time for dinner."

"I don't know who 'all' is yet. I will in time, but for now his job is to protect Helen and Jolene at all costs. I want your word."

"You drive a hard bargain, Jarvis. I admire your convictions, though I wonder about your stubbornness to do everything the hard way. You have my word."

He stood up and poured two glasses of Jack Daniels, something he drank like iced tea.

"To a successful conclusion to the case of your dead brother. I'm betting on you to win."

And now, on the plane, I rode next to what may have been the most dangerous man I'd ever met, not as if this was apparent at the moment. Rocky sat quietly listening to his music, his head slightly bobbing to the beat while reading a novel on his Kindle. We had gone first class at Brandon's insistence, for Rocky was a big muscular man who needed the wider seats. His hair was still long and today he wore it in a ponytail. His arms bulged at his short sleeve shirt, his skin tanned as if he lived in the sun. He had a scar under his eye, the origin of which I'd not learned. I sat there thinking of our last adventure together, in which he'd killed several people to save me, my friends and loved one, from a fate worse than death. It hadn't been the plan and I had been mad how it all came down, but happy to have lived through the experience. Now, he was here again. I knew Helen and Jolene would be safe from whatever dangers might await them once I started poking at the hornets' nest. He was tough, resourceful, and deadly when needed. There was little doubt in my mind he would stand and defend them to the end.

Landing without incident, we gathered our luggage and took a cab to Helen's house. I had called her the day before, informing her I would be coming into town. I didn't give details, so as not to frighten her. She was home, still taking time off from the ordeal. We walked in the door Saturday afternoon and I went over to give her and Jolene a hug. Both looked as well as could be expected twenty or so days after learning of Flynn's death.

"This is my associate, Rocky," I said. "We need to sit down and talk."

When Molly saw Rocky, she gave a low growl. He knelt down and put out his fist for her to smell and the growl turned to panting. He scratched her ears and, when she rolled onto her back, he rubbed her belly. *Who would have known, a trained killer was a dog lover?*

We all walked into the living room. Helen and Jolene sat on the sofa, while I took the easy chair. Rocky stood and Molly followed him, her eyes fixed on her new best friend.

"I'm back to finish the job," I stated. "I'm going to find out who killed Flynn. This may put you two in danger. Rocky is here to protect you."

Both looked over at him and he gave them a reassuring smile. He was relaxed, yet the muscles in his arms bulged as if he was flexing. Even though I had a lean, muscular build, no matter how hard I tried my arms would never get that large, and paled in comparison.

"Nothing will happen to you, I promise," he said reassuringly.

"You look formidable," said Helen.

"Believe me, he is. But for him to do his job, there are rules you need to follow. At no point are either of you to go out alone without him. He will drive you to work and to school, where you will be safe. He will pick you up from there as well. Never leave there with anyone else. If you need to go shopping, he goes too. If you both need to go somewhere, either do it together or I will take you."

"This sounds serious," said Helen.

"It is. I will be out stirring things up and I can't have you in the line of fire. Nothing is going to deter me from finishing this. But you two would be leverage for me to stop. With Rocky watching you, there is nothing for me to worry about."

I could see the fear on their faces. It was important for them to understand the circumstances, the potential danger, so as not to take unnecessary risks.

"Jolene, this also means no dates with your boyfriend, for now," I said. "No matter how much you want to see him."

"After what happened to dad, his parents told him to stay away from me," she said sadly. "In the end he had to break up with me."

"I'm sorry."

Molly broke away from her new friend and came over to me. I too rubbed her ears, remembering another smaller dog that had been stabbed on a previous case.

"If Molly goes outside, someone should go with her as well just to be safe. I don't want anything to happen to her either."

"Why would they want to hurt her?" asked Jolene.

"To make a point and to scare you."

These words were doing a fair amount of this already.

"The packages you told me about arrived yesterday," said Helen, changing the subject. "They are in the kitchen."

Rocky went and carried both of them out. Opening them up, he pulled out our needed weapons. Rocky had two 9mm Glocks, a sawed-off shotgun, and a Bowie hunting knife, freshly sharpened. I had my Berretta 9mm, two Smith and Wesson .38s, and a leather sap. Also packed away were several boxes of ammunition and four burner flip phones I had already setup. I powered on each of them and handed one to everyone.

"This is the phone we will use to contact each other. I've programmed the numbers into each phone to identify who you are calling. Use them only to call one of us and no one else. They are small, compact, and easy to use. Don't go anywhere without them. Unlike your current phones, the batteries last several days, making it easy to forget to charge them."

"Oh my, it looks like you are going to war," stated Helen.

"Hopefully not. We are just being prepared for the worse. Any questions?"

"How long will this last?" asked Jolene.

I gave the only answer I could.

"Until it's finished.

Chapter 30

After getting settled, figuring out sleeping arrangements, and getting supplies on Sunday, I was off Monday morning with my first task. I had to eliminate one suspect before moving on. Jealousy could have been the reason for Flynn's death, so I had to go that route first. Since I had his address, I would go pay a visit with Carlos.

He lived in an apartment off of Cottage Grove Avenue, in the center of town, south of the Drake University Campus. Once there, I saw his car parked and walked up the stairs to the second floor and began pounding on his door. It took several minutes before he opened it up, sticking his nose across the chain. He was shirtless and in his underwear.

"What the hell do you want?" he said.

I stepped back and kicked the door in. The chain gives you a false sense of security, and it tore off easily, driving him back across the room. I closed the door and locked it, pulling out my 38, pointing it at him. He put his hands up in the air.

"Take whatever you want," Carlos said. "I don't have much money, but you can have it all. I even have a little pot if you want it."

A woman came out of the bedroom with a pillow covering her naked body. It wasn't Casey.

"Grab your clothes and leave," I said. "Don't doddle, and come out here and get dressed."

She did as told and stepped out nervously, dressing. I was kind by not staring at her naked body. When finished she grabbed her purse."

"Leave your cell phone. You can get it later."

She tossed it on the table and ran out the door.

"Sit, Carlos." I said. "We need to talk."

His eyes lit up while sitting.

"Don't I know you?"

"I bought slacks and a couple of polos from you a few weeks back at Younkers."

"Yeah, now I remember. Hey, I'd don't make them, I only sell them."

I chuckled. "No, but you did threaten to kill my brother."

His expression gave him away, but still he lied.

"No, man, it wasn't me."

"Yes, it was, because he was screwing one of your girlfriends, Casey Gaines."

He wasn't sure what to do.

"Now he is dead and you are my prime suspect."

"Now wait. I wasn't involved."

"Did you beat him up because of Casey?"

"Okay yes, I did. But I wouldn't kill him."

"You said you would if he didn't stop."

"Hey, it's something you say. You know, to scare someone."

"Oh, you mean like this?"

I stepped forward, pulled back the hammer on the gun and aimed.

"Holy shit. Are you going to kill me?"

"If you killed Flynn, I will. Now, convince me you didn't do it in the name of love or lust or whatever you have with Casey. Apparently, it's not exclusive, from the sight of the naked girl who left here a minute ago. Or maybe Casey asked you to kill Flynn."

"No way. I had nothing to do with his death."

"How long have you and Casey been together?"

"Off and on a year or two."

"Do you know my brother is the second person to be killed who was involved with her?"

He looked away, as if to say yes.

"Both murdered during the time you were seeing her."

"Hell no! Her ex-husband was in a car accident, and drunk at the time."

"Interesting you know the details about it."

He paused and stammered his response.

"Sure, I mean, you know, Casey told me."

"You are lying about both of them and it's time for you to die."

I grabbed a pillow and pushed him down on the sofa, the gun pressed against his skull. He was yelling, but no one could hear him. He wasn't struggling any, only shaking in fear. I pulled the corner of the pillow up so he could talk.

"It was an accident and I didn't mean to. Please don't kill me!"

"Are you ready to talk?"

"Yes, yes!"

I pulled away from him. He was shaking and I walked over

finding an open bottle of Kentucky Bourbon. I poured a glass and handed it to him. He drank it all down. While I had been pouring, I pulled out my phone and, with a few taps and swipes, opened an app and held it in my other hand.

"Take your time," I said. "Give me the details of how you killed Flynn."

He looked at me. "No, it wasn't Flynn I killed; it was Taylor Gaines, Casey's ex-husband. I went to see him because he wouldn't leave her alone. I wanted to punch his lights out, like I did your brother, but he got away from me and jumped in his car. I chased him; we both were speeding and I clipped his bumper and he spun out, hitting a light pole. I panicked and left the scene."

"And how was it they determined he was drunk?"

"Casey helped me. Her father is powerful and used his influence to get the toxicology tests changed."

"Her father, the bank president?"

"No, her stepfather. Her parents are divorced and her mother remarried. He is some type of big shot."

"And Flynn?"

"I don't know anything about it. Yeah, I roughed him up some because I found out he was fucking Casey. But that is all."

"Get dressed," I said. "You have a story to tell the police."

"No way. I can't do it."

"You have no choice." I showed him the phone, hit stop, and played back part of what I recorded. Worry filled his face.

"I can pay you money."

"Nope."

I found his apartment phone and called Detective Frakes.

"Are you still in town?" he said.

"Yes. I'm cleaning up old business. I have a break in the death of Taylor Gaines," I said to him. "I have a confession; he wasn't drunk and it was a hit and run. I'm sitting with the person right now. You want to send someone to get him?"

"Give me the address and I'll be right over."

I did and then hung up the phone.

"Come on, I have lots of money I inherited from my parents."

"I know. I've read the story of how they died. I'm sorry."

"Ten grand and you erase the recording."

"It's not enough. Tell me a little more about your relationship with Casey, or I might beat on you some for resisting arrest."

Out of my back pocket I pulled out the leather sap and snapped it against his kitchen counter, making a dent in the laminate surface. The thump startled him.

"Crap! You can't use that on me!"

"Sure I can."

I started walking towards him, waving the sap. The sight of it had Carlos quivering more than ever.

"I don't want to hurt you, but I will," I said forcefully. "Do the right thing, for it may assist me in finding my brother's killer."

"Okay stop! I'll talk."

"Smart. Give me the lowdown on you and Casey. And don't leave anything out."

"If I do, then you'll erase the recording?"

"No, but I'll erase the part about her stepfather getting the evidence changed. It might be enough to save your life. If he is as powerful as you say he is, he'll learn you blabbed and won't be happy."

"Shit."

He did tell me all he could before Frakes arrived with some uniforms. And I lied about erasing the stepfather confession, which didn't please him any. Of course, I could have cared less as they dragged him off in cuffs while I gave my statement.

Chapter 31

Now, I was standing at the FBI office parking lot, waiting for Agent Wilson to leave for the day. The weather was warm and humid, so I loitered around outside, watching for him to walk out. I studied the area, so I knew where every camera in the parking lot was. He strolled out, so I pulled in behind with stealth and put my snub-nose revolver in his ribs as he reached the car door. I was tight against him, so the video couldn't easily tell who I was or what I was doing.

"Don't say anything," I said to him. "Your gun on the right hip, please pull it out slowly with two fingers and hand it to me."

He did as he was told and I pocketed it.

"Give me your car keys and cell phone, and climb back behind the wheel and wait."

I used the remote to make sure the doors were unlocked, climbed into the backseat and tossed him the keys while pocketing his Blackberry.

"Do anything stupid and I'll shoot you. We are going for a drive to farm country, so we can discuss some things privately."

"You are making a mistake," Wilson stated.

"I said to be quiet. Jump on I80 and head west until I tell you what exit to take."

He did as he was told, always watching me in the rear-view mirror. We drove a little while before having him exit. Off the ramp, we took a couple of back dirt roads and I told him to stop. He gave me the keys again. I stepped out, and he soon followed. I holstered my gun and punched him as hard as I could in the gut. He bent over and went to his knees. I stepped away, feeling a little less angry.

"That was for getting my brother killed," I stated. "Now we can talk."

Wilson put his hand on the fender to pull himself up, trying to get his wind back.

"You're getting soft," I said. "Been behind a desk for too long. I didn't think one punch would put you down so easily."

He coughed a few times before finding the air he needed to talk.

"You're right," he answered. "I'm glad I hadn't eaten yet. I'm sorry about what happened to your brother. Do you feel better?"

"Only a little. Now, I need you to tell me everything. Flynn never gave me the whole story. And then I plan to finish what he started. If you are on board, you can still get the credit."

"I'm not sure it will be fruitful to continue."

"He had the evidence in his hands, got cocky and got killed. He was doing something he shouldn't have been doing. Wasn't trained for. I fault you partially for this. I, though, can put them away or bury them. Tell me everything, so I can complete what he started."

"I can take some of the blame, but understand this was your brother's plan all along. He came to us with the idea for taking them down. All in exchange for clearing his debts and a finder's fee of ten percent."

"You're lying."

"No, it was all his idea. He had been working on it for a while. Took his time seducing the woman, knowing who she was. He was extremely confident he could get her in the sack and win her trust. He then talked with the IRS agent he was working with, who then contacted us. It coincided with work we were already doing, so we were interested."

"Helen called me when she became suspicious."

"When you stuck your nose in his business, he was concerned you'd stop him, so we plotted to exaggerate his money situation to make you think he had no choice. We arranged the visits with Helen and took his daughter for the ride, all with his blessing. We were selling them and you on his grand plan."

I wanted to slug Wilson again, but resisted.

"Flynn was pretty devious, but I find it hard to believe he would go to such lengths."

"Believe it. He did love his wife and daughter, though in an odd way. He really didn't want to lose them."

"So, they weren't going to be thrown out on the street?"

"Oh, he was in debt all right, but the IRS wants to collect money. Tossing them on the street and making them homeless wouldn't have accomplished anything. They would have come up with a payment plan where he could work it off. He wanted to exact revenge on the people who swindled money from him and his clients. But then you showed up and screwed everything up for him. And he knew you wouldn't leave it alone, so he leveraged you to assist him, or at least to think you were assisting him."

Now I wanted to slug Flynn, but of course couldn't. *How could he have been so stupid and arrogant?*

"So, was it Casey's father who cheated him out of the money?"

"No, his brother. He is running a variation on several investment scams, using ever-changing methods. He has several high rollers who claim twenty percent returns, vouching for the validity of his business. Then he takes the money, runs it through several accounts, pays out a few dividends here and there, especially when you first invest, suckering you to use those earnings and more. Then boom! The money dries up, with claims the businesses failed; the money magically disappears in an ever-changing trail of accounts that are difficult to trace. Since you are warned up front you could lose all your money, it says so in the fine print, it makes it challenging to take any action. It's an elaborate setup."

"What does this have to do with the Hedge fund of Casey's father?"

"Some of the money runs through the Hedge fund, then back out again, laundering it. The fund seems to be legitimate. But others are laundering money through it as well, namely one important fish. Have you ever heard of Alexander Toro?"

I shook my head. The name had no meaning to me.

"He is the head crime boss for this part of the country. Running guns, drugs, gambling and adult entertainment for any perverted indulgence you desire."

"Does he have the connections to tamper with evidence at a crime scene?"

"Most likely. Do you have information we can use?"

"Doubtful. Certainly nothing which will stand up in court."

Pulling out my phone, I found the recording of what Carlos said and played it back for him.

"Who the hell was that?"

I told him the name.

"Last name is familiar. Not sure why I remember, though. He's not from around here."

I told him what I'd found on the web.

"Yeah, now I remember. He is the only surviving family member."

"Be my guess. Any connection between Toro and his family?"

"Nothing I'm aware of, but I'll dig into it. Could be a

coincidence."

"Possible, but worth checking."

Wilson pulled out a handkerchief and wiped the sweat from his brow. He really had gone soft and spent too much time behind the desk in his air-conditioned office.

"Toro is all kinds of connected."

"When someone gets close to bringing him down, something happens to screw things up?"

"Exactly right. SOP when attempting to indict him. The FBI and the IRS have been trying to shut him down for years. Money goes through the Hedge Fund and through the brother's investment scam, they believe. We gather evidence, get some witnesses, and poof! It all blows up in our face. This would have been a key piece leading us to where the money has gone."

"So really, even if Flynn had brought you evidence, it wouldn't have been enough to bring them in."

"No."

"Did he understand this?"

Wilson looked away and remained silent.

"All he cared about was getting revenge against the brother, then?"

"Yes."

"Even if it meant ruining Helen and Jolene's lives?"

"We agreed to take care of them if something went wrong. All their debts to the IRS have been wiped clean."

"And the money they lost and the finder's fee?"

"Without results and someone ending up in jail, no, they won't get their money back."

I turned around and kicked the ground in frustration.

"How much did he lose?" I asked, facing him again.

"Over a hundred thousand."

"He told me he lost twenty thousand. Where the hell did he get so much money?"

"I don't know. Maybe you should ask his wife."

If they'd had that type of money at any time, it was news to me. The event with the James Brothers, though, was a clue. *Could there have been other investors?*

"Give me all the details and don't leave anything out," I said.

Chapter 32

We headed back to the FBI office and this time I got to ride up front. Once we arrived, he certainly could have had me arrested, but didn't, though he warned me the next time I wouldn't be so lucky. He shared as much detail as possible with me and I soaked it all up. Some of what he told me and I read was new. He allowed me to take photos of a few pages, so I could refer to them later. I left there feeling I'd made some progress.

I texted everyone I was arriving at Helen's soon, so Rocky didn't shoot me. I had missed dinner, so I grabbed a burger and brought it back with me. I sat at the kitchen table enjoying the bland, fatty food. Rocky retired upstairs to get some sleep, so Helen joined me.

"How do you like being babysat?" I asked.

"Reassuring, though annoying," Helen answered. "When you are with him, he is not much of a talker. Likes to read on his digital device. Seems totally engrossed in his reading, but appears to see and hear everything going on around him. Are you two friends?"

"No. We worked together last year and certainly aren't friendly, though not enemies either. He is quite good and we are lucky to have him."

"Where did he get the scar under his eye from?"

"I have no idea. From what little I know about him, I could hazard a guess it was from something dangerous he was involved him. Who knows? He could have got it from walking into the edge of a door."

Helen laughed, which was good to hear.

"How are you coping?" I asked.

"Good days and bad. I loved Flynn, even with his faults. I could be mad at him one moment and be lying in the throes of passion the next. I was certain we would be divorcing, until the final night I saw him, and he charmed me again. Now, I'll never know."

A couple of tears ran down her cheek. I offered her some of my fries, as if this would make her feel better.

"How about Jolene?"

"Not sure. She has been mainly stoic about the whole thing. She had some tears, though nothing earth-shattering. Has been more upset about the breakup with her boyfriend. It will be worse once school is out. I was hoping you would talk with her. She's always taken a shine to whatever you've said. You are the cool uncle."

"I will do my best."

"What about you?" Helen asked. "How are you holding up?"

"You saw me. I was in shock the whole week afterwards. Everything was a blur. Melissa helped all she could. Then, when getting back to work, another case presented itself and I knew I couldn't go further without finishing what Flynn started. That will be the final stage of acceptance, when I can move on."

"You think you can find out who killed him?"

"I do. I've already learned a few things. One item was quite surprising. How much did you know about Flynn's finances?"

"Not much. He handled most of it. I started looking into to it more and more when I became concerned about what he was doing. I was alarmed to see how little money we had."

"What about before this, going back a year or so?"

"I thought we were doing fine. Certainly, we weren't hurting for money and could buy pretty much what we needed. We paid cash for my car."

"Any ideas on where Flynn could have gotten over a hundred thousand dollars to lose?"

"Oh my! You must be kidding. No, I don't."

"Did he have a financial advisor he worked with?"

"I'm certain he did. Not sure who it was. Most information like that is kept at his office. Best place to look. He didn't like working at home, so he didn't keep anything here. Probably worried I'd find out about what he was doing. Did he really lose all of it?"

"From what I'm told, yes. Could have contributed to his death."

"Don't you get dead too," said Helen.

"Never going to happen," I replied confidently.

She smiled widely, which made me feel good.

"I'm going to retire for the night. Thanks for being here."

She leaned down and kissed me on the cheek and gave me a hug. I would keep from her the elaborate measures Flynn took in his mission to get back the money and to keep us all involved. No reason to hurt her and Jolene any more than what they already were going through. I finished my meal and, though I should have been exhausted, I wasn't, so I went into the living room and read through my notes and read some more of the documents I'd photographed. I had a much better idea of what I was up against. All I needed was to form a plan to bring Flynn's killer to justice. Even with all he had done, I still could not let this go unpunished.

All the evidence started with Casey and the men in her life – her father, uncle, stepfather and her lovers. Each of them played a part in this entire mystery. Love, sex and money were all factors. One lover was in jail, two others dead. But one former lover was still alive. I needed to talk to Samuel Rivera, who feared talking anymore about Casey. I had to get past his protection and convince him it was in his best interest to tell me. Threats would not work, and likely would get me hurt. I stayed awake until midnight, thoughts and ideas rolling through my head, before falling asleep on the sofa, my gun nearby. I was still without a plausible plan for my next move.

Chapter 33

I was up and moving around when Frakes called and wanted me down at his office. He didn't seem real happy, and I really preferred to be doing other things, but didn't want to lose my one police resource in town, on the chance I needed to fall back on him for information. He gave me the address of his office and I was there shortly after nine, sitting in a chair before him, trying not to show fear from his joyless expression.

"Carlos Depaolo claims his confession was coerced out of him," said Frakes.

"I reasoned with him," I replied.

"Says you put a pillow between your gun and his head and threatened to kill him if he didn't talk."

"His word against mine."

"Found the door chain had been ripped off. He says you kicked it in."

"It was already broken when he let me in."

"Girlfriend says you had a gun and told her to get dressed and leave. Took the cell phone so she couldn't call for help."

"She was naked and had a nice body. I didn't want her distracting him or me while we talked. I was courteous to her in my request."

"Even with the recording you gave us the DA figures we have no case."

"Still gives you something to dig into. Someone died who shouldn't have. Evidence was tampered with."

"True. We will dig deeper. You know how this goes, though. Neat and clean keeps the brass happy. Messy and dirty doesn't."

His office was large, with modern furniture and a view out the window. He even had his own coffee maker. He walked over to pour the black brew. He offered me some, but I declined. Coffee was one drink I'd never enjoyed.

"Are you still holding him?"

"Made bail this morning. Some big time hotshot lawyer flew in from St. Louis and threw around his weight. Somehow, a Polk County judge got involved and got things on the fast track."

"Pretty quick for some twenty-seven-year-old who works at Younkers selling men's clothes."

"I knew his last name was familiar. I'm sure you tracked it down. Last remaining living member of an Italian crime boss's family, gunned down seven years ago."

"Has ties when he needs them. Obviously not in the family business anymore. He offered me a bribe to erase the tape and let him go. Ten grand."

"Wow. Must have a nest egg somewhere. You obviously declined."

I nodded my head and left out the part about erasing a section of the tape for more information about Casey. 'Always hold something back from the police' was my motto.

"Anything else you care to share?"

"Only that he was Casey Gaines off-and-on boyfriend. She is whom Flynn was seeing and appears to be connected."

"She was the one you asked for information about, related to your brother's involvement with FBI Agent Wilson. Is she a suspect in his death?"

"A person of interest. She may know who and why."

"Any more detail you can give me?"

"Not much, because of the feds. I'm working on it now, unofficially with them."

"They may have gotten your brother killed. Why hold back? We could be of some help solving it."

"True. But I may need their pull, and I doubt you have their kind of clout. I will say Casey and her family are at the heart of the matter. I'm still working on several pieces. Carlos was one and I need a big favor to track down a couple more."

He rocked back in his chair after a sip of his coffee from his Iowa Hawkeye cup.

"I need to get into Flynn's office. Not certain what I'm looking for, but I need to check it. Can you get me in?"

"It's in Urbandale's jurisdiction and still an active crime scene, from what I know."

"I'm sure you have friends there who can get me in."

"I do. Though helping me doesn't mean they'll help you."

"How about if I say 'please'?" I said with a big grin.

He shook his head and picked up his phone, hitting one of his speed dial buttons. After several minutes of back and forth he hung up.

"She can meet us over there in about forty-five minutes."

"Cool. Enough time for me to buy you a couple of donuts and more coffee. What is nearby?"

"I prefer whole grain muffins. There is a bakery on the way which sells both."

"Cop who doesn't eat donuts. I'm surprised they let you in the police union."

"I'm in the closet. I hide my donut aversion from them. We'll take my car."

After getting what turned out to be a huge muffin and large coffee, which was significantly cheaper than prime rib, we headed over to Flynn's office. Once we arrived, we sat waiting until a plain clothes Urbandale car pulled up. Out stepped a fifty-something woman in a dark blue pant suit, flat black shoes, with shoulder length straight brown hair parted in the middle. She walked up to Frakes and they embraced as if they were old friends. He introduced her, as Detective Toni Bell acknowledged me. I vaguely remembered her face seen through the fog I was in the day I found Flynn. She had been at the scene and may have even talked with me.

"I'm sorry for your loss," Bell said.

"Thank you. I have a recollection of talking with you, though for the life of me I can't remember what you asked or what I said."

"You were pretty well out of it. Not hard to imagine why. What are you hoping to find?"

"I don't know. I'll pretty well know what it is when I find it."

"We've been over the place several times. No real hard evidence was found. Fingerprints and DNA, but nothing useful. The place was pretty messy."

"Any leads?" I asked.

"Nothing worth mentioning."

"So, it won't hurt me looking it over. I might find something worthwhile. I knew my brother fairly well and was here helping him with something which may have contributed to his death."

"Okay. You need to wear these gloves and cover your feet. I will be with you all the way. You find anything you must share it. Is this understood?"

Agreeing, I put on the latex gloves and foot coverings and entered the room. When I had found Flynn, I wanted to search the place before the police arrived but couldn't, for I was in shock. Searching would have been better before the scene was trampled by the army of police, detectives and paramedics which flooded the scene. But this would have to do. As with any search, I started in one section and methodically touched and looked at everything. I was in no rush and didn't want to miss anything. I'd been in his office several times, so had a good recollection of how it was. There was the main room with desk, filing cabinet, computer, one chair and a loveseat in the corner for clients to sit. I went through the chair and loveseat first, then the filing cabinet, and on to the desk. I went through all the drawers and found nothing of value. I powered on the computer and was prompted with a 'no hard drive detected' message.

"Looks as if someone removed the hard drive," I said out loud.

"Yes, this was our conclusion as well," said Bell. "Our tech guys opened it up and it was gone. Didn't have time to wipe so decided to take it and leave the computer behind. Easy enough to pocket it."

Once finished in the front room I went back to Flynn's office where he was found. It was larger with a desk, two client chairs, a sofa, a couple of filing cabinets, and a small refrigerator. I again went through it all coming to his computer on the desk and got the same 'no hard drive detected' message. I searched high and low for a flash drive, but couldn't find one. He had copied important evidence onto a flash drive, he had told me over the phone. In this technological day and age, everyone always had one or two lying around.

"Did you find any flash drives?" I asked.

"No," replied Bell from the next room. "We thought this unusual too. If they were here, they likely took them as well."

"I recall there being papers on the floor in here. Were they picked up?"

"Yes. The whole scene was photographed and then we checked every piece of paper. Nothing more than some old client files. We contacted all the names, but it led to nothing. Everything was put back in the filing cabinet."

"Where is the chair he was sitting in?" I asked.

"Lab boys took it, since it was covered in blood."

"What about his fingertips? From what I recall, several of them were cut off. Did you find them here?"

"No. This appeared to have happened elsewhere. From what we can tell, he was shot here with a small caliber .22 at point blank range. Bullet never exited his skull. Medical Examiner thinks he may have been unconscious when they shot him, if it's any consolation."

It wasn't, since he'd been tortured before they shot him. *The question was, did they get what they wanted?*

I pulled a chair around to the desk, so I could sit, and started going through the drawers again. Nothing jumped out and I was getting frustrated. I put my head back to think, looking at the old ceiling tiles, several of which were water-stained. It then dawned on me that Flynn used to hide things in the closet of his bedroom. Cigarettes, pot, booze, and even dirty magazines. There had been an opening to a crawl space in the ceiling where he could stash things. There was a small coat closet and a bathroom to check. Opening the closet, I stood on a chair, lifting a ceiling tile and pushing it to the side. I used my phone's camera flash as a light and looked around. I found a vinyl pouch with elastic around it and pulled it down after stretching to reach it. It appeared to have been recently placed there, as it was dirt free. As I stepped out of the closet Bell and Frakes were both there.

"What did you find?" asked Bell.

"Hopefully, something worthwhile. May I open it?"

"Sure. On the desk."

Inside were several sheets of papers. On some of them were names, contact information and dollar amounts. Also, was a ledger with more names, dollar amounts and plus/minus columns. A few of the names I recognized as friends of Flynn's, and even a few of mine from days gone by. Others I didn't know, but wondered if Helen knew them. Toward the bottom was a familiar last name, Wyche, but different first of Gabriel, with references as if this was who they had invested with, the business name Bank On It Returns. Yet Bank On It didn't provide any returns, showing only red for those who invested. It appeared I'd found a key piece of evidence about who had stolen Flynn and his investors' money. The evidence lined up with what Wilson had told me. Casey's uncle was implicated.

"What are we seeing?" asked Frakes.

"Maybe a motive," I answered.

Chapter 34

The previous day had been productive. I'd found something key in the case and Detective Bell had been happy enough to let me take photos of the documents. A couple of the familiar names I contacted immediately. One was an old high school friend of Flynn's who didn't like me much and had even beaten me up a couple of times. He was working at Mercy Medical Center near downtown, in their billing department. I didn't tell him who I was, only I was an old friend of Flynn's, in town after I heard of his death. I mentioned Flynn owed me money, and that immediately got his attention. We would meet in the cafeteria of the hospital.

I walked in, searched the room, and saw Burke. He had not changed much through the years, still round in body and face, about thirty pounds overweight for his 5'10" height. He was wearing a short-sleeved, white dress shirt and a horribly-colored striped tie. He didn't at first recognize me but, when I sat down and our eyes met, his face lit up with surprise.

"Damn, it's Jarvis Mann," he said with a hint of sarcasm. "The puny kid has grown up."

"Been a long time, Burke," I said.

It had been many years since I'd seen Burke. Probably the last time was at the end of his fist. The urge to slap him around was there, but I resisted, for I needed information. Of course, if he wasn't forthcoming, it was always an option.

"Too bad about Flynn. I was real sorry to hear about him."

"Didn't see you at the funeral," I said.

"No time to take off and couldn't afford to lose a day of pay. I would have been, otherwise. What are you doing here?"

"I'm here to talk."

"Well, I'm meeting someone for lunch, so it will have to be quick. Should be along any time now."

"Already here. I'm the one who called you."

"Why didn't you say it was you?"

"Wasn't sure you'd see me."

He shrugged.

"Need to ask you about the money you invested with Flynn."

"What money?"

"Come on, Burke. I'm a detective now, so I know a lot. It appeared you gave him money to invest and it was all lost. Maybe why you can't afford to take a day off for the funeral of your old friend. Or maybe you are still pissed at him for losing your savings."

He started to get up, but I grabbed his arm and pulled him back down, his plate crashing down, making a loud noise that turned heads.

"You aren't leaving until you tell me what I want to know."

"You think you can stop me?"

"We aren't kids anymore. You aren't bigger than me or tougher."

I punched him in the bicep, putting a lot of snap into it, and causing his arm to go numb from the blow. He started rubbing his arm and flexing his fingers from the pain.

"You didn't have to do that," Burke said.

"I felt like I owed you one from the past. Now are you going to sit and talk with me?"

"Sure, sure. What do you want to know?"

"How much did you invest with Flynn?"

He continued flexing his arm and took his cold can of soda and pressed it against his skin.

"Eight thousand. Pretty much all I had. They promised a twenty-five percent return."

"Did you see any of it back?"

"I got a couple of dividend checks the first two months after I invested. Both five hundred dollars. Flynn said to invest it back in again, so I did. Nothing more thereafter. I trusted the SOB and paid for it."

"So, were you mad at Flynn?"

"Hell yes, I was! I called him over, and over but he said to be patient. Then told me a few months back the money was lost on a bad deal. No way to get it back. I was furious. Even came to his work and threatened to punch his lights out. He told me he'd lost all his money as well, though he was working on a grand plan to get it back. I didn't hear anything from him after that. Been trying to dig myself out of the hole ever since. Girlfriend threw me out a month or so ago, saying I was a bum."

I wanted to feel sorry for him but couldn't, the long ago memories of him punching me fresh on my mind.

"Then you're a detective. Are you working on his murder?"

"Yes."

"Am I a suspect?"

"Not in my mind. I can't see you killing him in the manner he died. Though an Urbandale female Detective, Toni Bell, may be calling you to talk. Tell her the truth and don't be a dick, and you'll be fine."

"Sure, sure. Can I go now?"

"Yes. Remember what I said."

I didn't hold out any hope of him acting as an adult and treating her with respect, but I knew if he did something stupid she'd haul his ass in. I talked with a couple of other people in person who were on the list and all had pretty much the same story. Others I contacted by phone, and at the end of the day I counted over a hundred thousand in lost investments. This on top of what Flynn had lost made for a big payday for someone. Each had made a check out to Bank On It Returns. I called Agent Wilson at his office and asked what he knew about them.

"Yes, they are still around. Most of the money went to investments in businesses which didn't pan out, or so they say. Yet others, like Gabriel and his brother, their investments always paid off. They'd lose a little here and there, enough so no one got overly suspicious. Points to a few other high rollers, as I told you before, who did well to keep the illusion going. They have enough money flowing through, coming from sources unknown. This is what we were trying to track down and what Flynn thought he'd found. Have you located the evidence he had?"

"No. Still putting all the pieces together and learning where the money he invested came from. Apparently, he had his own group, and not one of them got any return of any kind."

"It's quite a scam. The question is will anyone testify?"

"Testify to what? Like you said, there was a risk and they lost, like many investors do every day."

"Why we need the proof your brother found."

I couldn't argue the point any more. I had to end the call with Wilson because my other phone was ringing. It was Rocky and he didn't sound pleased.

"I've been waiting for fifteen minutes outside the school and Jolene hasn't shown yet," he said.

"Have you tried calling her?"

There was a long pause, since it was a stupid inquiry.

"I withdraw the question," I said.

"Good thing. Goes straight to voicemail."

I nearly asked if he went into the school to look for her, but knew it wasn't an option, as his presence would likely scare everyone inside.

"Wait there in case she shows. I'm only about ten minutes away."

I hopped into the car and drove as quickly as I could, worrying and wondering what the hell could have happened to her.

Chapter 35

I wasn't ready to call Helen yet. I didn't want her to panic. When I arrived, I pulled up to Rocky in the Mustang. There was still no sign of her. I rushed into the school to check with admissions and, after arguing with them for a few minutes and showing them my PI ID, they checked, and she was at all of her classes except for the last one. The question was, what happened to her? I told Rocky to head back to the house in case she showed up there while I went to pick up Helen. When she came out to the car and I told her to not get upset, she did anyway.

"Oh my!" she yelled out. "You said she would be safe at school."

"She was. There is no reason to jump the gun on this. We need to think through where she could have gone. It could be of her own doing. I'm certain she was getting stir-crazy having to stay at home. What about girlfriends?"

"Well, she does have one girl friend, Kristen. I don't have her number, since I'm using this other phone. We can go home and get it."

"What about her boyfriend?"

"She said they broke up."

"Didn't seem all that upset about it. Could be she wasn't being completely truthful."

"You're right. Not outside the realm of possibility. I know where he lives and it's not far from here. Let's go and see if he is home."

When we arrived, we rang the doorbell and his mother answered. She knew Helen and didn't seem happy to see her.

"I don't want you around here," she said.

"Bev, is Andrew home?" asked Helen.

"No. Now please leave."

She tried to close the door, but I prevented it by leaning my shoulder into it. She wasn't strong enough to push it.

"Who the hell are you?" Bev said.

"Uncle of Jolene, who is missing. Could she be with Andrew?"

"Of course not. I told him to stop seeing her."

"Gee, and he always does what you tell him?"

She stopped for a minute before answering.

"Usually. Of course, Jolene could twist him to go against my wishes."

Helen was not pleased with the comment.

"Look Bev, I don't have time to argue with you," stated Helen. "Jolene is missing. She may or may not be in danger, but if she is with Andrew, he is in danger as well. Can you please let us in and try calling him?"

After mulling it over, she opened the door and we walked in. She grabbed her cordless phone and made the call, but got no answer.

"Did he say anything about doing something after school today?" I asked.

"He was going to hang out with friends and have dinner with them. I didn't question him on who. I only told him to be home before dark."

"What about his father? Can you check with him?'

There was a long pause before she answered, a sense of anger in her face she was trying to control.

"His father lives in another state and hardly talks to him. He couldn't care less. And my current husband and Andrew don't see eye to eye. He wouldn't have any idea either."

Brow-beating her wasn't getting us anywhere, so we went back to the house. The cell phones I'd purchased had GPS tracking, something I made sure of for this very reason. I called up the web portal and it showed the phone was offline. Either the battery had died or it had been turned off. Helen then called Jolene's female friend and she was reluctant to say anything. Helen put her on the speakerphone.

"Please, Kristen," pleaded Helen. "We need to know where she is. She isn't in trouble, but could be in danger. If you know something, please tell us."

"I really shouldn't," she answered.

"You know what happened to her father," I said, trying to scare her. "How would you feel if the same happened to Jolene because you wouldn't tell us?"

There was a long pause, though you could hear her breathing.

"Well, she was going nuts having to stay at home," said Kristen. "She told me she was skipping last period and meeting up with Andrew. They were going to an afternoon movie at Jordan Creek. It was a 4:30 showing, I believe. They wanted to be together. They are so much in love, but his mother is being such a bitch about them."

"Thank you, Kristen," said Helen. "We are relieved she is okay."

"I'll go get them," I said after hanging up, "and bring them both back here."

Jordan Creek wasn't too far away and I was there in about twenty minutes. I asked for the manager and showed him my ID and explained the situation. He agreed to allow me to check the theaters. Since the movie times were staggered, it was pretty easy to figure which one they went to if Kristen had the correct time. I walked in and they were in the back by themselves and appeared to be making out. I crept up the stairs and slid into their row a couple seats down from them. They sensed a presence, stopping their lip lock and looking at me. Jolene was surprised.

"Since you don't appear to be watching the movie," I whispered. "I figure we can leave now and go back to your mom's."

They both pouted for a minute, then reluctantly agreed, walking out with me. They were silent all the way home, her in the front, him in the back. Once in the house Helen walked up and hugged them both. She was mad, but happy the worry was over.

"Sit down, you two," I said. "We need to hash this out."

I motioned for Helen to come to the kitchen.

"Were they there?" Helen asked.

"Yes. They were in full make-out mode. Pretty obvious they haven't broken up."

"What should we do?"

"When you were young did your parents ever tell you not to see some boy ever again?"

She frowned.

"Of course, they did. They told me to stop seeing Flynn."

"How did that work out?"

"Out of spite I wanted to see him even more."

"Then I'd say you know the proper course of action here. Do you want me in there with you?"

She glanced over her shoulder and saw the two of them on the sofa, holding hands.

"No, I can handle it."

Out she walked while I took a seat at the table. I then realized Rocky was in there too, cooking, his hair pulled back into a ponytail, his gun holstered under his left arm. He had a couple of pots, one simmering and one boiling. The heat from the oven filled the room.

Whatever it was smelled exceptional.

"Hired bodyguard cooks as well," I stated.

"Needed to keep busy while we waited," Rocky replied. "I can cook a few things and my three-cheese Italian sausage pasta dish is one of them. Figured Helen would be busy tending to family matters."

"Smells good, I can hardly wait. Maybe you should put out a book: Rocky's Recipes for Rough Men."

It was possible he smiled, though I couldn't say for sure. After Helen was done, the three of them joined us in the kitchen and enjoyed the meal. It had been agreed upon that Jolene and Andrew could spend time together at the house. If they wanted a little alone time, it would be allowed for them to go to her room, but no sex. If they wanted to go out somewhere, either Rocky or I had to be with them. After dinner, I drove Andrew home and we talked some on the way.

"You really like Jolene," I said.

"She is special to me," Andrew answered. "I do love her and want to be with her all the time."

Missing Melissa came to mind. All those miles between us, literally and figuratively, were hurting us.

"I know the feeling. What about your mother?"

"She doesn't understand."

"She's scared for you, after what happened to Jolene's father. It's understandable."

"I'm almost eighteen. She can't protect me forever. I have to make my own decisions."

"I'd approach it from that angle."

"She won't listen."

"You have to try."

"And neither does Ben."

"Is that your step-father?"

"Don't call him that. He is hardly a father. I can't stand him!"

"I'm sorry. I didn't come from a broken home, but I've worked cases of families that were. I know it can be difficult."

"Between the two of them, I don't stand a chance, and can barely get a word in edge wise."

"I'll walk in with you, see if we can reason with them. I've dealt with tougher people than her recently, so I'm not scared."

He smiled as we pulled up. Together we walked to the front door and entered, braced for the onslaught. Maybe I should have been scared.

Chapter 36

My morning started poorly when Detective Frakes called me.

"Where are you at?" he said. "I need to pick you up and take a trip down to Drake."

This didn't sound good.

"I'm still at Helen's." I gave him the address. "How long before you're here?"

"Fifteen."

On the drive down, it was quiet in his car, other than the radio playing soft jazz, which always made me sleepy. We pulled up to an apartment building I knew, several police cars on the scene. After Frakes showed his ID, we walked through the door I had kicked in a few days earlier. There was a buzz of activity and it became obvious why. Sitting on the sofa was the dead body of Carlos. He had been shot through the roof of the mouth, the gun still in his hand. I'd seen enough violent death in my life and it was never pleasant.

Over strode a Des Moines plains clothes officer. He acknowledged Frakes.

"Is this him?" he asked.

Frakes said, "Yes" and then introduced us. Detective Culbert showed no emotion. Apparently, he's seen his fair share of violent death too.

"You're the one who recorded his confession?" he asked.

"I am. What happened?"

"From appearances, he killed himself. Killed a woman first, then one up through his mouth. Woman is in the bedroom."

Once in the room, I recognized her as the one I'd found with him the other day. She lay on the bed naked, blood on the sheets behind her head. A pillow had been used to muffle the shot.

"A murder-suicide then?" said Frakes.

"If not, then made to look that way. There is a note on the kitchen table. Looks like it was printed up on his laser printer."

"May I see it?" I asked.

Culbert called out and had the note brought to me. It was in a plastic bag. It said:

I'm sorry for the death I've caused because of my jealous rage.

May the angels forgive me for killing Flynn Mann, Taylor Gaines and Jill Westin.

"I'm assuming Jill is who is on the bed?" I asked.

"From the ID we found in her purse, yes," answered Culbert.

"A neat and tidy confession," I said.

"Our bosses will like it," replied Culbert.

"It stinks. In my mind, this was staged."

"Why do you think so?"

"For one, I know Carlos didn't kill Flynn, for he would have told me when I was questioning him. Two, why use the pillow to kill Jill?"

"Trying to silence the sound."

"True, if you planned to do it. If it was in a 'jealous rage,' like he said, I doubt he'd have taken the time to cover her face and shoot her. This seems more premeditated to me. Did anyone hear the second shot?"

"No."

"Time of death?"

"Sometime after midnight. Nothing conclusive yet."

"Gun?"

"Beretta 9mm. Probably a million of them in the world."

"Any evidence he owned a gun? Extra bullets, cleaning kit, holster?"

"Nothing yet."

"I'm not here to tell you how to do your job, but I'd look at this real hard before calling it a suicide. Might not be much to find, as they were likely pros. You know who he is? His family history?"

"Yes," said Culbert. "You think it's mob related?"

"Could be, though I'm inclined to think it's related to my brother's murder and my digging into it. He had a high-class lawyer fly up from St. Louis to bail him out. Could be worthwhile paying him a visit."

"I doubt my budget or my boss will allow me a trip down there," said Culbert.

"Nor mine," added Frakes.

"Fortunately, mine does, and has some sway."

"Wilson," said Frakes.

"Yes. I always wanted to see the new Busch Stadium and the

Arch. Now I have a good excuse."

Chapter 37

Agent Wilson agreed to cover the cost of travelling to St. Louis, but insisted on going as well. I didn't argue, as having an FBI agent throwing his federal weight around wouldn't hurt any. I wanted to drive. It was only about five hours there and back, but he insisted on flying and being back later that day. Before leaving, I checked with Rocky to make sure he'd be fine by himself. Upon seeing his nasty expression, I knew I needed to stop asking the obvious. We flew out on an early morning flight and landed at Lambert St. Louis International by 9 a.m.

A local FBI agent met us at the airport in a large black SUV that the government must have gotten a volume discount on. He handed a folder to Wilson, who then passed it to me. Apparently, he already knew the contents. It covered the lawyer we planned to visit.

Sydney Cay was fifty-five, wealthier than I'd ever be, with several houses throughout the Midwest and offices in St. Louis and Chicago. He owned a valuable collection of classic cars, was married, with three kids and seven grandchildren. He was the lead partner in Cay and Richmond Law Specialists, with an office in the heart of downtown, with a beautiful view of the Mississippi. His clients included several high-profile Missouri and Illinois politicians, and a couple of names I knew: the two Gaines brothers and Alexander Toro.

"I don't see any mention of Carlos DePaolo," I said. "Why did Sydney come all the way to Des Moines to bail him out?"

"We'll ask him," said Wilson. "His connection to Gaines and Toro is a clue."

"Got him bailed out quickly before he could spill anymore, and then had him killed."

"Be my guess. Men like Toro don't like people rolling on them. When he heard about the recording you gave the police, it was lights out."

"Seems silly to call attention to himself."

"Men like Toro don't care about anyone digging into their business. They fear no one. Why he is nicknamed Alexander the Bull. Keep pestering him, and you'll be the next one gored."

Right now, I didn't really care. I was in this till the end, though I would prefer it wasn't my end. I read through the rest of the papers when we arrived at the tall building. The driver double-parked while we went inside, his federal muscle no match for any ticket-writing meter maid. We rode the elevator to the fifteenth floor and immediately we saw the shiny brass letters announcing Cay and Richmond Law Specialists.

I had made an appointment, but didn't use my real name. I stuck with Smith, while still using Wilson for my FBI companion. Asking specifically for Cay, we were looking for legal advice for an issue with the law, we needed assistance with, money being no object. A leggy redhead led us to a meeting room with charcoal, oval, conference room table, conference phone and a view of the St Louis Arch. You could see some large freighters cruising the Mississippi, the liquid highway of commerce. She offered us coffee, tea, juice or bottled water. Wilson wanted coffee with cream and sugar, while I settled for water. I flashed back to my first glimpse of Melissa at Bristol and Bristol all those months ago, and the connection we had formed almost immediately. Feelings of how much I truly missed her, buried deep down.

We sat and waited for twenty minutes before Cay walked in. His suit was perfect: matching gray slacks and jacket, striped tie with diamond clasp. He was average height and build, in shape, with immaculate teeth and black, perfectly combed hair and graying temples. He smiled and introduced himself, saying he was sorry for being late. Another pretty woman joined him, introducing herself as Rita, his legal assistant. She would be taking notes of our conversation.

"Mr. Smith and Mr. Wilson, what can I help you with today?"

"Well Sydney, we have a delicate matter to discuss," stated Wilson. "Something you may not want Rita to be privy too."

"She falls under the same lawyer-client confidentiality rules as I do. You may speak freely around her."

"We have a hairy legal issue where we need you to come to Des Moines and bail out one of our partners who has been arrested for vehicular homicide. Seems there is a recording of him fingering one of our associates."

"A bull in a china shop type of confession," I added.

Sydney remained cool and calm, but understood what we were getting at.

"Rita, you can leave the room," he said. "Please put the 'Do Not Disturb' sign on the door."

After she left, Sydney lost some of his coolness.

"Who the hell are you?"

Wilson pulled out his ID and showed him. I left mine in my pocket. No reason to let him think I wasn't FBI too.

"Agent Bart Wilson," Cay said. "I thought I knew all the agents in the St. Louis office. You must be new."

"Out of the Des Moines office. Here to ask you some questions on your involvement with Carlos DePaolo."

"Wow, Des Moines office, pretty scary," Cay said sarcastically. "My involvement with him is confidential. Lawyer-client privilege."

"Has he been your client for long?"

"No."

"Why would someone in Des Moines hire someone all the way down here in St. Louis?"

"Because I'm the best."

"Doubtful he could afford you. He worked in a department store selling men's clothes."

"Pro Bono."

"Or maybe someone called you and told you to fly up and get him out of jail before his big mouth stirred things up."

"No comment."

"Did you know who his family was? Their crime history over in Italy?"

"Of course, I know all of my client's histories. Those accused of crimes need lawyers too."

"Speaking of crime, are you aware your client is now dead? It didn't appear you rushed up there to see what happened?"

"I understand he killed his girlfriend and then killed himself. Murder-suicide is such a waste."

"Yet, you aren't there to handle his matters, now that he has passed."

"I was his lawyer only on his legal problems. Someone else will need to handle his estate issues, if there are any. My specialty is criminal law."

"And the criminals who commit them," I said.

"So, he speaks too. Does Agent Smith have a badge?"

"Call me Smitty. Left it on my desk back in Des Moines. Luckily,

Wilson is here to vouch for me. What about your ties to Edward and Gabriel Wyche? They appear to be your clients as well."

"I have many clients, Smitty. I can't remember all of them."

"Really? They didn't call you to come bail Carlos out, since he was dating Edward's daughter Casey?"

He threw up his hands and smiled.

"And what about Alexander Toro? When I mentioned the bull in the china shop, you obviously knew who I was referring to. He was mentioned on the recording. Carlos claimed he arranged the forged evidence in a hit and run, to show the driver was drunk at the time."

"Gentlemen, this is getting tiring," said Cay while standing. "You have come under false pretenses, wasting my time. Do you know how many hundreds of dollars I charge per hour for a consultation?"

"Send us the bill," I said while standing. I walked over, looking him straight in the eye. "Tell the Wyche brothers and Alexander the Bull that Smitty is gunning for them."

"Would this be a threat?"

With a grin, I patted him on the back.

"Most definitely"

I strode out of there oozing confidence, even though I'd just painted a large target on my chest.

Chapter 38

Surviving another jet ride, I returned to Helen's knowing no one would be home yet, because Rocky would be out picking them up. When I arrived, a familiar old beat-up Chevy was parked on the street, the two James Brothers standing in the front yard. I pulled into the driveway and got out, hearing Molly barking in the house. They both approached me, each carrying an aluminum baseball bat down at their side, nervously tapping their legs.

"You both must have a game later," I said. "Though I don't see a glove, so you must be hitting only. Error prone in the field?"

"Funny as always," said one of them. "We are here for our money, isn't that right Bruce?"

Though I could still not tell them apart, I now knew which was which. They were dressed similar to before; Chicago cubs ball caps, baggy gym shorts, dry-fit tops and god-awful colored running shoes.

"Damn right," added Bruce. "And if we can't get it, we are taking it out of your hide."

"I'm not too worried since Cub fans couldn't hit the side of a barn door to save their lives."

Being a Cardinals supporter from days past, it was always fun poking at fans of *The Loveable Losers.*

"Really, is that so?"

Bruce took his bat and smacked the siding on the house, leaving a healthy sized dent.

"Poor defenseless house didn't stand a chance," I quipped.

"Man, this smart mouth doesn't get it," said Crispin.

In unison they continued moving forward. I backed up the driveway weighing my chances and options. The bats tilted things in their favor. Though I had an ace up my sleeve.

"Two against one and both with lethal weapons in hand. Not really a fair fight, is it?"

"We don't give a damn. After you sucker punched us the last time, we've been waiting to settle the score."

"If you think I sucker punched you, then you both have been drinking and smoking too much weed."

I could smell the booze and marijuana smoke on them even from a distance. Sometimes boys never grew up and remained immature even in their late thirties. These two happened to be large sized and wound up tighter than a spring, and higher than a rocket ship.

"Gentlemen, Flynn is dead. If you've come for money, then you are out of luck. There is no money to be had. You should walk away before someone gets hurt."

"You will be the only one to get hurt," said Bruce.

"We are going to break a bone for every thousand Flynn stole from us," added Crispin.

Molly continued to bark, now standing at the back-porch screen door, growling at the two brothers, when they came into her line of sight.

"Tell the dog to shut up or I'm going pulverize her too," said Bruce.

They'd pissed me off.

"Now you've gone too far," I replied.

Using my ace, I tilted the odds in my favor and pulled out my .38 and pointed at them both. Their movement came to a halt.

"What the fuck?" they both said in unison.

"Touch a hair on the dog and I'll kill you both. Is that clear?"

No dog was ever going to get hurt on my watch again.

"You wouldn't dare shoot us," said Bruce. "You don't have the guts."

Taking my gun, I aimed at their feet and fired. Together they each let out a squeal of fright that could have shattered glass.

"I believe that answered your question," I said. "Do you have any others?"

Behind them, Helen's car pulled in and out marched Rocky. The brothers turned and saw him, and I believe their hearts stopped. He walked over and snatched the bats from their hands, like it was nothing, and gave them a look that may have caused them to pee their pants. With the end of the bats he poked each one in the ribs lightly, but enough for them to flinch. The message was clear.

"Now boys, you have to understand that if you come around here again and threaten anyone at all, including the dog, your lives will likely not be worth a plug nickel. The gentlemen before you or myself will give you a beating you'll never forget. Are we clear?"

Both were still frozen in fear.

"Answer the man," said Rocky, poking them again, a little harder this time.

"Yes," they both said softly.
"I don't think Jarvis could hear you."
"Yes, we understand," this time loud enough for all to hear.
"Initially, I planned on getting you your money back, as I'm working on a solution. But now I'd say for the aggravation and fear you've caused this household, the cost of your loss will pay for us not having the police come out and put your butts in jail. The debt has been paid. Is that understood?"
They both acknowledged this time with no hesitation.
"Glad to see we've come to an understanding. Say a pleasant, mannerly hello to the ladies, stroll slowly to your car, and drive away calmly so the neighbors won't give you a second thought."
They did as they were told, glancing back in fright, giving both Helen and Jolene who stood next to the Mustang, a simple "Hi," and were gone never to be seen again.
"These might come in handy," said Rocky of the bats he was holding as if they were toothpicks. "The weight on them is about right for me."
"Oh my," said Jolene, as she and Helen stood beside Rocky. "Who were those jerks?"
"Classmates of your father, from way back," I answered. "The James Brothers, Bruce and Crispin."
"They were investment partners with Flynn?" asked Helen.
"It would seem so. I kicked their butt earlier in front of Flynn. It seemed they felt like I'd not played fair in the duel, and wanted to get even."
"I never liked those two," said Helen. "Do you think they'll be back?"
I looked at Rocky, who started to laugh.
"I think they have been significantly emasculated enough that it will be a long time before they bother anyone again," said Rocky.
I walked over to Molly and let her out the backdoor. She came running, sniffing the ground, going back and forth before peeing on the spot where the two James Brothers had stood.
"Atta girl, Molly," I said. "You show them who is boss around here."
We all started laughing, her tongue sticking out in a happy pant.

Chapter 39

The weekend was here and it was time to turn up the pressure some. I had wanted to track down Samuel Rivera since I'd gotten back to town, and was finally getting around to it. I needed to talk with him one more time to see what he knew. I called his office and, today being a Saturday, he was not in. Since he owned homes in several cities, odds were he might not be in town. I had his address and took a shot. It appeared he was there, as were a large group of people, for he was hosting a barbeque. The house was spacious, though not as big as I would expect a furniture mogul would have. Maybe sales of cheap furniture weren't in vogue.

The front door was open, so I let myself in. The front foyer and living area were crawling with male yuppies in shorts and flowered shirts, females in golf shorts and blouses open to show cleavage. Strolling through, I smiled and said, "Hi" to all I saw, making good eye contact as if I belonged. I'd have dressed differently if I'd known the dress code, but in my slacks and polo I didn't stand out too much. I saw his ape of a bodyguard and glided by, so he couldn't make me. I hit the kitchen and found a cold beer. Through the window, I saw that Samuel was cooking over a huge barbeque, larger than my kitchen. He was searing up burgers, brats, chicken and steaks, all the while being a jokester with all gathered around him. He dished out the cooked meat on demand. I moved outside, getting as close as I could, grabbing a plate. No reason I couldn't enjoy the meal too.

"I'll take a burger with cheese please," I said to him as I'd moved to the front of the line. "Well done, if you have one."

"No problem," he replied.

He glanced over and for a second tried to remember who I was. After a moment it dawned on him.

"Jarvis, isn't it?" he said. "Nothing has changed, so enjoy your burger and leave."

"So happy you remembered," I said. "I'm not here to cause problems, unless you won't talk. Fifteen minutes of private time is all I need and I'll be on my way and never bother you again."

He let out a big sigh. He was entertaining and didn't want a big scene. He looked around and called out, asking one of his guests to take over. He waved me on to follow him and we entered into what appeared to be the office he used to work from home.

"Make it quick," he said while sitting in his chair.

No reason not to eat, so I enjoyed a bite of the burger while standing. I wanted to be ready in case his bodyguard popped in.

"Tell me how you met Casey?" I said.

"How else? We met at a bar."

He named the bar and it was the same one I had followed her to.

"You went over, bought her a drink and you hit it off?"

"Most definitely. She was with two other friends. We made eye contact and hit it off right away."

"One thing lead to another…"

"Yes. I didn't have to work too hard. We got a hotel and had sex."

I'd finished half of my sandwich. It was quite good. Those with money always had the best burgers.

"You continued to see her?"

"For a few months, two or three times a week."

"Was it getting serious?"

"Not for her. She enjoyed the sex, but didn't care to get involved beyond a pleasurable time in the sack and me spending money on her for lavish gifts. I was infatuated."

"What happened to end it?"

"She did, when I said I wanted to spend more time with her. 'No thanks' she said."

"Was she seeing someone else?"

"She always was. Some hot guy who spoke French and Italian to her while screwing. She told me about him. Some younger stud. Drove me crazy."

"Yet you still wanted her."

"I was going through a tough time. My wife and I were separated, she was living in our home in Kansas City, me living here. It had been a long time since I'd felt the kind of passion we shared. I didn't want to lose it. So, I wouldn't leave her alone."

"You were stalking her?"

Turning, he stared out the window at his guests, his hand nervously tapping the arm of his chair.

"In a manner of speaking, yes."

"You wouldn't leave her alone, so some man paid you a visit."

He nodded his head.

"Pushed you around, punching you a few times, telling you to stay away from Casey or he would come back and do worse."

He didn't answer but even viewing his face in profile confirmed the affirmative.

"Called the police and filed a complaint."

"Stupid move on my part. I got a call the next day saying drop it or else."

"Which you did, and then you hired the man of granite to protect you."

"It scared me to death. I'm not a tough person, so it doesn't take much to put me over the edge."

"Nothing to be ashamed of."

"If anything, it knocked some sense into me. Got me to call my wife and see if we could work something out."

"How is that going?"

"Slowly, but we are talking. When I go down there, we have dinner and are friendly."

I finished the burger and washed it down with the remaining suds, managing to keep the grease on the plate and off of me.

"Did you know about Casey's family?"

"Some. I know her mother remarried a big shot criminal. I'm sure he is the one who sent the man to scare me."

"Do you know his name?"

"No. And I don't want to."

"What about Carlos DePaolo?"

"There was a Carlos Casey talked about. He was the young stud I mentioned before."

"He never came to threaten you?"

"No."

"Did you ever invest any money with her biological father or uncle?"

Samuel paused, uncertain how to answer.

"I'm guessing that is a yes. How much?"

"Twenty-five thousand."

"Casey provided the connection?"

Barely a nod, but it was there.

"Did you see any return on the investment?"

"At first, yes, but then nothing. I called and was told the money was lost in the market when the company went belly-up. I didn't have a lot of recourse and I was afraid to take additional action, so I wrote it off as a business loss."

"You aren't alone. Others have been bilked as well."

"Now you understand why I don't want to talk about it. I felt like a foolish old man who got conned by a hot, younger woman. I'm getting on with my life and will, hopefully, never do anything stupid like this again. Could you please leave me alone now?"

There was that look in his eye, the glimpse of genuine sadness. I felt sorry for him, having been conned by a woman myself last year. There was no reason to push it any further, as I'd gotten what I'd came for.

"Thanks for the burger, it was outstanding. You won't hear from me again."

I went through the kitchen and grabbed some water and walked past the Michelin man, waving, no expression of remembering who I was filling his face. I should have probably gone back to tell Samuel he needed to upgrade his protection, but didn't care to scare him any further.

Chapter 40

It appeared Casey was not only providing a little nookie, but also clients for her father. She seemed to be the doorway to finding Flynn's killer and I planned on opening it. I went to the bar that evening, hoping she would show, since she had lost two of her lovers over the last few weeks and might be on the prowl for more. Though she may not have had a shortage of them I planned on working my magic.

"I arrived at 7 p.m. and took a seat at the bar, nursing a beer to remain lucid. I had some chicken tenders, which were edible, and waited. At around eight, Casey showed and took a seat on the other side of the room. Shortly after, Jennifer and Kayla showed up, the three of them were laughing up a storm. If she was in mourning for her now dead lover, it didn't show. Knowing Kayla would remember me, I told the bartender to send a round of drinks to their table, with a note to Kayla asking how her love life was. When they arrived, I was pointed out, and raised my beer to them. There was some conversation before Casey waved me over. Once there, I smiled brightly and took a seat.

"Ladies," I said. "How are you all doing tonight?"

"Feeling good, since you arrived," stated Casey. "Kayla was telling me what a gentleman you were with her."

"How kind of her," I answered. "She was marvelous company and we had a lovely dinner together."

Kayla blushed, while the other two snickered. They had seen the note too.

"What she didn't tell us was what happened after dinner," said Jennifer.

"I won't kiss and tell," I replied. "I'll only say it was one of the more enjoyable evenings I've had in some time."

"What do you have to say to that Kayla?" asked Casey. "How many times did you enjoy each other?"

"No comment," she answered while laughing.

We talked and I studied Casey, showing my interest in her. I kept the drinks coming, along with food. I continued my control on the alcohol. Ninety minutes into the conversation and after a trip to the bathroom for the three of them, which took so much time I wondered if they had snuck out, Kayla and Jennifer said they had to leave.

"It's getting late for us," said Jennifer. "We have church in the morning and hubby was kind enough to let me blow off some steam for a while."

"Same here," added Kayla. "We'll leave you two alone to enjoy the rest of your night."

She leaned over and spoke softly.

"Thank you for the advice. It has done wonders for my love life."

"You're welcome," I answered, while giving her a short embrace.

The three of them exchanged hugs and ear whispers before Kayla and Jennifer left. Casey and I were alone.

"I hope I didn't bore and chase them off," I said.

"No, not at all," stated Casey. "They left so we could be alone and decide what to do from here."

"Did they have any suggestions?"

"They did, though nothing I hadn't already thought of. Kayla told us how you treated her. It was quite gentlemanly, noble, and rather sexy. It is a shame she didn't enjoy a seductive evening with you. Her loss could be my gain."

"Do you care to leave and explore this further?" I asked.

She mouthed yes, so I paid the bill and we decided to take my car. I opened the door for her and, when I slid into the driver's seat, she grabbed me and kissed me with a red-hot fire. I kissed her back with all my skills. It lasted for some time before she broke away.

"I wanted to make sure you understood what I'm looking for," she said.

"No question. Where shall we go?" I asked. "My place isn't available. What about yours?"

"I like doing it in a hotel," she said. "More exciting. We can check in as Mr. and Mrs. Smith."

I smiled at the irony.

"Is there one nearby you recommend?"

She named a hotel and it was the first one I'd followed her and Flynn to. *Maybe I should have asked if she got a volume discount!* I checked us in and got the room key card and rode up in the elevator, her hands and mouth all over me on the entire trip up. When we stepped inside she lunged at me again, her arms pulling me in tight, her hands squeezing my ass. She smelled good and could kiss as well as anyone I'd been with. Though my body was excited, I remained in control, with visions of Emily White and how that turned out still fresh on my mind. She spun me around and pushed me back on the king-sized bed and started to undress, by unbuttoning her top. The old me would have enjoyed all of her pleasures and then revealed who I was and used whatever means necessary to get information from her. But I was not that man anymore. I stood up, grabbed her before she finished unbuttoning, and threw her on the bed, her bra covered breasts popping out her open blouse.

"Wow, I like a man who takes charge," she murmured.

"I don't think you'll like how I'm going to take charge at all," I said.

My words confused her.

"What?"

"You were involved with my brother and now he is dead. I'm here now to find out everything you know about it."

The pleasure in her eyes turned to anger.

"Who the hell are you?"

"Jarvis Mann. My brother was Flynn Mann and I believe you know something about who killed him."

She sat up and started buttoning up her top, and tried to stand, but I pushed her back down again.

"You aren't leaving until I get some answers."

"Who the fuck do you think you are? You can't keep me here against my will."

"Actually, I can. And with a phone call I can get an FBI agent down here who will lock you up until you speak. We can do it easy and talk nicely to each other, or we can make it more difficult."

I pulled out my phone and called up the number to show her. The anger had now turned to fear.

"Please don't."

"All I have to do is press the call button and get him on the line. Should be able to lose you in the system for a day or so."

"You wouldn't dare."

"Like hell I won't."

It took a minute, but her eyes changed from fear to phony passion.

"Come on now," she said seductively. "We paid for the room and you're a good-looking guy. I can provide you pleasure like you've never had before. I've been told I provide the best blow-jobs any man has ever had."

"Lady, I don't want your mouth anywhere near my crotch!"

The anger of my words startled her. Panicked, she looked for her purse, but I grabbed it and checked inside. Among all the womanly items, a wallet and her cell phone, was a 22 caliber pistol. Finding it loaded, I removed the bullets and then gave it a quick sniff. It did not smell like it had been fired recently.

"Do you have a permit for this?"

She looked away without answering.

"Flynn was killed with a 22. Could this be the gun?"

Silence still. I pocketed it and the bullets for testing later. I doubted this was the gun, as she didn't seem the killer type. But I was going to run with the leverage it provided.

"I guess we take this gun and test it and see what the FBI says. Probably three to four days they could hold you now. Same change of clothes and no shower for that long will certainly be unpleasant. Would you agree?"

She pouted, but remained defiant. Now it was time to find out how much she really knew.

"Hard to believe you are out picking up men so soon after Carlos' murder," I said.

There was a look of shock on her face.

"You are lying."

"No, I'm not. Did you see it on the news or read about it in the paper?"

"I don't care for either. Too depressing."

"Well then here, look at this."

I pulled up my phone, opened the browser and found one of the local TV stations website. It was still big news and was easy to find. I opened the page and handed to her.

"Oh my god!"

She read through it and started to cry. It seemed sincere and genuine, though I had been fooled before by women. But it appeared she didn't know about it. She handed me back the phone and cried for ten minutes, sobbing into her palms.

"It would seem you didn't have a hand in his death," I said. "And I'm sorry to be the one to tell you."

I grabbed some tissue and tossed it to her.

"I was wondering why he hadn't called."

"Now the question is, what you know about Flynn's death?"

"I don't…I mean I can't…"

"Come on now, Casey, it's time to tell me everything you know or I'm dragging you down to the Feds and let them have at you. They won't be as kind as I'm being."

She was beat. You could see it on her tear-stained face.

"What do you want to know?"

"Start at the beginning. Don't leave anything out. I have all night to enjoy a pleasant conversation with you."

Chapter 41

I got her to tell me all, or at least concluded I'd rung all the available data out of her. I took her back to her car at the bar and she left without a word. Heading back to Helen's, I had much to mull over, but fell asleep in the bed upstairs before all I'd gathered overtook me.

The next morning, I awoke and found Rocky again cooking, this time making a full-sized breakfast of omelets, pancakes, bacon and sausage. His large body moved easily around the kitchen and I imagined the heavily-armed cook working for Roni, and snickered. It was hard to mock him too much. His meal had me in cholesterol heaven. He could kill you slowly by clogging your arteries, or quickly at the end of a gun. I preferred the slow method, for I'd witnessed his skill with a weapon and it was lethal.

Once we finished eating, Helen mentioned something I'd forgotten about, Flynn's motorcycle.

"The police returned it yesterday," she said. "They found it in a parking lot several miles from his office. They had impounded it, but found nothing of value, so they said I could have it back. It's out in the garage."

I needed to stretch my legs and walk off some of the meal, so I grabbed the keys and headed outside, Molly hot on my tail as she hugged my leg step for step. I opened the old-style swing-up garage door and saw the bike. It was dirty but still in marvelous shape. It didn't look as if it had been wrecked. Only abandoned. I found an overhead light, so I could see it better. He had saddle bags and I searched them, knowing if anything had been there of importance the police would have found it, but I like to be thorough. I meticulously started at the front of the bike and checked every area. Molly found a comfortable spot after sniffing carefully and sat down. I took the keys, warning her I was about to start the bike, but the loud roar was familiar, so she sat undisturbed. It started right up, and I turned on the lights. I'd often wanted a bike like this one, but never could afford it. I revved the motor and desired to take it for a spin. Helen walked into the garage and smiled.

"You look good on it, Jarvis," she said. "I never liked Flynn riding it because I thought it was dangerous, but the times I rode on the back were pretty fun. I'd say take it for a ride, but one of the rear brake lights is out."

Turning the unit off, I left the key on to see. Sure enough a rear brake light was out. I found a screwdriver and removed it. The bulb was missing, but inside was a small flash drive. I showed it to Helen and she put her hand over her mouth.

"How did it get in there?" she asked.

"Flynn put it there for safe keeping," I answered. "The shrewd devil occasionally did something smart."

"What's on it?"

"Let's go in and find out. But I'd hazard to guess it's the files Flynn found on their network."

Helen brought me her notebook. I plugged the drive into the spare USB port. When I tried to access the data on the drive I was prompted for a password. *What the hell could it have been?*

"Did he have a standard password he would use?" I asked Helen.

"Oh wow, I can't say for sure. He was so secretive about things of that nature. I know for basic items he wasn't concerned about he would use Jolene, Molly or my name in certain combinations."

"I don't believe he's used something easily guessed like those," I said. "Possibly something I would think of, figuring I'd be the one to find it or, if the police did, they would come to me. Not sure if he thought that far in advance, but hiding the drive makes me think he did. Now I need to figure it out."

Think Jarvis, think. There had to be something, some clue he left or gave me. My mind ran back over the last conversation we had on the phone. *Didn't he say something I was supposed to remember later?* I squeezed my eyes closed and let my mind roll back in time. There was something, a word or phrase, which seemed out of place when he said it. Something he normally didn't say when we talked or hadn't heard from him in sometime. Then it hit me.

"Dollar sign Smitty 723," said Flynn on our last call.

I was so perturbed and confused over the words that I really hadn't put it together. He had hesitated before saying it. When I questioned what he said, he stated, "Remember". And sure enough, I now did. A dollar sign, Smitty which had been my fake name as a kid and 723 the street number of our home in Old West Des Moines where we were raised.

"I think I figured it out" I said out loud. "Flynn said it in our last conversation. Something I'd only deduce. Damn, he sometimes could be pretty sharp!"

"What is it?" asked Helen.

"It could be several things. It's a matter of figuring the combination."

So, did the dollar sign replace the S in Smitty? I tried $mitty723 and it didn't work.

Then I tried $smitty723 and no go.

Finally, $Smitty723 and I was in.

"Hot damn!" I yelled out.

Molly got all excited and I reached down and hugged her, while Helen came around and looked over my shoulder to see what was on the screen. There were several folders containing many files of varying formats; spreadsheets, databases, MS Word and PDF. I began combing through them. There was much to look at and most of it didn't mean a damn thing to me, at least the data files. But there were several text-based files showing names of customers through the years, some of which I recognized and others I didn't. Flynn's name, along with several others who had joined him in pooling their money, was shown. One memo from Gabriel Gaines to his brother said to bring in more clients or their scam could collapse. This appeared to be the smoking gun. Now, it was a matter of what to do with it. I quickly made copies of everything and stored it to the cloud and emailed it to my lawyer, Barry, in Colorado. I, like my brother, was not ready to share this with the FBI. But I did plan to expose what I'd learned to the two Gaines brothers.

"I need to go shopping," I said to Helen. "Where is there a computer store nearby?"

Chapter 42

I was ready to stir things up. With enough to work with, the time was right. My time with Casey had been revealing. Whether she ran to her dad or step-father for help afterwards didn't matter to me. But after what she learned about Carlos, she might fear them and keep quiet. No matter, for today I would stoke the fires even more. After dropping Casey's .22 off at the FBI office for testing, I was going to pay a visit to Edwards's girlfriend, Tina Bailey. She liked to work out at Anytime Fitness in Clive, Casey had informed me. According to Tina's Facebook page, she was there now, sweating into her spandex. She was an internet poster child who enjoyed flaunting what she was doing every second of the day. It wasn't far, and I was in the door with a flash of my ID, and a little name dropping, and was standing in front of her staring as she ran on a treadmill.

Dressed all in workout clothes that hugged her toned body, she was moving at a steady pace. Her long auburn hair was tied back, her face showing little strain from the run. She was probably only an inch shorter than I was, and well-built, with all the right curves and proportions, which moved seductively, especially during exercise. I gave her a low-wattage smile which was charming, but not so she would jump over the front of the machine and wrap her legs around me, as would happen with the high-wattage version. Her concentration was good as she smiled back, maintaining her speed. She was used to men staring at her at the gym.

"Can I help you?" she said, her breath as if she were standing still.

"Tina, how have you been?" I said, as if we were old friends.

"Great," she responded with a bare look of uncertainty.

"Man, you look fabulous!"

"Thank you."

She slowed the machine down until it stopped. Grabbing the towel on the hand rest, she dried off her face and stepped off, looking me in the eye.

"You don't remember, do you?" I said.

"I'm sorry, no I don't."

"Not surprised, as it's been some time. We went to Hoover High together."

More information gleaned from her Facebook page.

"What was the name?"

"Smith. Pat Smith. My friends called me Smitty."

"And we were friends?"

I looked down, giving the timid by-golly look.

"No, not really. I sort of had a crush on you. I don't think you ever really paid attention to me. I was too shy to come up and talk with you, since you were the school hotty."

She smiled brightly.

"My loss. Not sure if I recall the face though."

"I've changed quite a bit. I was a gawky teenager. Overweight, with acne. I was a late bloomer."

She looked me up and down, slyly admiring what she saw in my six-foot frame.

"Apparently. I doubt I'd have missed you looking as you do now."

"Thank you. And I will say you look even better today than in your teens."

"Believe me, I have to work at it. Sweat like a pig to keep my form."

"I'm sure it's a rush for you to see men admiring your body."

"Yes, it can be a turn-on."

"Like now?"

"Maybe."

"Damn, I certainly wished I'd had the courage in high school to talk with you."

"Who cares about then, when we have now."

There was a hint of excitement in her eyes.

"So true. Can I buy you lunch when you are done toning your body?"

"Well, I normally run another couple of miles, but what the hell! Let me shower and I'll meet you outside."

"Sounds great. I'll try my best to keep the vision of you showering at bay."

She laughed and maybe even blushed a bit.

"Play your cards right and who knows…"

Walking away, she looked back and I smiled full wattage, knowing I had her, though she didn't come running and wrap her legs around me. Around thirty minutes later she was outside, in white shorts and a tank top, which barely contained her bra-less chest. She jumped in my car and we found a nearby sports bar which served food. We walked in together, finding a small two-seat table. I decided on a beer. She wanted a wine cooler. We added a basket of popcorn chicken to fill the food void.

"Hard to believe you are here with me," I stated. "I figured on a pretty thing like yourself being married or with someone."

"Does it matter if I did have someone else?" she said with a wicked smile.

"Not really. Though I wouldn't want some jealous husband coming after me."

She stopped to drink her red wine cooler and enjoy a couple of bites of chicken, a hint of desire flushing across her face.

"Well, I'm not married. And my guy is busy playing golf with his brother. A normal Sunday for him."

"Wow, his loss! And what do you do on Sunday?"

"Well, as you saw, I work out, then take a hot steam and do a little shopping."

"I guess you skipped the steam after the work out."

"There is still some time for steam if I so desire."

Under the table her hand grabbed at my inner thigh and began stroking. I must say it felt good, and for now I was going to let her enjoy herself. I put my hand on top of hers, sliding it further up.

"May I ask what your guy does? I want to make sure he isn't a cop or something before contemplating my next move."

"He is some stuffed shirt banker. He wouldn't and couldn't hurt a fly."

"So why are you with him?"

"Money mostly. Spends a lot to keep me happy. And I give him what he wants."

"Which would be?"

"Well I'm pretty enough to go to social gatherings and be his smiling hot girlfriend he can show off."

"Is that all?"

She leaned over and spoke into my ear.

"No, I let him fuck me however he desires. And believe me when I say this, I'm willing to give you the same for an afternoon you'll never forget. I suspect you would be way better in the sack than he is. And from what I can tell right now, endowed better too."

It was pretty clear where this was leading. I took her hand and moved it to her inner thigh, sliding it up until it reached her zipper. Her eyes closed. Pleasure was overtaking her. Again, the old me would have taken her and then flaunted it in Edward's face.

"Gee Edward, I had sex with your girlfriend, once in the shower at the gym, once in the bathroom at the bar, and then one last time in the car. Oh, and by the way, she had more orgasms with me in one afternoon than she's had with you the entire time you've been going out!"

While I guided her hand to stroke herself, I looked her square in the eye, her breathing getting heavier and heavier, her excitement building and building until her body began to shudder and shake in climax. With my other I pulled out a business card and tucked it down her shirt. She looked up, surprised and uncertain what I'd done. I leaned and whispered in her ear.

"I'll be sure to tell Edward how I mind-fucked you today," I said. "I'm certain he'll be thrilled to hear his girlfriend had an orgasm while sitting in a bar with the man who is going to put him in jail."

I threw down two twenties for the drinks and food, walking away satisfied in a separate way than she was, the moment before the horror of my words filled her mind.

Chapter 43

I was neither angry with myself nor proud of the games I'd played with the two women. They both were easy targets I had taken advantage of, but I didn't really care. I was on a mission now and nothing would get in my way. If either of them reported back to the men responsible, it would not matter. I had learned enough and was about to light the fuse on the power keg that would blow things wide open.

One of the items Casey had shared with me, which Tina had confirmed, was the Wyche brothers played golf every Sunday, with a standing reservation at the Urbandale Golf and Country Club for noon, and would finish up between three and four. Then, they'd enjoy a drink or two at the bar, along with a meal. Today I planned to pay them a visit with lit match in hand.

When I arrived at the club, I made my way into the dining room and took a seat. A waiter came by and took my drink order and I watched the room. It was a little after three, but it had been raining some today, so golfing would be on the slow side. I had been provided pictures by Agent Wilson, so I knew who to look for. At around 3:30, they came in and took a table with two other gentlemen, probably part of their foursome. I called over the waiter again, wrote down a note, and asked him to give it to either of the Gaines brothers. When they read the note, they looked my way and I waved. I wasn't certain if they would join me, but what I wrote should have gotten their attention. They each talked back and forth, then Gabriel excused himself and sat next to me.

He was not a big man, probably 5'9", maybe 160 pounds, with receding, blonde hair and nice tan. His golf clothes were expensive and more traditional, with plaid knickers, tall socks and argyle sweater. I wanted to ask him if he had a leprechaun on his shoulder, but resisted. I gave him a warm smile as he sat down, something he didn't return, as his eyes bore through me like acid.

"What the hell is the meaning of the note you wrote?" he said, softly, but with angry tones.

"I figured 'Hi sailor' wouldn't work," I replied. "Something a little more direct would solicit a response."

"A note 'You killed my brother and now I'm coming for you'

would, indeed," Gabriel said. "Of course, I have no idea what you are referring to. I'd suggest you leave before I call the manager. I carry a lot of weight around here."

"I'm certain you do, but I couldn't care less. Bring over the manager and I will show them some things you won't want others to see. Documents, pictures, and even say a few things about your niece, Casey, and your brother's girlfriend, Tina."

I pulled out my phone and brought up a document and then handed it to him. He looked at it with little apparent reaction, though you could tell he recognized it. He handed me back the phone quickly.

"No idea what this is," Gabriel said.

"Sure you do. But if not, then I'll start going around and showing others here, starting with the two men in your foursome. Now, to prevent this, have your brother join us so we can discuss this nice and calmly."

Waiting for a few moments, he stared, maybe in hopes of scaring me, but failed. He shook his head and went over and whispered in his brother's ear. He looked shocked and didn't care to leave his table. Gabriel said some more words and then got tense, before he agreed.

Edward appeared to be the older of the two, dressed in slacks and a golf shirt, with blonde hair though, unlike his brother's, his wasn't thinning. He was a bit taller and thicker, and appeared to be nervous. He didn't look to be the alpha in this relationship.

"Okay, say what is on your mind," stated Gabriel. "And make it quick so we can return to our guests."

"Prospective clients," I said. "Or maybe patsies would be a truer term."

Gabriel made a mean face, while Edward was startled. I decided to direct all of my conjectures his way.

"Edward, I know what has been going on here," I said, loudly enough so they could hear but others couldn't. If I was losing them, my vocal pitch would increase. "The stealing, lying and the killing. All so you can afford this fancy lifestyle you and your brother live. Nice for you and the wives or girlfriends, or both. A couple of movers and shakers like you two probably keep a little sweet honey on the side. Pussy on demand."

Edward was getting nervous. His hand was shaking as he took a long draw on his wine he'd carried over. My next words wouldn't help any.

"Speaking of which, Tina says 'Hi Eddie.' We spent some time together at lunch after her work out, and I provided her some stimulation. It didn't take much to get her off. Apparently, she's a little backed up, since you don't measure up when it comes to satisfying her."

Edward blushed, as if embarrassed by his shortcomings.

"Don't be crude," stated Gabriel.

"Oh, come now, Gabe, I'm only speaking the truth. Her words, not mine. A hot gal like Tina would only be with an old man like Eddie for one reason, and that would be the money he spends on her. You and Eddie here are living high on the hog. Of course, it's tainted money, since you're stealing from people and running money for Alexander the Bull."

When I said the name, it startled Edward, and he spilled his glass and nearly fell over backward in his chair. Gabriel put his hand on his brother, grabbed the glass, but didn't show anything but disgust. The waiter came over and cleaned up the wine and refilled the glass, which Edward immediately drank from.

"Let me tell you what I know," I stated. "I know Eddie here has a Hedge fund, all on the up and up, pulling in a pretty good return for its investors. Money from Alexander Toro's criminal business is laundered through this fund: dirty money in, clean money out. Giving him a way to hide it from the feds and keep his enterprise operational. I don't really completely understand all this fancy accounting, but I'm certain a math whiz with the bureau would."

I was on a roll now and wasn't about to stop.

"Gabe here ran his own investment dealings, pulling in money from people with the expectation of huge profits. But only a few profit, while others see very little if any of their money back. Gabe is one, Alexander another, and maybe a collective of ten other investors. People like my brother and his friends get the shaft. You tell them the businesses you invested in failed or went bankrupt and their money is lost. You point to the contract which says you could lose some or all of your money in the deal, which is pretty standard. Yet it's a scam, a house of cards which will soon collapse on itself, for there is no more money coming in to replace what you are taking out. Maybe you plan to close up shop, cut and run, maybe start up something else when the timing is right, and the funds you are living off of dry up."

Edward had finished his wine and called for more, while munching on an appetizer he had ordered when sitting at the other table. Gabriel continued to nurse his Scotch and ice, his expression rarely changing.

"The thing is, all is good until my brother comes along. Flynn never was good at leaving things alone. He was in a money bind, thanks to his poor investment in your scam, which he'd dragged several of his friends and clients into, and needed a way out. So, he started looking into things and found a weak link, and this was Casey. She liked men, and seemed to want to be with several at one time. Flynn has always been a playboy at heart, even when married. Good looking and smooth talking, it didn't take much to get Casey in the sack. Hell, she was ready to jump my bones if I'd let her. He worked her for several months, biding his time before asking her about getting him a job with her dad, which is you, Eddie. You met for dinner and he charmed your pants off, almost as well as he did your daughter. Flynn could run a line of bullshit with the best of them. He was in, now, and all he needed was to find something, which my persistent brother did. Problem was you learned about it, somehow. Maybe your systems inform you when files are accessed. Could be it was a carrot you placed there to lure him out, figuring you could get it back. You two probably aren't complete idiots. Once learned, you knew trouble was around the corner. You called in your buddy Alexander the Bull and he sent some men after poor Flynn. Tortured him, beat him up, cut off several of his fingers, and when it was all done shot him in the head."

This part I didn't care to relive, but needed to use it for effect. Edward was now sweating profusely from his forehead and through the pits of his gold shirt.

"One thing about Flynn was, he wasn't stupid. He had the evidence, but knew it would do him no good if you found him with it. He hid and password protected it, putting it somewhere he hoped I would find it. Maybe even had a copy you did find, thinking it was the only one. Well, gentlemen, I did locate it and I have it all right here. This flash drive shows you all of what he found. It, of course, isn't the only copy. I've made sure my lawyer has a duplicate, and copies are stored in cloud servers waiting to be shared with my friends at the FBI. I think you'll find the evidence here is sufficient to bring you down, or at the very least get the IRS to look more deeply into your books and operation. 'Probable cause' I believe is the term they like to use."

"Let's say what we have here is what you claim it to be," said Gabriel. "What will it take to make it go away?"

"Nothing short of confessing to my brother's murder, coming clean on your money stealing operation, and rolling over on Alexander Toro. Short of that, we have nothing to talk about."

"Then why the grandiose show in front of us if you don't care to make a deal?" said Gabriel. "If you have all of this, why not go to Agent Wilson and see what happens?"

I slid my chair over to Edward and put my arm around him.

"Because I want it all," I said, looking him straight in the eye. "I'm going to get you for all of it. No ifs, ands, or buts. I'm going to bring you all down and make sure my brother didn't die in vain."

I could feel Edward cringe at my words and I moved my lips to his ear.

"And I wanted to see you sweat," I said loudly so everyone could hear.

I stood up, grabbed a cloth napkin, and tossed it to Edward.

"It would appear I succeeded."

Chapter 44

There was little doubt I'd put myself in the line of fire. This was fine, because this was what I was hoping for. Putting Helen and Jolene in the crosshairs as well didn't thrill me, but Rocky was skilled and they were in good hands. All we needed was to be prepared.

We had spent time going over the house, the weak points and the best place from which to fight. The ladies knew, when told, they should take Molly, go upstairs, lock the door, and hide in the cast iron tub. Helen was given a small snub nosed .38, to be used, only if directly threatened. There was a basement, but the two windows had bars over them, making entry challenging. The front and back door by the kitchen were solid wood from a time long since passed, when doors were made this way with good deadbolt locks that were difficult, but not impossible, to breach. There was a large window in the living room where the couch sat, a pair of smaller windows on the driveway side, easy to smash or shoot through. The kitchen had a tiny window you could access from a small porch where the doorway existed. If there was time and money, we'd get all of the windows barred, but for now we'd have to deal with it. The best protections were the stairwells leading upstairs and to the basement, and the archway connecting the living room and windowless office. Also, a coat closet by the front door provided some cover, as did the small half bathroom. Each night one of us rested on the sofa, while the other slept in Jolene's room, while she shared a bed with her mother. That night I dozed in a recliner, my gun sitting close by. Molly slept on the floor next to me, ever vigilant for any sound out of place, one of her strengths even in her later years.

Sleeping as well as could be expected on a ten-year-old recliner, I awoke and used the restroom. When walking back I saw Molly's head rise, her ears flopping at something outside. Jolene was coming down the stairs and I motioned her to stop. I walked over to the front window and peered through a crack in the dark curtains. It was barely light out. I saw an overgrown SUV parked across the street. The windows were tinted, so I couldn't see who was inside. The engine was running and, for all I knew, it was a neighbor's car. Of course, I'd memorized all the vehicles which came and went, and this wasn't one I'd inventoried. Molly started to growl when four men stepped out in unison. All were dressed in black with masks over their faces, each carrying a weapon capable of firing multiple bullets per second. I spoke to Molly to come and took her to the stairwell.

"Take her upstairs, grab your mom, and lock yourself into the bathroom as we discussed," I stated firmly. "Get Rocky down here right now."

Smartly, she didn't hesitate and ran up the stairs. I put on my pants, made sure my Beretta was ready, the shoulder holster with extra magazines, and my .38 as backup in a holster on my belt, leather sap in my back pocket. Rocky came down, shotgun and Glock at the ready, his knife on his belt.

"How many?" he asked.

"Four with automatic machine pistols. As we discussed, you hold the fort here while I take the kitchen. Do what you must, but I'd like one alive, so I can talk with him."

Rocky didn't argue, though I knew he would shoot to kill, especially with the amount of firepower coming at us. I made it to the kitchen, making sure the door was bolted, tipped over the table so it faced the door, and got low in the stairwell to the basement, ready for any noise or movement. Since they didn't know the layout of the house, we'd use it to our advantage. If they saw the table, they would assume someone was using it for cover. Rocky would do the same thing with the sofa, which he would move with ease. Now we waited, time on our side.

The waiting game was easy for me. I had plenty of time. I thought of my life the last year, the highs and lows, love and death. Melissa, Dennis, Bill, Ray, Raven and Kate had been the positives. Emily, Leather, Marquis, Grady, Mack, Roland, Dirk, Merrick and Jack were the negatives. Then there was Brandon and Rocky, which bled over into both, for which I was thankful and fearful at the same time. Several of the bad people had died. Most had deserved death, but a few – like Ariela, Jack and Dona – hadn't. They had done bad things, but should still be alive today. Not directly my fault, but certainly I'd done little to prevent it. Those events continued to swirl around me, jump in and out of my thoughts, never leaving me for too long. Maybe it was making me a better detective and person. It for damn sure didn't make sleeping at night easier.

Now two more deaths, Flynn and Carlos, with more likely to happen now. These men would not leave without killing me and everyone else in the house. Standing up and saying "Hey, let's talk about this before we shoot it out" wouldn't work. They were here to do a job and kill. I had goaded the bad guys into action, so I had expected no less. Mine was to prevent it, those I was protecting to live another day.

The moment was at hand. I heard them working the backdoor, finding it locked. There was a long pause, then I heard the sizzle of a fuse. A loud pop went off and the door flew open. Another pop came from the living room, both timed to open simultaneously. No one stepped in, and I waited, having a clear line of sight. A head peeked through the doorway and back again. In came one man high, another behind coming in low. They saw the table and fired into it, the noise loud, the table never standing a chance. The high man walked over and looked to see no one there, then turned and I fired, squeezing off three rounds, taking out his legs, his scream of pain filling the kitchen. The low man rolled and I fired three more rounds, catching him in the shoulder and neck. He fired back, but I was protected by the stairwell, his aim high anyway. He tried to get up and run out the backdoor, but I fired again into the back of his head and he fell down the porch stairs.

I crawled out of the stairwell and saw the man I'd shot in the legs clutching his wounds. His machine pistol was nearby and he tried to reach for it, but I pointed at him, ready to fire again, so he stopped. I slid it away from him and waited. Rocky walked in, dragging one of the other men, having shot him in the side and hand, a wide grin on his face.

"One to talk to like you asked?" he said. "The other is dead."

Checking on the one outside I found him dead as well. We had to talk with them before the police arrived. We needed to be quick.

"Which one of you cares to tell me who sent you?" I asked.

Neither responded at first. Over by the archway to the living room, leaning against the wall, was one of the aluminum baseball bats Rocky had taken from the James Brothers. He grabbed it and tossed it to me. I pressed the end of it into the leg wounds of the one I'd shot. He yelped in pain, but still nothing.

"The first to talk lives," said Rocky. "If neither of you speak, then I'll shoot one of you at random."

Both remained quiet, other than the loud breathing from their pain. Rocky took his gun and killed the man he was holding, shooting him in the head. The other on the floor saw this and cringed. I then pointed my gun at his head.

"You have ten seconds," I said. I could hear sirens in the background and started to count.

"Alexander Toro hired us," he said.

"Who were you supposed to kill?"

"Everyone in the house I found."

"Did he say why?"

"No. Kill you all and then burn down the house."

I pulled out my phone and called Frakes.

"I need you here right now. We are about to be stormed by the West Des Moines police and I need a friendly face."

"What happened?"

"Alexander the Bull made a run at us at my brother's house and lost. I have three dead bodies and one still alive."

"Crap. I'll be right over."

I was really screwing up the violent death average for the greater Des Moines area.

Chapter 45

A couple of squad cars arrived, so Rocky and I surrendered our weapons. I dropped Frakes name to keep them from shooting us. When he showed up, they let us loose and I went and got Helen and Jolene, for they weren't supposed to leave until they heard from either of us, and had been told to shoot if anyone opened the door that wasn't us. The place was crawling with tech people going over the scene, and they had plenty to do. Three dead bodies, one in the living room, one in the kitchen and one out the back stairs. The fourth man was being attended to by paramedics, with strict orders not to leave him alone. Since the sofa and table had been shot up, we moved outside to talk. Frakes wasn't thrilled with the carnage, but seemed impressed with our accomplishments.

"Wow, four guys with automatic weapons and you took them all down," he said.

"Yes, and left one for questioning," I answered. "Don't you dare leave him alone or he won't live long, either in jail or if he gets out."

"Did you get any answers from him?" asked Frakes. "He is not saying a word to us at this point."

"He told me what I suspected. It has to do with my brother's murder. They were here to kill all of us and burn the house down."

"They have no ID on them. We will run their prints and see what we come up with. I doubt they work at QuickTrip as clerks. No plates on the SUV, though I'm certain it was stolen and will lead us nowhere."

Standing outside, Helen and Jolene seemed be holding up well enough. They had Molly on a leash as she sat in the grass panting and taking in all the activity.

"Detective Frakes, this is Helen, Jolene, and the one lying on the ground with her tongue hanging out is Molly."

"Good to meet you, ladies. I'm sorry for your loss and what happened here. It would appear you are in good hands, though. If you'd like to walk Molly, you may."

"If they walk, either Rocky or I must go with them."

Frakes looked over at Rocky, uncertain what to make of the imposing figure creating a large shadow from the rising sun.

"Sure, the four of you can leave while I talk with Jarvis," stated

Frakes. "Do you need a weapon?"

Rocky had firm grip on a baseball bat and smacked it a couple times in his open hand.

"No," he said with a smile and they walked away.

"Quite a mess. You know since you came into town the homicide rate has sky rocketed."

"I'm not sure they qualify as homicides, as we were defending ourselves. The homicides would have been if they had succeeded. Fortunately, we were able to thwart them."

"I don't expect any trouble for you here. We are going to be here a while. The place is pretty shot up and both front doors blown off. You won't be able to occupy the home until we are done and the damage repaired. Do you have a place to stay?"

"Other than a hotel, no. You don't happen to have a safe house we can borrow with police protection?"

"Hell no. This is West Des Moines and we don't have the budget or need for such things. Check with your FBI buddy, Wilson. He is the one with the resources. I'm only a simple Midwest detective who mostly deals with domestic violence and rape."

"Consider it good on-the-job training for if you want to move to big city crime."

"I like it fine right here," said Frakes. "Give me all the details of what took place this morning and don't leave anything out."

I covered my last forty-eight hours; my questioning and semi-seduction of Casey and Tina, the confrontation with the Wyche brothers, especially Gabriel. And the black SUV pulling up and the four men assaulting the house. I left out the part about finding the flash drive. I was still holding this in reserve. Frakes took it all in, making notes as I went along.

"Dogs are something else how they can sense danger," stated Frakes. "If I were you, I'd keep her handy. I doubt this is the end of it."

I agreed and, when the others returned, Frakes took them one at a time, learning what they knew. I stepped away and made a call to Wilson. It was Monday morning, so he should have been at his desk. He answered on the first ring.

"I'm hearing rumblings something may have happened at the Mann household," he said.

"It did. Four men came and tried to kill all of us. We prevailed."

"What caused them to come after you now?"
"My persistence in pestering them."
"You mean being a pain in the ass! I'm well aware of this talent you have."
"It's a finely-honed skill."
"Impressive, you besting four heavily armed men. Did any of them survive?"
"One did and we talked to him before the police arrived. Alexander Toro sent them. I'd say you should talk with him quickly. I doubt he'll be alive long."
"I'll have my men intervene and take him away."
"He'll be heading for the hospital. I shot him several times in the legs. Frakes says they are taking him to Mercy Medical Center-West Lakes. I'd put a guard or two on him."
"Done. Ballistics came back on the .22 and it's not the gun which killed your brother."
"Legally obtained?"
"Yes, it's registered to Casey Gaines. All on the up and up."
"No surprise there. It's what I expected. We need a favor."
"Oh boy, I can hardly wait."
"The Mann house was shot up. We need somewhere to stay and I'd rather not put them in a hotel. Too confining if they try again. You have any safe houses in the area?"
There was a long pause before he spoke.
"Maybe, though I'm not certain of its availability."
"Start making calls. We need somewhere and I can't go out and rent a house in twelve hours."
"I'm not sure I can find something that quick."
"You are the FBI. You can do anything which needs to be done. Make it happen."
He wasn't happy with me bossing him, but I didn't care. After hanging up, I called back to Denver, looking for some advice. It was still early there, but I knew he would be hard at work as always. He answered his cell phone on the second ring.
"Jarvis Mann, you are still alive," said Brandon Sparks. "How are things going in corn country?"
"Well enough, though a quartet of men tried to kill us all."
"It would appear they failed. I'm sure Rocky did an admirable job as always."

"He did as I expected him to."

"What are you needing now?"

"Information, since you are connected in ways I'm not."

"Another favor, it would seem. They are piling up on my side. Are you certain you want to be indebted to me any further?"

He was right about this, but I had little choice.

"The person I'm interested in is Alexander Toro. It would seem our paths have crossed and he likely is the one who killed my brother."

The line went completely silent.

"Are you still there?" I asked.

"This mess you are in is related to The Bull?"

"It is."

"Don't do anything else. I'm flying to Des Moines."

With his statement, the phone went dead. It appeared as if we'd have company for dinner.

Chapter 46

Agent Wilson, after some fussing, got us set up at a home in the western part of the city. It was new and modern, on a decent chunk of land, with four bedrooms, big garage, and some privacy provided by fencing and huge trees. We packed up as many items as we needed, when the police allowed us, and moved in. The ladies needed to do some grocery shopping, so we hit a nearby Hy-Vee and spent $350 dollars to stock the place. Once settled, we were all tired, and relaxed as best we could from the stressful day. Molly was loving the new home, inside and out, smelling all her nose could handle until she finally crashed. As dinnertime approached, my cell phone rang and it was Brandon.

"Let's meet somewhere and talk," he said.

"Didn't take you long to get here."

"Having a private jet speeds things up."

No surprise he had one in his stockpile of possessions.

"How about Roni's Italian Bistro? I know the owner and she says it's fabulous."

"I'll find it and meet you there in an hour."

As I drove over, I wasn't certain why I picked Roni's restaurant. I did want to see the place, try the food, and enjoy a quiet meal after the grueling day. Inside, something was nagging at me to see her again. The distance from home and the craziness of the last twenty-four hours all contributed. With Brandon there, I was sure I'd be safe from any temptation, since this was a business meeting.

When I arrived, the place was pretty busy, but had room for two, so I didn't need to name drop. Brandon showed up a few minutes after, dressed in his normal upscale casual, expensive black jeans, boots and collared, long sleeve shirt. He shook my hand firmly, sitting across from me. When the waitress arrived, he ordered his Jack Daniels with no ice, a bottle of expensive wine, and some breadsticks. I settled for a foreign beer on the waiter's suggestion.

"You know the owner," stated Brandon. "Looks like a delightful place, and doing quite well, it would appear. Is she here?"

"I'm pretty certain. She rarely isn't here. Works in the kitchen supervising."

"How do you know her?"

"Old girlfriend from high school."

"One who got away," said Brandon, drinking his JD moments after the waiter set it before him.

"I ended it with her. She wanted commitment and I didn't."

"Yes, the Jarvis Mann foible. Always interesting seeing changes in people after fifteen to twenty years. Some become more handsome or beautiful with time, others not so much. Where does she fall?"

"Still beautiful, possibly more so. Time has been kind to her."

"I sense temptation."

I shrugged, as if to say maybe.

"I won't tell, if so. I may get a sense of the attraction for myself, as a lovely lady is heading our way right now."

Roni arrived, dressed for restaurant business, one-piece cyan dress, with gold belt and white heels. I stood, as did Brandon, and she gave me a hug and shook Brandon's hand after an introduction, which he held for what appeared to be an eternity, cupping hers in both of his.

"Good to meet you," Roni said. "Are you and Jarvis old friends?"

Brandon smiled and sat down, leaving me to answer.

"We are acquaintances," I replied. "He is here to provide me support."

"Is this related to the Flynn and Helen problem?"

I nodded.

"I heard something on the news and tried to call Helen. Is everything okay?"

"For now, she and Jolene are safe."

"And you?"

"I'm good and will be even better after a satisfying meal. What do you recommend?"

"Well, I know you are partial to spaghetti and meatballs, if the past is any clue. Our steaks are also out of this world."

"Spaghetti rarely disappoints me. What about you, Brandon?"

"Chicken Parmesan sounds good," he said. "Will you be cooking it for us?"

"No, but I will supervise and make sure it's perfect. Anything else?"

"I'm always looking for solid investments. If the food is good, maybe we can have lunch someday to discuss if you have need for a silent partner."

"I'm always open to possibilities," she answered with a glorious smile.

She called over the waiter and gave him our order, and then walked away. Brandon watched her the whole time, and I felt a small pang of jealousy, though I was uncertain why.

"Lovely woman," said Brandon. "I did not notice a ring."

"Divorced. Her business is her love."

"I know the feeling. Doesn't mean there isn't a fire down below which needs attention."

I couldn't argue the point and wanted to change the topic.

"The biggest item which needs attention right now is this business with Alexander Toro. When I mentioned his name, you didn't hesitate to jump on your jet and fly out here. I assume you know him."

Brandon ate a breadstick and finished his JD.

"I know of him, but have never met him. He is maybe the most powerful man in the criminal world of the Midwest. He is also extremely ruthless and territorial."

"More so than you?"

Brandon smiled.

"I am a pussy cat compared to him."

"So, this tells me quite a bit. The question is what can I do?"

"I've arranged to meet with him. You, Rocky and I are going to fly to Illinois tomorrow and see if we can come to an understanding."

"I can't leave Helen and Jolene unprotected."

"They will be safe. He gave me his word he would try nothing further until after we meet."

"His word is good?"

"Through the channels I went through, yes. You can trust his word."

"Still, I'd feel better if they weren't alone."

"I brought my two men who provide protection for me when I travel. They will stay with them until we return. I'm certain you and Rocky are adequate protection for the trip."

I smiled at his humor.

"So, what time will we leave?"

"Sharply at 7 a.m. We are to meet at around nine or so."

"What is there to discuss? If he killed or had my brother killed, he must pay the price."

"I don't know what understanding you can come to. But you must go with an open mind. For if this is to continue, you will all die, and it will likely not be pleasant."

"Like what they did to Flynn?"

"I've heard worse. The stories going around say that Alexander the Bull has no qualms about inflicting as much pain on his victims as possible. He generally is a witness to the torture, and often even partakes in it. My sources say he took a hacksaw and severed a man's leg, forcing him to watch, a tourniquet in place above where he cut it off, so he didn't bleed to death. It seems he was being kind to your brother by only cutting off his fingers and beating him up before killing him."

Kind was hardly the word I would use. Maybe Alexander had a soft spot for his step-daughter and went easy on Flynn, or at least easier than normal.

"So why are you doing this?" I asked, fearing the answer.

"Isn't it clear I like you, Jarvis?" he said. "The world is more enjoyable with you in it. I would miss having you around."

I wasn't sure if I should take it as a compliment or be worried I'd become his PI boy-toy.

"Well, business hasn't been boring since you came into my life."

The food arrived and all tasted good. Brandon enjoyed his wine and meal, while I filled myself with pasta and meatballs. About ten minutes in, Roni came over to check on us.

"So, how is everything?" she asked.

"Excellent," I said, after wiping sauce from my face.

"Outstanding," added Brandon. "I do believe we should talk of options."

She smiled widely and handed him her card.

"Call me anytime and we can discuss," she said while putting out her hand.

Brandon stood up, took the card in one hand and took her hand with the other, pulled it up and kissed it gently. There was some heat between them. I imagined more than a business meeting in the offing. The pang of jealously returned and there wasn't a damn thing I could do about it but order another beer.

Chapter 47

We were up and in the air bright and early the next morning, flying in Brandon's Learjet, headed east. My nerves on the smaller plane weren't any better than on the big ones. I was always happiest when fully in the air or on the ground. Take offs and landings were always nerve-racking for me.

The flight was quiet and quick, maybe ninety minutes flying time. Rocky was busy reading his Kindle and I wondered what exciting books he read. If it was a saucy romance, it would ruin my ideal of him. Brandon talked on the phone nearly the entire flight and I wondered how he could hold a cell connection going several hundred miles an hour in the air, when mine dropped when standing completely still. Maybe he paid for priority service.

When we landed at a small airport west of Chicago, a limo waited for us with food and drink in the back. I settled for water, while Brandon had his JD and Rocky chose a beer. Food was basic: some cheese, chips, crackers and dip. I wasn't real hungry. Nerves from the flight and the impending meeting ran roughshod in my stomach. Expectations were uncertain, other than that we would meet and discuss. If there was a way out, I was open to options, but anything short of putting my brother's killer in jail would be hard to accept.

After forty-five minutes of drive time, we arrived at an old manufacturing plant, parking in a cracked and weed infested parking lot. We were the first to show up, sitting and waiting in the air-conditioned back. The day was warm and humid, so I was glad I'd put on the extra layer of deodorant.

"When they arrive, we'll step outside and wait," stated Brandon. "Let me do the talking at first. And don't do anything silly to provoke his anger. Simply a meet and greet. This is not the time for you to spring to action. Give me your word you will keep your gun holstered."

"So long as they do," I answered.

"They will. If they don't, I doubt it will matter much. He will likely have more firepower than we do."

I turned to look at Rocky and he smiled.

"It would have to be an army," he said.

The buildings of the plant looked as if they hadn't been used in years. Doors were broken and open, windows missing or cracked. A weathered sign hinted of it once being a meat processing facility. There was farm land all around, with this year's crops beginning to sprout. A set of rusted train tracks ran to the main line miles down the road. I had no cell service when I checked my phone. There was not another soul nearby, so if it all went south we would likely die here, which wasn't comforting. I couldn't imagine Brandon coming here if he thought there was danger, so I took him at his word all would be safe so long as I didn't start something.

In a cloud of dust, four large Chevy SUVs came down the road. Two pulled up facing us, a third parked behind, the fourth pulling sideways behind the third. Several men got out of the front two, guns at their sides, waving for us to step out. Brandon got out first, followed by Rocky, and then myself. We walked side by side, the sun and humidity baking us, about fifty feet before they waved us to stop. I felt exposed, with thoughts of the O.K. Corral coming to mind and I wondered which of the Earp brothers I was.

From the middle SUV stepped out two men, one heavy-set and older, the other younger, lean and a bit taller. The heavy-set gentleman took the lead and waved for the armed men to spread out. He took short steps, his feet in expensive, black dress shoes, and a well-tailored white suit holding in his girth. His bald head glistened in the sun, sweat starting to form. He looked to be pushing sixty and labored from the building heat. He stopped about twenty feet in front of us, the younger lean man a step behind and to the right of him.

"Alexander, it is good to meet you," said Brandon.

"I am here because of the respect I have for you," replied Alexander.

"And I for you."

"I know of your long-haired friend as well," said Alexander. "His reputation is stellar. What name are you going by now?"

"You may call me Rocky," he said.

"If I'd known I was sending men to face you, I'd have sent more. I know you are formidable."

"You would have required quite a few more," said Rocky with a smile.

"Yes, I'm certain of this. Though no man is unkillable."

"No one has succeeded yet. I may be the very definition."

Alexander laughed. At least he had a sense of humor.

"And you would be?" he asked of me.
"Jarvis Mann."
"Oh yes, the PI from Denver. The one who is pestering my business."
"It is my highly honed skill."
An expression I'd been using a lot lately. Another business card slogan, though he did not laugh at my words, which was not a good sign.
"Brandon, we can stand here all day and discuss resumes," stated Alexander. "But it is too hot to lounge around and socialize. I am here to listen to what you can offer me to resolve this conflict."
"Well, it seems you have sent men to kill Rocky, Jarvis, and members of the Mann family. We would like this to stop."
"It will stop when he stops nosing into my affairs."
"He believes someone needs to pay for the murder of his brother."
"Is that so? And who do you expect killed your brother?"
"You did," I said boldly. "Or at least ordered his death."
"Strong words. Do you have evidence of this?"
"Working on it. Also, the deaths of Carlos and the woman in his apartment. You are responsible for ordering them as well."
"My understanding is it was a murder-suicide."
"The Des Moines police don't think so. It's only a matter of proving it, which I will help them do in time."
"Continuing will get you killed, along with your other family members. Is it worth this potential cost to wage this vendetta?"
"I run a close second on the unkillable meter."
"I can snap my fingers right now and these men will gun you down before you can pull your weapon."
"We had an agreement, Alexander," said Brandon. "No shooting. We are only here to talk this out. Jarvis understands this as well, don't you?"
I nodded, for I knew that in this current situation, I couldn't win.
"Then let us talk," said Alexander. "Jarvis here must understand there is nothing he can do but walk away and leave the past in the past. Take the information he has found and bury it. Leave my family alone. Don't come near it again and he will live with no fear from me."
"And if I don't?" I asked.

"I can't make it any clearer than this; you, your sister-in-law, niece and anyone else who stands with you will die. This includes the unkillable Rocky. As I respect Mr. Sparks, I will give you seven days to take care of any personal business and for you to leave Des Moines, never to return. You have my word no attempts on you or your family will be made during this time. You leave and we will never bother you again. If you are still around at sundown next Monday and continue to bother Casey, her father, and her uncle, we will hunt you down. Messing with those in my family and in my business, is tantamount to declaring war on me. If the mood strikes me, I may have them bring you to me, so I can cut you up into little pieces, which I spared your brother from."

"What about all you've done to my family, in killing my brother?"

"Don't you see he was nothing? Only a fly speck needing to be washed away. None in your family is of any consequence to me. The same can be said of Carlos and his lover. I am Alexander the Bull, and I call all the shots."

There it was, he admitted to killing Flynn. I had no doubt, but I now know for certain. I was at the O.K. Corral, warned to be out of town by sundown Monday, a western cliché. I wanted to pull my gun and shoot him right then and there, but knew I'd be dead before I got off a round. with the firepower in front of me. I turned and walked back to the limo and crawled inside, thankful for the cooler air, though uncertain what my next move would be.

Brandon and Rocky joined me, and the limo pulled off back to the airport.

"Well, that went well," said Brandon.

"I know for certain he killed Flynn," I said. "And I know he sent the men to kill us. Now, I have seven days to decide what to do next."

"If I were you, I'd do as he said and leave town. Add it up as one in the loss column. No shame in losing."

"If they had killed your brother, would you?" I asked.

Brandon leaned back in his seat, a fresh glass of JD in his hands.

"Probably not. But of course, you aren't me. And, with respect to your talents, which I know are good, you aren't capable of winning this one. And I can't stand with you this time and provide support. You are on your own from here on if you plan to continue."

He was right. This was my battle and I had to decide if the price was worth it. *What to do, what to do?* Jack Daniels wasn't one of my favorites, but I was going to learn to like it. I reached over, grabbed the bottle, and poured myself a full glass. Drinking was what I was going to do until a better idea came along.

Chapter 48

I was not good at holding my liquor. A couple of beers here and there was all I normally drank. Hard to say how much JD was flowing through my veins. I only vaguely remember the flight back, the drive to the safe house and then somehow was now sitting at a bar. I wasn't sure how much time had passed. Through the window I could see it was getting dark. I scanned the room and it appeared familiar. Then it dawned on me: I was at Roni's Italian Bistro. I pulled out my phone and checked the phone log and found I'd tried to call Melissa. I had a vague memory of not getting her. It was a Tuesday and, depending on the time, she was likely working or at school. Anger and disappointment had filled me when I couldn't talk with her. I missed her and missed being with her. I needed companionship to pull me through, to help me find a solution. Right now, the only answer I had was I had drunk too much, certainly more than I was capable of. I headed to the bathroom, found an open stall, and threw up. After ten minutes of emptying my stomach and cleaning up, I felt marginally better and came back, hoping to get some food. Standing there before me was Roni, looking sad. Apparently, she knew I was there, yet I didn't recall talking with her.

"Feel any better?" she asked, her hand on my shoulder.

"I need food. Something plain an empty stomach can handle."

"I can whip up something," she answered, then spoke to the female bartender. "No more liquor for Jarvis. Sierra Mist on the rocks."

She walked away while I sipped my soda. In a few minutes she returned with plain pasta and cheese ravioli.

"I'm assuming you can still feed yourself?" she said with a grin.

"Ha, ha. I'm sure I can handle it without stabbing myself."

I slowly ate, in hopes it would stay down. I knew it would help some, but only time would clear the booze from my system.

"How the hell did I get here?" I asked.

"Brandon dropped you off."

"Really."

"Yes, he wanted to talk business, which we did. He is quite charming."

"Did you close the deal?"

"Not yet. He wanted to have dinner tonight."

"You two have plans?"

"I told him not tonight. I needed to make sure you were okay."

I felt a pang inside, but it wasn't from the booze or the food. I was flattered she wanted to see me through this, since it was hardly my finest moment.

"I'm definitely feeling the effects of too much Jack Daniels."

"My experience says when you drink like this something is troubling you. Do you need someone to talk to?"

I nodded.

"Let me check on a few things and we can go somewhere quieter to converse."

I finished my pasta and soda, feeling more human than earlier, though still not myself. She returned in about fifteen minutes and led me outside to her car, helping me in, buckling my seatbelt and kissing me on the top of the head. She drove carefully and soon we arrived at her place. She got me inside, seated on the sofa, returning with some ibuprofen for my throbbing head. She had changed out of her work clothes and was sitting next to me in shorts and T-shirt. She smelled wonderful as she turned to look at me.

"Tell me what is bothering you? I'm all yours for the evening."

"This damn business with Flynn," I stated. "I'm in so deep and I don't see a way out. If I quit on it without bringing his killer to justice, I will have failed."

"Certainly, you've failed before," she replied. "It can't be the first time a case hasn't finished the way you hoped."

"No, I've been down this road before. But it's personal. Not only have I failed Flynn, but Helen and Jolene as well."

"So where are you at now with it all?" Roni asked.

I spelled out the details of my meeting with Alexander the Bull, the timeline he laid out, and his ultimatum. She listened to every word I said, no judgment in her eyes, no concern or fear. When I finished she reached out her hand and held mine.

"Take your time to decide," Roni said. "In the end, you have to do what is best for Helen and Jolene. Helen loved and hated Flynn, all at the same time. I'm sure finding his killer is of some importance, but being able to live her life without fear for her and Jolene is paramount. Don't let your pride get in the way of making the right decision here. It seems you have no choice but to walk away."

"It all makes sense, but it's hard to let go."

"Though I'd be sad you can never come back to Des Moines, I'd be even sadder, even crushed, if you were to die, knowing there was no possibility of seeing you again. You must let it go. If not for yourself, then for those who care for you."

I felt the heavy burden hit me as I slumped over onto Roni's lap. I wanted to finish what Flynn had started, bring his killer to justice. But it wasn't going to be. I had to walk away, no matter how much I hated to. I wanted to cry, but the remaining booze in my veins held the tears in check. I rested on her lap for some time, feeling her hand gently running through my hair, then I heard her speak.

"Well, I hate to say it, Jarvis, but you smell," she said. "You should take a shower and maybe brush your teeth. It will make you feel better."

She got me up and led me to the bathroom, pointing out where everything was. She provided a fresh toothbrush and robe and, though it felt odd, I stripped before her, so she could take my clothes and launder them. I stepped under the water and enjoyed the stream. It cleared my head some as I rinsed my stench and troubles away, my mind a blur on what I was doing here. I had minty breath and soapy aroma when I stepped out of the bathroom in the robe. Roni was standing there waiting for me, also in a robe. She grabbed my hand and led me into her bedroom. She put her arms around me and began kissing my neck and ear. Her lips moved to my mouth and I found myself kissing her back. I wanted to escape it all and she was there for me to get lost. The kissing became stronger and more passionate. She opened my robe, removing it, pushing me down to the bed. She opened her robe, her naked body before me, and she crawled on top. My mind said no, though I couldn't for this moment say why, my body taking precedence, aroused and ready. All my anger and concern were gone as I plunged deep inside of her, escaping the hell that had occupied my last month, releasing a passion with a woman I shouldn't be with, though I couldn't see myself with anyone else at the moment. There was no regret at the first or second climax; we would enjoy this night. Regret would come later with a throbbing headache in the morning light and the realization of the mistake I'd made and the trust I had broken.

Chapter 49

When I awoke in the morning I felt like a cad and hungover like I hadn't felt in many years. It was not a good combo and I really wasn't sure what to do. I could try to sneak out, but my clothes were still in the washer or dryer and I had no idea where they were. Being a detective, I could have searched for them, but for some reason didn't make the effort. I crawled out of bed naked and found the bathroom, and more ibuprofen to ease the pounding.

Looking at myself in the mirror revealed a worn-down man with more guilt to deal with. Guilt for not being able to find my brother's killer and for sleeping with someone else when I was in a committed relationship. I could spin it all I wanted, but this was a major screw up. Sure, I had been drunk earlier, but I knew what I was doing when she pulled me into the bedroom. I could have put an end to it, but didn't. Deep down, I was afraid I had wanted this. Maybe to give me an excuse to end it with Melissa. No matter how much I tried to tell myself, the facts were I was in many ways like my brother when it came to relationships. Even with a good woman, it never seemed enough for me. It was a failing I couldn't seem to overcome.

Roni stepped into the bathroom, hugging me from behind, her lips kissing my shoulders, her naked body pressed against me. I tried to remain calm. I turned around and kissed her softly, for it seemed the correct thing to do.

"Can a girl get a little privacy?" she said. "Then you can join me in the shower if you'd like, and afterwards I'll make some breakfast."

Out I walked, finding the bed to sit on. When she finished, she called me in and we showered together, each of us washing away the night of desire. I wished for colder water to ease my blood flow. We stepped out without getting further aroused, dried off, and she retrieved my clothes. Once dressed, she made a nice breakfast. I wasn't sure what to say and she was quiet herself. I could see contentment in her eyes.

"I believe we should talk about last night," I said finally, the silence killing me.

"I agree, but I must get off to work soon. It's was nearly eleven and it would seem we would need more than a few minutes."

I hadn't noticed it being so late.

"Yes, I agree," I said. "I have some things to work out with Helen and Jolene. I promise to call you when we have more time. It may be a day or so, but I vow to reach out to you."

"No worries, Jarvis. Last night was wonderful. But it doesn't have to be life-altering. I know you needed a release and I was happy to provide it. Let me finish getting ready and I can drop you wherever you need me to."

She left the room and I called Rocky to see how things were going.

"Where have you been?" he asked.

"Sleeping off a lot of booze," I answered.

"Alone?"

"No comment. How are Helen and Jolene?"

"Fine. They were both worried about you. I told them you had some thinking to do and you were fine."

"Thanks for explaining to them and covering for my inebriation. Need you to come get me. I'll be at the Merle Hay Mall in about twenty minutes."

"Never thought I'd be a chauffeur in Des Moines, Iowa."

"If it's any consolation, you are the toughest driver in the Midwest."

It wasn't, and he cursed at me before hanging up the phone. Roni walked out in her work day clothes, ready to leave. We went to the car silently, as was the drive. When dropping me off, she reached over to kiss me softly.

"Don't worry, everything will work out for the best," she said.

I turned on my main cell phone. It had been off for a day now. A familiar chime informed me of a voicemail and, tapping deeper, I saw it was from Melissa. I couldn't bring myself to listen to it, standing outside the north entrance feeling like an ass, both happy and sad thoughts rolling through my brain. I needed to push all to the side. I had more important items to work on. Rocky pulled up and the two ladies got out to join me. I had suggested shopping and maybe some lunch, but Rocky didn't care to shop, so he would go off and do his own thing, returning when we were done. *Maybe he was tracking down some new cooking recipes.* Inside, the ladies stopped at various stores, mostly fashion and spent some money. Helen and Jolene seemed to have grown closer in the tragedy. It was good to see, for my connections to them in Des Moines would have to be severed, at least when it came to visiting. This saddened me. They were all the family I had left.

An hour, a few hundred dollars, and several bags later, we sat in the food court for some fast food. Partway through the meal, I finally broached the subject.

"We need to talk about where we are in our current situation," I said.

Both of them turned their full attention to me.

"Rocky said there may be a solution, but you'd need to let us know what it was," said Helen. "From his tone, it didn't seem ideal."

"It's not, from my perspective," I stated. "I know who the person is behind Flynn's murder. Unfortunately, I will not be able to do anything about it."

"Why not?" asked Jolene.

"Because he will send an army of people to kill you and me, and there won't be anything I can do about it."

Both women sighed.

"He is a powerful man, who can do unspeakable things to you both. I can't have that. With my connection, he agreed to leave you both alone if I stopped pursuing this case and left town within seven days, never to return to Des Moines again."

"You believe this will work if you leave?" asked Helen.

"My associate, who is a powerful man himself and brought us together, says he will keep his word."

"He is the one who killed Dad?" said Jolene.

"Yes, he admitted it."

"He can't get away with it. He must pay and go to jail for his crime. You promised you'd catch him."

"I did and I'm sorry. This man is too connected, his reach brutal and precise. He failed in his first attempt because he didn't understand what he was up against. He is likely not to fail again."

Jolene looked away in anger.

"Honey, you have to understand that in this world, some people get away with certain actions simply because of who they are. It's not fair or right, but it's part of the society we live in. I'm not happy about it either. And if there was any way I could complete the task without putting you both in danger, I would. But, so far, no option has presented itself."

"You are scared of them and are going to run away, never to see us again!" yelled Jolene.

The words rang true, yet still I lost my cool.

"They will torture you and your mom in ways you can't imagine," I said in anger. "In a manner where you'll beg for your life or beg for them to end it, because the pain and humiliation is beyond what you can bear. Do I need to spell it out in more detail!"

She started to cry, so Helen moved over to console her, giving me a stern stare in the process. I felt like a first-class heel for spouting off, but needed to get my point across. I was running away; and I was scared. Scared for them and myself. If there was a magic wand to correct it all, I'd use it. In this case, no miracle potion was forthcoming.

The two ladies went to the restroom to clean up. I stood around waiting till they came out. Jolene stepped forward and hugged me tightly.

"I'm sorry, Uncle Jarvis," she said into my chest. "I know you aren't scared of them and you did all you could. I'm going to miss you."

"Believe me, I'll miss you both as well."

Her forgiving me was cleansing. It wasn't the magic wand, but it was a start, the beginning of cleansing my tortured soul. I'd found a miracle potion after all.

Chapter 50

The rest of the day, and the next, were spent getting things ready for me to leave. Helen's house was released by the police, the bullet damage repaired and ready to go several days before our seven-day window closed. Insurance would cover the damage; no physical memory of the carnage would remain.

I'd called FBI Agent Wilson, letting him know the pursuit was over, something he wasn't thrilled about. He yelled endlessly at me on the phone, threatening to sue me for the money spent and to throw us out of the safe house. I told him to go ahead, I didn't care. The threat was over and we could go to a hotel if needed. A couple more choice words from him and I hung up, not wanting to hear anymore. Another punch to the gut owed, but I would resist, since I didn't need to be arrested.

Detective Frakes called to let me know the remaining shooter had been out on bail but failed to show for his arraignment. We both knew he would never be seen again, and either was dead or somewhere far away from the Midwest. The likelihood being the former, the body never to be found, punishment by The Bull for his failure. Another mystery to the cold case file, along with my brother's murder.

"I'm leaving town," I said to Frakes. "I won't be back."

"You are ending the quest for your brother's killer?" Frakes asked.

"I know who it is, but can't risk bringing him down. I must leave it be or those I care for will pay."

"I'm sorry to hear this. We'll continue on our end. I don't like leaving unsolved murders, but it doesn't look good we'll ever get them."

"Even if you could, you would never bring him to justice. The Bull is too much to wrangle."

Once done with the call, I told Rocky he could move on as well, but he decided to hang around until I left, as he had nothing better to do at this time. It wasn't his fight, but you could see he didn't care to run from it either. For now, he was hanging out, reading his Kindle, always one eye out for any potential danger.

While he was still around I decided to go to the cemetery and visit three graves, two together and one by itself. My parents had died within the same year, bringing a grief I'd not encountered before. My father was a tough man who refused to allow me to go down the wrong path in my teen years. "You must be responsible for your actions and become the man you deserve to be," he often said during those trying times when I didn't care what trouble I'd caused. I'd pretended not to hear him, but it still sunk in, buried deep somewhere in the back of my mind. I was better for it, though still prone to silly mistakes. Part of being human and my humanity often got the better of me. I left flowers on all of their graves, telling Flynn I was sorry I couldn't complete what he started. Sorry he had died unnecessarily, sorry his stubbornness and human fallacies had got him killed.

While driving from the cemetery, my main cell phone rang. It was a number I didn't recognize, appearing to be an Illinois area code.

"Mr. Mann," said the voice on the other end I didn't recognize. "I have a proposal you may be interested in hearing. I'm hoping we can meet somewhere private to discuss."

"Referring to?"

"I would prefer not to divulge over the phone. I am in town and can meet you today."

"You have to give me a clue before I will agree."

There was a long pause.

"It is in reference to a death in the family."

"I am no longer working the case."

"I believe I can assist you in finding a resolution which may be satisfactory to you in that regard."

"And who would this be who could provide this?"

"Again, I would rather not say over the phone. I can tell you I'm in a position to bring a certain horned creature down."

Interesting to say the least. It could have been a trap, but curiosity got the better of me.

"Where and when?" I said.

"Walnut Woods State Park. In two hours, we'll meet at the Limestone Lodge. I will be in a black Ford Taurus rental car. I will be alone. Please come alone too. If you don't show, or bring someone with you the opportunity will be lost."

The line went dead and I contemplated my options. *Ignore or pursue.* I was being tempted by the lure, bait which could get me killed, though a lead I had to explore. I called Rocky on my burner phone.

"I've got a meeting with someone in two hours," I said. "If for some reason I don't get back to you by this evening, I need you to take Helen and Jolene back to Denver and tell them they can never return. Can you do this for me?"

"What are you up to?" said Rocky, sounding perturbed.

I told him of the call.

"Do you need backup?"

"No, he said to come alone."

"Could be a setup."

"I know, but I'm planning on getting there early and look around. If it doesn't look right, I'll leave."

There was a huff in Rocky's voice, but he agreed. I headed to Walnut Woods, which was south of West Des Moines, the Raccoon River bordering it on three sides. It had once been remote from any houses, only farm land nearby. But now, with city growth all around, it didn't seem so far away. Still, the thick walnut trees, many standing a millennium, had the feel of living in the great outdoors. The moist air, smoke from campfires, and mosquitoes confirming it.

Either with courage or stupidity, I finally listened to Melissa's voicemail on the drive over. She sounded joyful and happy, having finished the semester of schooling on a high note.

"I know you are busy, but I couldn't help calling you to say the semester is over and I aced everything. I did so well I'm going to take the summer off. I hope when you are done we can finally take the beach vacation we had planned at Christmas. No need to call me back. I'm sure you are neck deep in your case. So you know, I'm going to start looking at options for us. I still have the string bikini to model for you. With the diet and exercise, I've already started, I'll look marvelous in it, and even better when you slip it off of me. Love you!"

Not believing I could feel any worse, I was wrong again. *How was I going to handle this? What could I say to her?* It was too much to chew on right now and I had to shove it to the outer reaches of my mind. One problem at a time.

I arrived, finding a parking spot, and began strolling the walking paths around the lodge. Being a Thursday, it wasn't real busy, a few cars out and about, with people hiking. No one looked suspicious, or ready to jump out and shoot me. The trees provided good cover and the likelihood of a sniper was minor. I had grabbed a sandwich on the way over and enjoyed it while waiting. When I finished, I tossed my wrappers into a nearby receptacle. I saw the black Taurus pull up. Out stepped a familiar figure, though I didn't know the name. It was the man who stood two steps behind Alexander in our meeting in Illinois. His face looked tense as he walked over to me, searching around for danger. He was dressed casually in jeans, a sweater, tennis shoes, with a ball cap and sunglasses. It was a minor disguise, but effective, for I wasn't totally sure it was him until he removed the sunglasses.

"Jarvis Mann," he said from a few feet away. "Let's go for a walk."

He didn't appear to be armed, but I had my .38 in a hip holster covered by the tail of my shirt. I walked beside him until we were deeper in the woods, no one around to hear him.

"You were in Illinois at the meeting," I stated.

"Yes. I'm his second in command."

"Dangerous, you coming to meet me."

"Why I chose this location. I need to be certain you are not wired."

I pulled up my shirt, so he could see.

"I am armed."

"Yes, I noticed when walking up. There should be no reason to use it. May I pat down your lower region?"

I nodded, and once he was sure no one was approaching, he did a basic search.

"Satisfied?" I said.

"Yes. One can't be too careful when contemplating what I'm about to propose."

"Which would be?"

"There are some within the organization who feel a change in leadership is necessary. I have come to offer you a way to avenge your brother's death. Put an end to this messy situation."

"Which would be?"

"To kill Alexander, so I may take over his operation."

I let out a low whistle, in surprise.

"Why would I do this for you? It seems if you wanted to do it, you could simply do it without my help."

"There are factors involved. I do not wish to get my hands dirtied. I am a business man, pure and simple. Killing is something I don't care to flaunt on my resume."

"Yet you work for him and know he has no qualms about killing."

"Alexander is from the old school where every violent solution is at the end of the gun or worse. I've seen what he has done to his enemies and even friends. Killing family members, women and children, like his threat to those close to you. Actions like his are frowned upon. It is unpleasant and unnecessary within our profession. It calls unneeded attention to the organization, especially when it comes to the FBI. If we worked more quietly, under the radar, our business would still thrive and the Feds would attend to more pressing matters like homegrown terrorism. We wish to succeed without bloodshed, or at least only as a last resort."

I could hear the birds and the locust songs through the woods. Their sounds were calming, as was this man's words. It made sense, yet I still wasn't sure I believed it.

"Others in your organization agree with this?"

"Yes."

"But you want me to take him out?"

"Yes. We would assist in arranging the place."

"I'm not an assassin by trade."

"Did you not kill several people last year single-handedly?"

I didn't correct him.

"To protect and save the life of my friends."

"Is not the death of your brother reason enough?"

"It is, to a degree. But I have his family to worry about. If I leave it alone they will not be harmed."

"What if I were to tell you this isn't the case. Even if you leave, they still will be harmed."

"He gave his word?"

"He has been known not to keep it. As I said, he is of the old school. When someone betrays you, then you kill their entire family. You don't want their children to grow up and hunt you down. Plans are in place to take you out one at a time."

"Why hasn't he acted upon it yet?"

"Because of his agreement with Mr. Sparks. He respects him, and fears him as well. He is not wanting a blood war among organizations. Also, this man Rocky is quite formidable. Once upon a time people under his protection were killed and he spent months tracking down the killers, taking them out one by one. I believe that is where he got the scar under his eye. He is a ghost Alexander would rather not deal with. It figures when you leave he'll feel his job is finished, with no more obligation to protect. Toro will take out your brother's family first and then finally come gunning for you. You would never see it coming."

I stopped walking, thinking over what I'd heard. The hope was my leaving would end this. Now it sounded as if this wasn't the case. Of course, he could have been baiting me to do his bidding.

"How do I know I can trust what you are saying?"

"My word is not enough?"

"I don't even know you. For all I know, you are drawing me in where Toro can take me easily."

"I may be able to arrange for you to talk with someone who can confirm this. Who has an interest in his demise as well."

"Who?"

"Are you familiar with all the players? Casey, her father, Edward, and Uncle Gabriel."

"Yes."

"One key part in all of this is Casey's mother, Kellie. She is a strong woman who has been beaten down by Alexander ever since he married her. She wants out, but sees no way, other than his demise."

"Alexander touted family as being important to him."

"Oh, they are important as a means to an end. He treats his wife like crap. But she can explain better than I. Would you like to talk with her?"

She was one part of the family tree I had not engaged with. Meeting with her wouldn't be any more dangerous than meeting with this man whose name I still didn't know.

"Absolutely," I stated. "When can you arrange it?"

"Right away, for your time will soon be up."

Yes it will!

Chapter 51

I finally learned his name and gave Max Groves my burner cell phone number. He would arrange a meeting, but it would have to happen somewhere remote. Kellie Toro lived in St. Louis, but he couldn't chance flying her out. Her protection was on board and would drive her. The decision was to meet halfway Sunday at ten, since Alexander was in Chicago to watch his favorite team, the Cubs, play baseball from his expensive suite seats. Keokuk, Iowa, which sat on the southeastern border of the state, was the locale, the small town of ten thousand hugging the Mississippi. It was about three hours' drive time for me, so I left early. The plan was to avoid anywhere too public, so Bluff Park was chosen, a stone's throw away from the mighty river, where the mosquitoes were the size of small birds. The wonder of GPS and mapping software provided precise directions, allowing me to arrive early.

Everything I was doing was a calculated risk. Danger was part of the job, but I wasn't sure if I'd ever get completely used to it. One case after another brought me to the point of risking it all. I longed for the simple cases of cheating husbands and wives without connections to gangsters. I longed for a simple insurance fraud case. I was more successful than ever, with money in the bank, though not happy in my success. I loved the challenge, though not the overwhelming stress and fear. I longed again for a string bikini beach vacation with Melissa, as she had proposed in her voicemail. Now, with my infidelity, it would appear that, unless she would once again forgive me, a sun and surf trip might be solo.

Waiting in the cooling air conditioning of the Mustang, as I wanted the muscle car in case a quick escape was necessary, a large, white SUV pulled into a parking space a couple slots down from me. I sat and waited for the passengers to get out, one large man and a smaller, older woman. They walked over to an open picnic table, where she sat down while he scanned the area. I stepped out slowly and walked towards them. The large man stopped me. I had left my gun in the car, chancing I wouldn't need it. Once he was satisfied after frisking me, I went over and sat across from her.

Kellie Toro was an attractive, fifty-something woman with bleached blonde hair, a robust tan, well-proportioned body, with too much makeup and bright, cherry-red lipstick for my taste. She was dressed all in white; blouse, knee length skirt and heels. Big square sunglasses adorned her face, a flowered scarf protecting her hair from the wind. When she removed the sunglasses, I could see why there was so much makeup, as it was hiding bruising around her eyes and cheeks. I doubted I'd get the clichéd story where she ran into a door.

"I assume you are Jarvis Mann," she stated.

I pulled out ID to show her.

"I'm Kellie Toro. Max said I should talk with you and hopefully convince you to go forward with his request."

"From the condition of your face, I believe I know why," I said.

"There is more that isn't showing. My husband is an animal. The world would be a better place without him."

"May I ask why you married him?"

"Why else for a woman like me? Money and power. I have all I want, all I need, other than love and devotion. I put myself in a position where I had no other option."

"How did you meet?"

"Is it really necessary to know this?"

"I am a detective, so I'm curious and cautious. Also, I've heard similar words from a woman in the past, where it wasn't the truth. I'm trying to get a sense of the situation and how it came to be."

She looked uncomfortable, shifting her body on the hard bench. She let out some air, her eyes meeting mine.

"We met while I was still married to my ex-husband, Edward. They were cooking up some type of business deal. Edward and I had what you would call an open relationship, from his perspective. He was screwing any skirt who would have him. When the opportunity arose, I would bed whatever stud I could find in revenge. Alexander and I were introduced and I thought what better way of getting back at him than by sleeping with a business partner. He was strong, powerful and a voracious lover. He dominated me, at first, and I truly enjoyed it. He would spend lavish amounts of money on me. Soon after, he told me to get divorced, so we could be married. He would make sure Edward wouldn't contest it. Next thing I know, we are on our honeymoon and I'm on top of the world, living with all the tea in China, if you know what I mean."

"Though it didn't last?"

"No, he soon became completely demanding, overbearing and violent. Many times, for no apparent reason. I'm always walking on egg shells around him."

"Toro wasn't already married?"

"His wife had passed recently under suspicious circumstances."

"Toro had her killed?"

"That was the rumor. She couldn't stand him either, and had a boyfriend. Needless to say, when he found out, he had them both killed, and not pleasantly, or so was the word on the street."

"Do you have any children?"

"Yes, a boy who is now eleven."

"How does he treat him?"

"When he isn't hitting him, he is pointing out any faults and failures. Grades, sports, even cleaning his room. When he does well, not a positive word is spoken. Alexander says it was how he was raised, and that it made him a man. He wishes him to be tough and mean, so he can someday run the business. In my mind, it's what made him a monster and I don't want my son turning out like him."

"Do you have a picture of your son?"

She reached into her pocket book and pulled one out.

"Good looking young man," I said. "Can't imagine anyone treating their kids like that."

"I know deep down he hates his father. We've talked many times about him."

Reading her face, her body language, told me all I needed to know. Though I'd been fooled before, I was certain she was telling the truth.

"What about Casey?"

"I understand you've met her."

"I have."

She let out a long sigh.

"You know what she is like, then. She is a woman now and can make her own choices, many of which are the wrong ones in my eyes. It's been some time now since we've spoken, as she no longer wishes to listen to her mother. Her father and stepfather are who she has doing her bidding."

"She uses them?"

"And then some. When she wants something, like money, a new car, maybe a boyfriend out of the way, she calls Edward first. If he isn't willing, she'll come and snuggle up to Alexander and slobber all over him. For all I know, she would screw him to get what she wants. It makes me sick to think of it."

I shuddered at the thought. Casey was much like the woman who had shot me before Christmas last year. One of my many terrible mistakes.

"She seemed surprised and upset about Carlos being killed. I don't think she was expecting it."

"I don't believe I knew him."

"He was her international lover. Alexander essentially admitted to me he killed him and another woman he was with, when we met. This wasn't her bidding to have him removed."

"It's possible. But there are others she has had scared off when she is through with them."

"Yes, I've met and talked with one. He was beaten up and had to hire protection."

"Certainly her doing," said Kellie. "I long ago gave up on saving her. But my son can be saved, and I'll do whatever it takes."

"So, what do you want me to do?"

"Put an end to it. Kill the SOB."

"I'm not an assassin. I have my reasons for wanting him dead, but cold-blooded murder is a reach for me. A road I'd rather not travel down."

She reached back into her pocket book and pulled out a bundle of money, the moist breeze off the mighty river causing the end of the stack of bills to fan.

"I can pay you. Here is five thousand dollars upfront. I can get you more when the job is done."

I looked at the money long and hard. But I wasn't in it for the money, though I did want to get Helen back the money Flynn lost.

"What recourse do you have to return the money stolen from my brother?" I said. "Gabriel, and likely Edward, were responsible. If you can get it returned to his wife and daughter, and the others Flynn parlayed into investing, I believe we can work something out."

"Yes, I can. Take this as a down payment and I can get Max working on getting the rest when this is over. Do we have a deal?"

There wasn't much more I could hope or wish for. So, after agreeing, we talked for a while longer, going over several other items, until we came to some working conclusions. When finished, I pulled out my burner phone to call Max.

"I've been convinced, so I'm in," I said. "We've talked it over, and here is what I have in mind…" and I spelled out assorted options with him which brought goose bumps to my skin.

Chapter 52

The plan was in place, with the remaining hours of Sunday meant to get everything in order. Monday was the day of reckoning. I had affairs to get organized, final requests, and personal items to clear before leaving. The list was long, so I wasn't about to doddle.

Calling my lawyer, Barry, who was always thrilled to hear from me on a weekend, I made further arrangements with him in case of my demise. All the remaining money I had would go into a trust fund for Jolene. If something were to happen to her and Helen, then the information Flynn had found would go to the FBI and the press anonymously. I was essentially giving him a verbal will over the phone.

"Will I be able to bill you for this work?" asked Barry.

"Absolutely," I replied. "The question is will I be alive to collect from."

"Well for my financial sake, let's hope so," said Barry with a chuckle.

"Gee, you are a sentimental guy, Barry."

"I would miss you if you didn't come back. Who else can I do work for and not get paid? You are my biggest tax write-off. Without you, I might actually have to pay taxes next year."

All I could do was laugh before ending the call. It was nice to feel wanted, though in an oddball way.

Then I called Melissa.

"How are you?" she said.

"Doing as well as can be expected," I replied. "The end is near. It will be all over in a couple of days."

"You will have caught his killer?"

"Yes."

"He will be arrested soon?"

"He'll be going down tomorrow."

"I'm so happy. So, I'll be able to see you soon."

"Absolutely."

"Did you get my voicemail?"

"I did. It made my day. I'm so proud of you for passing all your exams and acing this semester. And I can't wait to see what you have planned for our trip."

"It will be the three S's; sun, surf and sex. Hawaii, here we come!"

It was the trip we should have taken last Christmas, before I got shot. I didn't want to tell her it might not happen again, for several reasons.

"Being apart has been hard," I said. "Hopefully some time together can put us on the right track again."

"I'm sorry for how I've been these last few months. I tried to put all of it behind me; the shootings, your encounter with Emily, her seductive and violent moves on you. I've been buried in my work and school, trying not to think about it. But it's difficult. I truly want to work it all out together."

"I understand. I'm to blame for much of it. I wished it never had happened, but I can't turn back time."

I wasn't sure if I was talking about Emily or Roni in this case. Probably both, though she wouldn't know it. There had to be better days ahead for us, but at this point I couldn't see it and it showed in my voice.

"You sound odd," she said after a long pause. "Are you okay?"

I didn't like lying, but didn't want to worry her any.

"I'm just tired. Been a long, hard case. Thoughts of you in your bikini as we walk hand in hand make me smile. I miss you."

"I miss you, too. Are you certain you're okay?"

"Getting better every day I get closer to coming home. I love you."

"I love you too."

The call ended and I felt weird, strangely incomplete. There was unfinished business there I would need to attend to, if I got out of this alive. But the other was Roni. I needed to speak with her one last time to find out where this was going. Sunday's were a busy day for her, but she agreed to carve out some time for me. I stopped by her restaurant before dinner rush and we left together to take a walk on this hot, humid and sunny day.

"I have to say some things," I said. "Things happened between us I'm not pleased with myself about. Though pleasurable, they really shouldn't have happened."

"You were drunk and depressed," she replied, "needing an outlet for all that had happened. There is nothing to feel sorry about."

"But I shouldn't have slept with you, made love to you. It was wrong of me to do so, in that current state and in relation to my current relationship back home."

She stopped and turned to me, reaching her hand out to take mine.

"Jarvis, I'm as much to blame as you were. You are a wonderful person, who I deeply cared for all those years ago. I was quite sad when you broke it off with me at the end of our senior year, but I got over it. This was a curiosity of seeing a long-lost love all these years later, wanting to connect personally and physically. I shouldn't have taken advantage of you in your current state, but I'm not sorry it happened. You have nothing to worry about from me or fear of me being the other woman who will try and wreck what you have back home. I'm not looking to start any type of relationship and run off to Denver with you, as I offered after our senior year. I'm no longer that teenage girl who needed a man to feel fulfilled."

There was happiness flushing her face, for she had found herself. If only I could do the same in my personal life.

"I feel I've failed her again and I'm not certain what to do."

"To be honest, I wouldn't tell her. It will only ruin what you have. So long as you aren't chasing every pretty woman you encounter and it's only a one-time thing, I'd leave it alone."

"Would you want to know if you were her?"

She paused to contemplate, taking her time before responding.

"It's a hard question to answer, because I was her with my ex-husband. I didn't want to know, and even was in denial of what he was doing. But when I found out for certain, it was extremely painful. Of course, with him, it wasn't one-time. It was habitual in many ways."

The problem was it wasn't a one-time thing for me either. And, much like my brother, I was worried it would happen again. Ultimately, I had the responsibility to be faithful, but didn't seem to have the gene in me to remain so.

"Jarvis, you are a wonderful man," said Roni. "You aren't perfect by any stretch, but you have a good heart. Your lady back home is lucky to have you. Be sure to think this through carefully before telling her and destroying all you built together. This indiscretion shouldn't kill what could be a lifetime of love and happiness."

I pulled her towards me and gave her a big hug, knowing I'd likely not see her again.

"Thank you," I whispered in her ear. "If I never see you again, I'll always remember you fondly."

"As will I…"

She gave me one last kiss, turned, and walked out of my life; likely for the last time.

Once back in the car, I had one more call to make and then would return to spend a final evening with Helen and Jolene. If it was going to be a last supper, I wanted it to be a good one, a night of happy memories and good times, before the real world reared its ugly head the next day.

Chapter 53

Even with the thick thunder clouds holding back the heat of the sun, the humidity clung to me like a wet shirt, which was exactly how my white Colorado Rockies t-shirt felt. Standing there, I nervously pulled at the fabric, waiting for the dust trail in the distance, signaling the parade of gas hogs heading my way. They lined up as before, two in front, one in the middle, another in back, the same formation of men getting out; armed protection for their leader I was there to encounter. Alexander Toro moved closer to me, a look of uncertainty in his scowl.

"Where is Brandon Sparks?" he growled. "I was told I would be meeting him."

Unlike the last time I stood there alone, my fully loaded Beretta, my companion, was sitting in a hip holster, the strap unbuttoned, the magazine fully loaded with fourteen revenge rounds. I had wondered over and over what I would do, what I would say as he stepped within my range. Would it be a profound wisdom in words or pure action? I felt a couple of rain drops as I looked towards the heavens.

"Looks like rain is coming," I stated with a smile.

"Excuse me?"

"Farmers could use the moisture as it's been so dry lately."

"I drive all the way out here to get a weather report," yelled Alexander over a clap of thunder. "Where the fuck is Sparks?"

"I'm here to show you I got out of town before sundown Monday like you told me to," I answered. "Prove to you, so you'll leave Flynn's family to live in peace."

"You are trying my patience, Jarvis Mann."

"But you were never going to leave them or me alone, were you? You gave your word, but it was a load of crap. The only question would be if you would make it quick and painless or would you torture us like you did Flynn?"

Alexander gave a sort of half laugh and growl. I could tell by his eyes the rage seething underneath.

"It is of no importance now what I had envisioned for all of you," he bellowed. "I had planned to make it quick and painless. Now the three of you will each suffer."

"I was right: you weren't going to keep your word."

"Why would I keep my word with a pest like you? I squish bugs whenever I feel like it without a single concern over the consequences. I'm Alexander the Bull and I can do whatever the fuck I want! We might as well start the party now. Grab him, men, and if he resists shoot him, but don't kill him."

Alexander started to turn around, but no one moved. His men lowered their guns and stepped away, Max as well moving out of the line of fire. The Bull glanced at his men uncertain what was happening, swearing at them to act. Adrenaline was flowing, my blood pumping, feeling a rage I'd not experienced before. I took a couple of steps forward and punched him in the gut with every ounce I could muster. He gasped and doubled over, but remained standing. Grabbing the shirt collar, I raised his head and punched him with equal force in the nose, smashing it, blood streaming down his face. He backed up several steps, still on his feet, and I pulled my gun, firing once, nailing him solidly in the right collarbone. The force of the bullet pushed him backwards and he dropped to his knees and then back onto his butt, his hand clutching at the bleeding hole in his shoulder. It was not a fatal shot, though I hit him exactly where I wanted too. A few more rain drops hit the ground and, with gun still in hand, I walked over, squatting down next to him, tossing him a handkerchief.

"A present," I said. "It was my brother's. You'll see it has his initials on it. You can use it to apply pressure to either of your wounds."

Alexander didn't look scared, but certainly didn't appear comforted by the gesture. He checked all the faces of those he thought would protect him and found no solace. No one was about to save him. I was told he didn't carry a gun these days, but I checked him anyway, finding no weapon.

"Right about now you are probably wondering what the fuck happened," I stated. "I believe the term is *coup d'etat*. If you are unfamiliar with the term, it's something the people do to overthrow a brutal dictator. Normally his end is rather unpleasant."

"Max, you did this?" Alexander asked, his tone in a snort through his busted nose.

There was no smile on Max's face, or words from his lips; only contempt for the man he had worked for.

"Since he fields all your calls, then yes," I said. "Like before, we knew if you were told Brandon Sparks wanted to meet with you, you'd be there. You respected him, maybe even feared him. We used this ruse to bring you out here one last time."

His breathing got heavier, his ire building along with fear.

"You are all traitors!" he yelled out. "When others find out what happened, you all will be dead!"

"I'm sorry to say no one likes Alexander the Bull. You think you can do whatever the fuck you want, and for some time now that has been true. Killing for the sport of it, hurting those who once loved and maybe even admired you. But no more. You are a horrible person and the world will be a better place without you in it."

I stood up, raising my gun, pointing it at his head.

"There is a hatred burning inside for what you did to my brother. Rage like no other I've ever felt. You could have just killed him and be done with it. But you made it personal by beating him and cutting off his fingers. I brought a pair of sheering clippers with me to do the same thing to you. Imagining the look on your face as I slowly cut through the skin, bone and tendons. But I'm not a monster like you are, so I left them in the car. Though it did feel awful damn good to punch you and put a bullet in your shoulder."

"You don't have the courage to do it anyway," said Alexander.

I laughed.

"It doesn't take courage to brutalize or kill someone. Courageous people aren't made like that. No, to do it takes an angry fire deep down inside, and I have plenty of feelings like this towards you. And I could do it in a heartbeat, but I promised someone who hates you even more, that they could be the one to do it."

I put my left hand in the air and waved. From the side of the building pulled out the stretch limo I had arrived in. Parking behind me, out stepped Rocky from the driver seat, in jeans, boots and a t-shirt, his powerful Glock filling the shoulder holster. He was big, scary and imposing, as an enforcer should be, all eyes upon him, a mixture of awe and fear, as he stood for a minute gazing at the scene before him. The drama building, everyone wondering what was next.

With a wry smile, he turned and opened the back door, and out stepped Kellie Toro, dressed in fashion blue jeans, black boots and sheer tan blouse open enough to see some chest skin. In her gloved hands at her side she held a small sub-nosed .38 we had been practicing with earlier in the day, a few more windows shot out from the abandoned building behind us. She moved forward to within a few feet of Alexander, raised the gun with both hands like I taught her and sighted down the barrel.

"What are you doing, Kellie?" stated a shocked Alexander.

"This is for our son, to prevent him from becoming a monster like you," she said calmly.

She squeezed the trigger, slowly and precisely six times, aiming center mass, the sound of each shot filling the air. The bullets hit their mark, one after another. He was likely dead after the third one, but she used them all. His dead body, lying there motionless. I confirmed it when I checked his neck for a pulse. Kellie stood there looking at the bloody corpse before her, neither happy nor sad. She handed me the gun, then peeled off the gloves, tossing them to me as well.

"Feel better?" I asked.

"Not yet, but I'm getting there," she replied. "My happiness will be complete when I get back to the jet and hug my son."

She turned and headed back to the limo. Rocky stepped over to open the door for her, a bigger smile spread across his face, giving her a high five before closing it behind her.

"You'll take care of this," I said, while throwing the gun and her gloves on the body.

"Yes, I will," replied Max. "He died of a heart attack will be the official reason for his death."

"Not far from the truth. I believe he had one right when he knew it was her who was going to kill him. Never in a million years would he have foretold this ending."

I turned and walked back to the limo, Rocky still standing outside, his arms crossed, hair blowing in the wind and rain which was coming down a little harder now. He put out his fist and I bumped it with mine.

"Feeling better?" he asked.

"Not yet, but I'm getting there," I replied, echoing Kellie's earlier words. "When we get back to hug Helen and Jolene and tell them the ordeal is over, my happiness will be complete."

I pulled out the burner cell phone to use it for the last time, and once I got a signal called to let them know I was coming home again.

Chapter 54

It's always good to be home.

I'd been back in Denver about ten days now. Home had always been Des Moines growing up, but now my home was at the base of the Rocky Mountains. Home was where the heart is, but I truly didn't feel at home until I was in the Mile High City. It was a relief to be finally free of the confrontation with an evil man. A price was paid in the loss of my brother, which I would never forget, the sight of him sitting in his chair dead, a person so alive and cocksure days before. It was an ache I would relive till my final days.

We had returned back to the airfield, with the jet waiting for us, Helen and Jolene, along with Brandon and his pilot. The ladies were relieved when they heard from me, even more so when they saw me and got the good news. Max would make good on his promises. Their money was gradually returned, along with that of the other investors on the list. The two brothers were now broke and out of work, the Feds investigating them on various fronts. Max would pull the plug on the funnel of money from Alexander's organization, breaking all connections, moving it to other places to launder. I personally didn't care where this was. I could only worry about my little corner of the world. Crime and violence would always march merrily along, no matter what I did.

Now I was indebted to Brandon more than ever. I cringed at the possibly of what it could lead to. For now, it didn't matter, as I required his resources to accomplish my mission. He even had a smile when it was over, since he had formed a new alliance with Max which could pay off. He would be a mentor of sorts and possible associate in business, some of it even legitimate. And he'd found a new partner in Roni, investing in her restaurant and maybe even a little bit of monkey business too with my sexually liberated former girlfriend. Deep down, I was happy she had found her calling in life.

I was sitting outside my home/office, contemplating the events, waiting on a delivery. A call had come from a freight company saying they had a large package for me, which I needed to be there to sign for. I sat on the hood of my car wondering what it could be, enjoying the Colorado summer, without the humidity. *Damn I loved the dry heat.* A semi-truck with short trailer pulled down the alleyway and parked, blocking the road. The driver and his partner popped out and came to me with paperwork.

"Jarvis Mann," the larger and taller of the two asked.

"You've got him," I answered after flashing ID. "What do you have for me?"

"There is an envelope for you to open and read. We'll put the item onto the lift gate and bring it over."

I opened the seal and found the letter, a title, and a set of keys. It was from Helen and Jolene.

Dear Jarvis,

We can never say how much we appreciate all you did for us, including for Flynn. Nothing will ever clear the thoughts of his death, the horror we felt at losing him. But we will always be grateful for the extra mile you went to eliminate his killer and retrieve the money stolen from us. As a token of our gratitude, and knowing full well Flynn would want you to have it, we are giving you his Harley Davidson. Ride the wind in good health and fortune. We will always care deeply for you and hope it's not another seven years before we see you again.

Love, Helen and Jolene...

The two men rolled the bike over to me, removing the vinyl, waterproof cover protecting it. The Harley Softail was perfectly clean, freshly polished and waxed. I thanked the men, took the keys and sat on it, starting her up, the loud full-throttled roar fulfilling in my ears, echoing down the alleyway. I would ride on in my brother's name, on two wheels in his memory.

Flynn was about twenty years old when he came home with his first motorcycle, showing it off to me and our parents. Mother looked worried but knew she couldn't convince him otherwise. Dad studied it, examining the design, a thumbs up in appreciation. I would soon turn eighteen and would be leaving home to go to college a year later. Flynn looked so cool on the small Harley Sportster, black with glistening chrome, crimson gas tank and the famous Harley engine rumble. He was wearing black leather pants and jacket, his sunglasses giving him a slick look I never forgot. He smiled at me and revved the throttle.

"I'm going to get lots of ladies with this baby," he said proudly.

I recall mother blushing at his words, my father silently proud of his ladies' man son.

"Can I ride on the back?" I asked.

"Forget it. Chick's only on the back with me. They'll be holding on tight and I'll be loving it. Whispering in my ear while we motor around town. There is this one sweet thing I hope to cajole in to riding with me. Her name is Helen and she is going to be Hell-On-Wheels." He leaned over and whispered in my ear. "A sure-fire guarantee I'll get in her pants with this baby."

We both laughed and I knew some day I'd have a bike exactly like this one. But it never happened, as money was always too tight. The years had passed, my yellow and black Mustang being my chick magnet...

The bike felt right. I knew how to ride, how to shift and brake, as Flynn had taught me way back when. I would be rusty and needed to get a motorcycle license. But I didn't care. With the helmet, jacket and gloves also shipped with it, I filled the tank and took her for a spin on the back roads, getting myself up to speed. Twenty-five minutes of riding and I was off to Melissa's for dinner. A date with her and a moment in time I'd been dreading.

We had spent a few days together since I'd returned, a couple of passion-filled nights, yet guilt continued to haunt. Even though Roni felt it would do no good to tell Melissa of my indiscretion, I felt a burden which wore on me, and I could no longer hold back. When I pulled up, she walked outside to see my new ride, a smile on her face.

"Wow, a new toy?" she asked, standing there in shorts and a tank top.

"A gift from Helen and Jolene," I replied.

"You look good on it. The leather jacket is extremely sexy."

I dismounted, placing the helmet on the seat. I came over and gave her a hug. I struggled with the words, what to say, how to put it. I needed to be honest, knowing full well the possibility of what the end result would be, another vacation to the islands in jeopardy, another relationship with a woman ending badly.

"Melissa, I need to tell you something," I said. "Something

happened in Iowa, a moment in time I will always regret. I made a mistake with someone and broke the trust between us…"

I admitted my transgression, the tears and anger began to flow, and our relationship was forever changed.

Thanks for reading ***Blood Brothers***. I hope you enjoyed it and would love if you would leave a review on Amazon to help an Indie Author.

For now, you can always check out the other books in the ***Jarvis Mann Detective Series*** of which there are 8 total to read. ***The Case of the Missing Bubble Gum Card, Tracking a Shadow, Twice As Fatal, Dead Man Code, The Case of the Invisible Souls, The Front Range Butcher*** and ***Mann in the Crossfire***. All are available on Amazon in eBook, Paperback and Kindle Unlimited.

https://www.amazon.com/R-Weir/e/B00JH2Y5US

Be sure to check out my new series, the first book ***The Divine Devils***, winner of the ***2021 Killer Nashville Silver Falchion Award for Best Thriller***. And coming soon, ***Fallen Star: The Divine Devils Book Two.***

If you want to reach out, please email me at:

rweir720@gmail.com

Follow R Weir, Jarvis Mann, and Hunter Divine on these social sites as I appreciate hearing from those who've read my books:

https://www.facebook.com/randy.weir.524

https://www.facebook.com/JarvisMannPI

https://twitter.com/RWeir720

https://www.instagram.com/rweir720/

Thanks for reading. Stay Safe, Happy and Healthy!!